Don't miss Zach's first three adventures:

THE PLUTONIUM BLONDE
THE DOOMSDAY BRUNETTE
THE RADIOACTIVE REDHEAD

The FROST-HAIRED VIXEN

JOHN ZAKOUR

DAW BOOKS, INC.

DONALD A. WOLLHEIM, FOUNDER

375 Hudson Street, New York, NY 10014

**ELIZABETH R. WOLLHEIM
SHEILA E. GILBERT
PUBLISHERS**

http://www.dawbooks.com

First Paperback Printing, December 2006
1 2 3 4 5 6 7 8 9

DAW TRADEMARK REGISTERED
U.S. PAT. OFF. AND FOREIGN COUNTRIES
—MARCA REGISTRADA
HECHO EN U.S.A.

PRINTED IN THE U.S.A.

To Little Harris (lieutenant shorty pants) and to everybody else who still believes.

Acknowledgments

I'd be totally remiss if I didn't acknowledge my old writing partner and second favorite cousin Larry Ganem. It was a great experience working with him while we were writing the first three books. While it's certainly easier and faster to write a book alone (I had way fewer "disagreements" with myself) without Larry around there was nobody around to shout, "No! No! No! You've gone too far with that. I'm totally rewriting it." Hopefully the reader won't mind that there is now nobody to pull me back from the edge of absurdum. Plus, now without Larry around I don't have anybody else to blame if something goes wrong. The old, "Larry wrote that part . . ." excuse won't fly any more. I always say, "A person should be accountable for his own actions." I guess now I really have to practice what I preach more.

I am eternally grateful to Betsy Wolheim, DAW's Commander-in-Chief, for giving me the chance to write this book on my own as well for publishing the first three books. Betsy is fairly patient woman (for an editor) with a great sense of humor. Interestingly enough, Betsy was constantly pushing me back *towards* the edge of absurdum. My guess is that I was overcompensating for not having Larry around and playing it extra safe (by my standards) so I needed Betsy to give me a little kick in the pants. Thanks, Betsy!

I also have to thank my agent Joshua Bilmes, because quite frankly he'll whine if I don't. Seriously, Joshua does a great job of explaining the business aspect of writing to me preventing me from selling my books or "magic beans." Joshua is also "A-Number-1" at talking up my books and getting foreign publishers to buy them.

Aaron and Rebecca Goldweber also get a big thank you for their help with early editing with the book. That's the other spot I missed, Larry. Larry took actual writing classes in college so he knows things like the difference between a comma and a semicolon. Aaron and Rebecca are ace editors so they know these arcane facts too.

I of course have to mention all my real-life friends and family who are and were "inspiration" for characters in this and past books. The list is fairly long and just as boring but it's always nice to see your name in print: Carolina and Natalia Padilla, Tom Rickey, Ron Pool, my sister Mary Erdman and her husband Steve, Shannon Codner, and of course, my wife Olga. I'm sure you can all pretty much figure out who you are. If I left anybody out, sorry, I'll mention you twice in the next book.

Finally, I really have to thank my wife Olga and my son Jay, for putting up with me while I wrote this book. I'm hard enough to deal with on a regular basis but I imagine I'm even tougher to handle when there's a deadline bearing down on me. Thanks, I love you guys! (PS: Note to Jay: don't worry, you're going to be a character in a book soon enough.)

Chapter 1

The holographic name on my door reads Zachary Nix-ion Johnson, PI. That's mostly correct. My name is Zachary NIXON Johnson. That's what you get when you let your fiancée's brother program your door. Sure, the door would be easy to reprogram but I can't hurt my future brother-in-law's feelings. I look at it like this: it separates me from the crowd even more. Besides, most people either call me Zach, or Johnson, or in the case of the New Frisco police force, *that damn Zachary Johnson* (and that's when they're in a good mood).

You would think being the last freelance private detective on a planet with 15 billion beings, every day would be an action-packed adventure. Only this is 2061, the peak of the over-the-top-information age. A time when everybody has access to more information than any human, meta-human, or even bot could ever want or need. For the most part, clients only enlist my services when the information they need is particularly "sensitive." In other words it's so dangerous any sane person who avoid it like .10 credit sushi.

Somehow, some way, whenever trouble does teleport to my front door, it's always of the earthshaking variety. That's just my lot in life, my pile of spam to sift through. I've learned to accept that I will either be figuratively bored to death or some person, mutant, robot, android, alien, animal, and yes, once even a vegetable, will literally try to kill me. I find it's best if I don't ponder it too much.

Today, though, was a quiet day. Quiet days may not be the stuff of great adventure, but they are the stuff that let me recharge for upcoming great adventures. Life's like a rollercoaster ride; the highs wouldn't be nearly as fun without the lows. I was sitting in my office on the New Frisco docks, enjoying a nice game of holo-backgammon with my annoying but mostly trusty holographic assistant, HARV, who had me on the ropes.

"Looks like I'm going to backgammon you again, Zach! Which means you'll owe me ten more credits!" HARV said, not even trying to hide the joy in his voice.

"That's only because you're the one who rolls the dice, HARV." I felt I should remind him of that. I turned away from the shimmering board HARV was projecting onto my desk. I slid open one of my desk drawers.

"What are you doing?" HARV asked, annoyed that I had turned my attention away from his impending victory.

I started rummaging through the open drawer. "I'm looking for my real backgammon board. The one with non-computer-generated dice!"

Though I couldn't see HARV, I was certain he was shaking his head and rolling his eyes.

"Zach, Zach, Zach," he said softly, using his *what am I going to do with you, dense human* tone. "Remember, you sold that one last month at a charity auction of e-square-Bay to generate some extra money for Electra."

I stopped my rummaging and looked at HARV. "Oh, that's right."

"Of course that's right," HARV said very indignantly. Since he was a hologram HARV could appear in any form he choose. Over the years he has picked some dandies, from cowboy to ace detective to hot babe (I like to block out that one, except when I can use it to my advantage). Today he was in his favorite mode, snooty, aging English butler. In this form he was mostly bald with patches of graying hair running along his temples and circling around the lower area of his head. His eyes were just wide enough to make it clear when he was giving condescending looks. His nose would hardly be noticeable accept he accented it with a little handlebar mustache and usually had it sticking up in the air. He was wearing a better-than-tailor-fitted gray, Ralph Lauren-C (that C stands for clone) suit and black bow tie. I think HARV enjoys acting as a butler because even when he's serving me he still gets to look down on me.

"Zach, first you make such a big deal about me finding one for you. Then the nano you need a few extra credits you sell it off," HARV moaned.

"I wanted to make a special contribution to Electra's clinic," I said. "After all, she puts up with a lot."

"Now that may very well be the understatement of the century," HARV said.

My last big case six months ago was kind of a washout for me. I was acting as bodyguard for teen pop "singing" sensation Sexy Sprockets. It seemed like a simple enough job, protect a very beautiful but not overly (or even remotely) talented singer from a crazed cult that wanted to kill her. When you're me, crazed cults are a walk in the park on a sunny day. Of course, when you're me, it's never just a crazed cult. The crazed cult was actually an overzealous supporter of the Governor of New California, as the powers that be wanted to make sure Sexy never made good on her plans to retire and run for governor. Turns out protecting Sexy was the easy part.

Long story abridged for HV: Sexy's slimy and totally dishonest (and those are his best points) manager was augmenting her latent psi powers to force teens to love her music. That was, of course, until the manager met my psi assistant Carol. Carol had far more mental powers and potential than Sexy. The scumbag manager decided to focus on her, augmenting her powers. The process didn't go as planned (it never does) and turned Carol into a vastly powerful psi who could dominate the minds of everybody. She became so powerful she started to bring down the house—literally. Carol created a telepathic, telekinetic maelstrom that ripped the roof off of Frisco's very expensive public auditorium (lovingly called The Fart) and threatened, at the very least, to tear the province of New California apart. Luckily, I was able to bring to Carol back to Earth (by getting shot—trust me, you don't want to be me) and thus saving the day.

After that, everybody lived happily ever after—everybody except me. There aren't many lawyers left in the world since the great lawyer purge (at least those who openly practice law without being called greeting card salesmen), but those who are jumped on the case and down my throat. They sued everybody and anybody even remotely related to the case. They sued for: destruction of personal property, mental anguish for forcing the concert to end early, mental anguish for not stopping the concert sooner, compound mental anguish for not stopping the mental anguish soon enough, the rise in the cost of liquid hydrogen, and bad cases of acne. You name it they sued for it. My insurance company covered a lot of my expenses (then sent me death threats and really hiked my premiums). Sexy picked up most of my remaining tab. The whole ordeal soured Sexy on running for governor. Instead, she ran for World Council rep and won easily. She now represents the Western United States, thus proving politics is even more accepting of the strange, unusual, and mostly useless than the music industry.

I ended up making fifty-two credits and got to put "saved the world again" on my resume.

HARV looked me in the eyes. "You're fixating on the Sexy Sprockets case, again."

"Maybe," I said. "It's the reason I needed to sell my real backgammon board to get the cash for Electra's clinic."

HARV rolled his eyes. "Zach, let it go. You saved the world, made a few credits, and didn't get killed despite numerous attempts. You should be happy." He pointed to the board. "Now back to more important matters. My victory."

I don't know why HARV took such great joy in constantly beating me at backgammon. It worried me a little. I decided it was best not to think about it too much. I knew when the chips hit the fan, HARV had my back—eventually.

"I can't help thinking that you might load the dice," I said.

HARV glared at me. "You're acting like a typical human, trying to blame your computer for your inadequacies," HARV said. He pointed to the shimmering board. "By the way, I just rolled you a nice two and a four."

I looked over the board. There are times when a

two and a four can be a handy roll. This wasn't one of those times. In fact, it was a roll that would leave me wide open.

"Thanks, HARV. You're all silicon . . ."

"Hey Zach, my chips just let the dice fall where they may. You don't have to be me, the most advanced cognitive processor on Earth, to generate a random number between one and six."

He looked at me.

I glared at him.

Until just a few months ago HARV and I actually were linked together—literally. He was connected through my optic nerve to my brain stem. Yes, it was as uncomfortable as it sounds. It was an experiment developed by my very brilliant and almost as mad friend Dr. Randy Pool. He wanted to see how a human/computer nano link would benefit man and computer, but mostly computer.

Having HARV hooked up to my brain gave me instant access to all the knowledge and information HARV has access to, which is nearly everything. Our link allowed me to communicate silently with him. It also let me project holograms from my eye lens. The link for better or for worse gave HARV easy access to the chemicals in my brain allowing him to juice me up from time to time.

Randy would always insist this was beneficial to me. I have to admit there were instances when it came in handy that HARV could crank up my adrenaline, norepinephrine, and even the electrical currents of my body. Still, I couldn't help feeling like a supercomputer's personal guinea pig/biochemistry lab. Plus, I could never turn HARV off (though Randy could), so HARV was constantly with me, droning on inside my head like a whiny, electronic Jiminy Cricket. After a while I got used to it, but I never totally accepted it.

HARV, for his part, got to interact with a human brain on a constant basis. Randy's theory was this would be good for HARV, as it would help him grow to be more than was designed to be. He would become greater than the sum of his nano chips. If you ask me (which nobody did), it was working. Before our link, HARV had only a very rudimentary sense of humor. He could recite a joke easily enough, but he couldn't *tell* a joke. He was unable to comprehend what made funny funny. In the time we, for lack of a better word, were "bonded," he grew—upgraded. HARV is loath to admit this.

Randy recently removed the chip set for modifications. He insisted he needed to add more shielding to it. Not for me, mind you, but for HARV. He was worried that my personality was tainting HARV too much. I'm pretty positive he wanted HARV to be more human but less like me. Randy e-mailed me a couple of days ago (or was it weeks?) saying the upgrade was complete, and I could have it stuck into my brain at anytime. (Though Randy used much more technical terms than "stuck into my brain.") I've been purposely avoiding it. Why? I'm not really sure.

Having instant access to HARV, who has instant access to pretty much all the information in the world, is undeniably handy when you are in my line of work. Plus, the ability to project holograms from the eye lens has come to my rescue on more than one occasion. I also must admit that HARV's ability to supercharge the biochemical reactions in my brain, thus stimulating other parts of my body, has gotten me out of a dicey situation or three.

There can be no question having a computer connected to your brain does come with an upside. But the universe is filled with checks and balances so with that up naturally comes a downside, which admittedly has a lot more gray area. I don't like sharing my brain with another living consciousness. I guess it's not so gray after all. In this world where everything is connected to everything else, our brains are our last oasis. The place where we can be alone with our thoughts. When HARV is hooked up to me or I am hooked up to him (as he likes to say), my thoughts and I are never alone. That's why I planned on delaying sticking HARV back in my brain until the need arose. (Not to mention that the process is far more painful and unpleasant than being examined by an angry mutant proctologist with big hands.)

"After this game, you will owe me one hundred credits," HARV said proudly.

I looked up at HARV. "Why do you care? You're a computerized hologram. You don't need credits."

HARV furrowed his balding brow. "It's the thought that counts."

"You don't think. You just simulate thinking," I said, knowing it would really rattle his e-chains.

"There's nothing simulated about my thinking," HARV said, his narrow eyes tapering to slits as he scowled at me. "You don't have to have an organic collection of white and gray matter to think."

"That's what you think you think," I said.

HARV crossed his arms and looked away from me. "Quit stalling and make a move!"

I won't deny that I was pleased when Carol's voice and image superimposed itself over HARV. Not only did it let me put off the game, but Carol was a lot easier on the eyes and the mind than HARV. She was back to her old self, a cut above normal humans. She could still stop traffic with her looks or her brain, but she was no longer bordering on godlike.

"Zach, you have a visitor," she said with excitement in her voice. In her time with me, Carol has seen everything from amorous aliens to zany killer bots made of zinc. She handles it all coolly and in stride. I was worried at the prospect of someone who could get Carol this wound up.

HARV looked at me looking at Carol. "If this was a threatening situation don't you think Carol or I would have warned you by now?"

"Carol, yes. You, I'm not so sure," I said.

HARV gave me a slight grin. There was a gleam in his eye—literally. "Touché, Zach, but you worry too much."

"When you're me, there's no such thing as worrying too much. Remember how the networks wanted to try to kill me week after week for a reality show?"

HARV gave me a dismissive wave. "Oh please, that was just the Faux Network. They didn't want to kill you that badly anyhow. Then they wouldn't have a show."

"What about that time when the grandma assassin tried to strangle me with her pantyhose in Ultra-MegaHyperMart?"

"Well, you did have seventeen items in the fifteen-item line. You can't blame her for being mad. If it wasn't for me augmenting your muscles, she might have killed you."

"It's only because she was bionic."

HARV smiled. "Of course, there was that time you got attacked while guest umpiring a girls softball game between New Vegas showgirls and cocktail waitresses. Only you could turn a fun charity event into a fight for your life. That was great the way that Melissa girl took you out . . ."

"Hey, she hit me with a blindside tackle."

HARV's smile widened. "Then when that Jody girl jumped in, pelting you with softballs."

"They aren't soft at all. Especially where she was hitting me."

"Oh Zach, don't be such a whiner. It's not like you weren't wearing your underwear armor."

"Which is exactly my point," I said, pointing at HARV. "How many other people do you know that need to wear carbon-steel-reinforced underwear?"

"Don't forget computer-enhanced. Those two ordinary little waitresses would have been using you for home plate if it wasn't for me."

"They weren't ordinary, they were mutants for Gates' sake. They both played in the Female All-Tackle Mud Rugby League before they became New Vegas waitresses."

"I understand that league makes an excellent training ground for cocktail waitresses."

I started rubbing my temples.

"Zach," Carol called over the holographic-intercom. "It's not only bad business but rude to keep clients waiting."

"Trust me," HARV said. "You'll be okay."

"Whenever you say that I never am."

"At least in the short term. I guarantee it. If you die, I'll forget about those credits you owe me."

"You're not going to tell me who it is?"

HARV just gave me his patented (really it is) sly grin.

"Okay Carol, send them in. HARV, turn off the game."

"This isn't going to save you from losing," HARV insisted.

"Quit being a Pentium, HARV. Go to stealth mode before I find a way to unplug you!" I ordered.

"Fine," HARV huffed.

HARV and the backgammon board disappeared. My wall screens changed to a nice black background. Without the shimmering holographic computer or the information-filled interactive wallscreen, my office looked like it was yanked out of some hundred-year-old, classic PI flick. It was an office of a guy who won't take spam from anybody. Besides my antique wood desk and my leather chair that tilted back just the right amount, there was a chair across the desk for a client and a coat rack in the corner by the door. It was all simple and spare with no clutter. I liked it that way.

Some people would even say I'm a throwback to simpler times. I take that as the ultimate compliment. Even though it's never meant to be. The old days, when we relied more on our guts and instincts and less on massive amounts of data and statistics, were better days. Today too many people suffer from information overdose.

"I'm recording this in my journal as a victory," HARV mumbled just audible enough for me to hear it clearly, drawing me back to the present.

I took a deep breath to clear my mind. I was pretty certain HARV was right (as usual); whoever it was didn't have hostile intentions. Experience has taught me that most assassins don't politely wait in the reception area before they kill you. Still, these are strange times. It was possible, however unlikely, that my guest was a very polite trained killer who had mentally overpowered Carol and somehow managed to reprogram HARV into thinking he wasn't a threat. When you are in my line of work and the universe has tattooed "kick me hard" on your butt, there's no such thing as being too paranoid.

I spun around to greet the door as it started to open. I was ready to move my wrist in just the right way that makes my trusty Colt 46 version 3-B pop from up my sleeve into my hand, just in case. I tensed. I took a deep breath and held it. A woman sauntered into the room. This wasn't any woman. For starters, she had more curves than a road up the Alps, only these curves were in all the right places. She was wearing a light red syn fur, micro-minidress trimmed with fluffy white cotton. The entire outfit was accented by her hot red boots with three-centimeter-high heels. On anybody else it would have looked ridiculous but on her it looked sensuous, like she was born, or in this case created, to wear it. Her hair was a frosty white that danced down over her shoulders. Her skin was creamy smooth like virgin snow. Her green eyes twinkled, giving her the appearance of the perfect blend of wise, caring, and oh so voluptuous. I exhaled. I relaxed. I had no choice. There was something warming and calming, yet extremely arousing about her. She was both yin and yang.

"Mr. Johnson, how nice it is to meet you in person."

It didn't take my keen mind to detect who this woman was. "Santana?"

"In person! Ho ho ho," she said. "Sorry, I couldn't resist throwing in the 'ho ho ho.' Though my marketing elves insist that's so last cen."

I stood up and held out my hand. "What brings you this far south?" I asked.

I was familiar with Santana—after all, everybody on Earth is. Santana and her team of highly skilled elves and bots have been operating for over twenty years now. The World Council created them as a way to "instill joy and unity into the entire world's population." Santana is the CEO and all around head honcho of the North Pole Organization. It's their job to coordinate the Holiday, the time of year when everybody in the world is given three gifts.

To my knowledge she had never been in New Frisco. For her to be down here, knocking at my door, something had to be terribly wrong. I noticed that while her lips may have been smiling, her eyes weren't, at least not really. This wasn't a personal visit just to see if I was being naughty or nice.

Santana shook my hand. She had a strong, firm grip, like a person who works for a living, which belied her soft look.

"Mind if I sit?" she asked. "This synthetic fur doesn't breathe well this far south."

"Of course not." I replied, as I motioned to the extra chair across from my desk.

She sat. She wiped a bit of sweat from her brow. "I'm not used to this heat. It's never like this at home." She shrugged. "Still, it comes with the job. It's a clean job but somebody has to do it," she said with a forced smile. She had something to tell me, she was just having trouble getting it out.

"Uh, Santana, I'm sure you came here to discuss something besides fashion."

She smiled. Her smile brightened the room, like a halogen star on top of an old Christmas tree. "I see you're all business." She took out a paper computer from her pocket, unfolded it, and typed a quick note. I hoped she was putting me on the nice list. She finished typing the note then put the computer back. She smiled again. The smile downgraded to a frown. "Zach, I have a problem."

"Go on," I said in my most professional, concerned voice.

"This isn't easy for me to say." She paused again.

"I've noticed."

She took a deep breath. She quickly blurted out, "There's been a killing at the North Pole. I think somebody is trying to destroy the Holiday."

"A killing at the Pole?" My voice was dead serious, though I was having trouble believing what I was hearing.

Santana shook her head. "Actually, there have been two killings. Elves M-778 and M-892."

"Two killings?" I couldn't hold back the surprise in my voice. This type of thing wasn't supposed to happen at the Pole. It was the happiest, safest place on the planet, a haven from the real world. I took a breath to maintain my composure.

"Are you sure the elves were murdered?"

Santana paused for a moment. "Well, I'm not a professional at this sort of thing, but I'm reasonably certain. M-778 was found squished under a five-hundred-kilo bag of toys."

"That could have been an accident, " I interrupted.

"I thought so at first also. But elves aren't prone to accidents. Furthermore, from what we could make out from his mangled body, both his hands and feet were tied. Once I saw that, I ruled out accident."

"Good deduction." I agreed. "What about the other elf?"

"M-892 was poisoned while taking a late-night snack and drink."

"Poisoned?"

"Somebody had mixed wine in the elf's eggnog punch. Wine is deadly to elves."

I couldn't help thinking that wine, if consumed in high enough quantities, could also be deadly—or at least trouble—to non-elves. I managed to keep this thought to myself.

Santana continued, "Luckily, we found M-892 before the next meal cycle or we would have had a major problem on our hands—lots of dead elves. Our operation and the Holiday surely would have been ruined. We're fortunate our lab works so fast and efficiently."

"Have you mentioned any of this to the police?" I asked.

Santana shook her head. "I couldn't. For one thing, the Pole doesn't come under any jurisdiction. For another, if word leaked out that somebody was trying to destroy the Holiday, the public would panic."

"Good thinking." I agreed.

"That's why I came to you, Zach. My elves and security bots are good, but they aren't up to solving a murder mystery. They just aren't designed for that. I need you to find out who is trying to sabotage the Holiday. You have to stop him. The happiness of billions is in your hands. If the Holiday is canceled, the very structure of society itself could be ripped apart. Will you take the job? I'll pay whatever your normal rate is."

I stopped and thought about what she said. At a quick mental glance, I thought this talk of society being ripped apart seemed exaggerated. On reflection, it wasn't totally far-fetched. The entire world had come to depend on the Holiday. It was a time when everybody, regardless of anything, received three gifts from the North Pole. One gift they picked from the Pole's extensive catalog and two specially selected fun gifts were chosen by the Pole's crack staff of elf consultants. If something happened to offset this, who knows how that would impact the world?

My decision was never in doubt. "Of course I'll take the job." I hesitated for a nano then continued. "Since the job's for such a good cause, I'll even do it for half my normal rate."

Santana smiled. For the first time since she had entered my office the twinkle in her eyes matched the one in her smile. "You're a good man, Zachary Nixon Johnson."

"Let's hope I'm good enough."

"Ona Thompson and Sexy Sprockets rave about

your service. You saved the day in their cases. I'm sure you can get equally pleasing results with my case."

"It's your job to be optimistic, Santana."

"Yes, I suppose that is part of the job. Like my elves, I'm made to see the bright side." She smiled again. "You'll start immediately?"

"Yes, I believe my calendar is free. I'll need to make a trip up to the Pole."

Santana nodded. "Yes, of course. We have a bi-monthly seven-day, six-night tour of our facilities. The group is limited to ten people, and we're booked years in advance, but I do have a certain leeway to add an extra person now and then. The tour started yesterday, but I can get you in." She stopped to think for a nano. "So somebody on the tour is involved?"

"I wouldn't bet against it. Particularly if the deaths coincided with the arrival of your visitors."

Santana nodded.

"Would your fiancée Electra like to join you? It might help make the trip look more like a vacation." For a gal whose job it was to supervise a bunch of elves and deliver presents to people, Santana had a pretty good mind for this.

"I'll ask her. She's always complaining that I never take her anywhere. She'd be a help examining the bodies. Though, I don't know how much she knows about elf physiology."

Santana stood up from the chair. "Good. Then I'll count on you for sure. If Electra wants to go, just have your computer call my elves." (Now that's a phrase I never thought I'd hear.) "We'll squeeze her in. The more the merrier."

"No problem, Santana."

"You realize that you have to port to the North Pole."

I was trying hard not think about how the only way
I could get there was to have my molecules scrambled,
then descrambled, and hopefully put back exactly how
they were before they got scrambled.

Santana saw the look on my face. "I know how
much you deplore porting."

Deplore was way too mild of a word. I hate teleporting even more than I do flying while being audited
with Yoko Ono's greatest hits playing in the background as telemarketers try to sell me life insurance.
I inhaled slowly. My logical side knew that porting
was perfectly safe. Studies by scientists who have far
too much time on their hands have shown that the
odds of being killed by porting were far less than the
odds of getting struck by a bolt of lightning while
wearing a rubber suit on a clear day. Despite that, I
couldn't help imagining my top half being sent to the
Pole while my bottom half went to Hawaii. However,
duty called.

I took another deep breath. "No problem, Santana.
The fate of the Holiday is more important than my
fears. Hopefully all I'll lose is my luggage."

Santana smiled. "You don't have to worry about
that. No luggage is allowed at the Pole. We supply
everything! It's part of the price of admission. This
way everybody is equal."

"Sounds reasonable in a Marxist kind of way."

"You do understand what I mean by no luggage,
don't you Zach?" she said leaning forward. It was a
movement that was much sexier than it should have
been.

"Santana, you're paying me five thousand credits a
day. Of course I understand what no luggage means.
It means I don't bring anything with me. Believe me,
I can handle it."

Santana just stared at me. Those big, all-knowing

eyes knew that my brain still hadn't made the connection.

She helped me out. "At the North Pole, everybody
dresses in the same green or red elf suits. Except for
me, of course." She paused, hoping that now I would
see the problem.

I held my hands out. "So I have to wear an elf suit
for a couple of days. I'll survive. As long as nobody
takes pictures or anything."

Santana continued to give me that *aren't you forgetting something?* look. If she wasn't Santana, it would
have been an *aren't you forgetting something, stupid?*
look. "I'll give you a hint, Zach. The suits don't have
a lot of extra space to hide things up your sleeve."

Now it hit home. "My gun! I can't bring my gun!"

"Very good, Zach. You really are the best."

I couldn't tell if she was being sarcastic or overly
optimistic. I chose to believe the latter. "I can live
without my gun. I don't even like the thing. It's just
with some of the characters I deal with a sidearm is
sort of a necessity. I don't really see myself having to
shoot any elves at the Pole though."

Santana just smiled. "Body underarmor is also
restricted."

"No problem, " I told her. "It itches when it gets
too cold. I don't suppose you allow personal computer
communication links?" I asked semi-rhetorically.

Santana shook her head. "Sorry, Zach. While at the
Pole, you have nothing to rely on except your wits!"

She stood up and pointed to a button on the buckle
of her belt. She turned and started to walk away. She
was engulfed in a pool of energy then disappeared.

"What the DOS?" I said.

My wallscreen sprang to e-life. HARV's holographic
form appeared before me.

"From the energy readings I would compute that

was a PPTD, a portable personal teleporting device," HARV said with more than a bit of awe in his voice.

I shook my head. No good could come from portable personal teleporting. I turned my attention to HARV. "What are your initial thoughts on the case?"

"Nothing to rely on but your wits!" He smiled. "Too bad, I always liked the Holiday."

I ignored him and started running through potential culprits in my brain. When a problem like Santana's arises, my first instincts are to check out the big corps. These days there are about four of them that control most of the action on Earth: ExShell, HTech, Enter-Corp, and UltraMegaHyperMart. ExShell is the energy giant; their motto is, "We sell you the sun." HTech specializes in building high-tech devices; their motto is, "Everything is better in bits." EnterCorp controls much of the entertainment industry; their motto is, "We make fun more fun." UltraMegaHyperMart is the largest chain of retail stores in history; their motto is, "If we don't sell it you don't need it." (They allege that 99.9999 percent of the population has purchased at least one item from one of their stores or from their net site.) Of course while all of these megacorps may claim to specialize in a particular area, they are all far to greedy not to dip their toes (and feet, knees, and most of their other body parts) into one another's pools of potential profits.

"Enough chitchat, HARV. Find out if any of the big corps would profit from the demise of the Holiday."

HARV churned for a quarter of a nano. "Done. All of them make far more profit after the Holiday than they do before. It seems the free gifts given by the Pole spawns a frenzy of buying other gifts."

"Dig deeper. Find out if the Holiday upset or re-arranged the apple cart. Maybe one of them makes less more than the others?"

HARV looked at me confused (it's never good a sign when you confuse a supercomputer). "Less more?"

"Companies are greedy. Maybe one of them is jealous that the others grew more than it did."

HARV shrugged. "You humans are strange. I suppose that is possible."

"I also need a breakdown of everyone currently touring the Pole."

"That will take a bit longer. The Pole's computer defenses are quite good."

"Ask Santana for them."

"That's no fun."

"Just do it, HARV." Randy may have been on to something with his concerns that HARV had the potential of becoming too much like me.

"Fine. Done. Her elves say they will have the information for me within hours."

"Why so long?"

HARV shrugged again. It's unnerving to see a supercomputer shrug. "I didn't ask because I'm sure they wouldn't answer. They were quite chipper and peppy though." He paused for a nano. "DOS, I find them even more annoying than I do humans."

"Is it possible for an elf to go bad?"

"I am analyzing the psychological profiles of the elves now."

A picture of a smiling elf face appeared on my west wallscreen.

"It's highly improbable for an elf to 'go bad,' as you put it. While they can be quite irritating, they are built for nothing but kindness and goodness."

"Highly improbable, but not impossible. Correct?"

HARV looked at me and shook his head. "Of course it's possible. Elves are organic sentient beings created by humans. 'Nuff said."

"HARV, you just said '*nuff*."

"Did not."

"Did too."

"Zach, I assure you that while the word *'nuff* may be in my vast vocabulary database, I would not use it."

"Review the last minute."

HARV rolled his eyes. He frowned ever so slightly. "I must have been relating to the person I was interacting with. It's within my parameters you know."

I smiled at him. It wasn't a big smile, just one noticeable enough for him to catch.

HARV shook his head. "I am deleting that word from my database and I will fervently deny ever using it. It's your word against mine. Who do you think the world will believe?"

"How did the elves get to the Pole?" I asked, tipping the conversation back to business.

"They were cloned in New Brazil then teleported directly to the Pole via a special teleporter programmed solely for delivering elves."

"Hmmm."

"What are you thinking, Zach?"

It was a well-publicized fact that the World Council created the elves, and for that matter Santana, in their labs. The WC has extensive resources and capabilities. For better or for worse, they have their hands buried into every aspect of everyday life; in some parts they are buried clear up to their shoulders. Yet the elves were a special job, the kind of job that would take a mind too smart to work on a government salary. They had to have had a consultant. Somebody like my buddy Randy, but Randy would have only been fourteen at the time. He was probably good enough to do the job then, but Randy's an electronics guy not an organics guy. I couldn't see him working outside of his field. I was fairly certain that would go against some sci-geek union rules.

"I'm not sure yet. Do me a favor, though. Try to get the name of whoever led the elves project."

"The elves were made by the Council; they are hush-hush about that kind of thing."

"I'm betting they had help—outside help. I want to find that help and talk to it, if possible."

"Okay, but that could take some time. Information of that type can be tricky to find. Sort of like looking for a specific grain of sand on the beach during a hurricane."

"I have faith in you, HARV." I got up and stretched out. "Net with Randy and tell him I'll be coming by for the thingy."

"The thingy? You want me, the most intelligent cognitive processor in the known worlds, to say *thingy*?"

"Yes," I reaffirmed. "That is correct."

"Do you stay up nights thinking of ways to humiliate me?" HARV asked.

"Nope, it just comes naturally," I told him.

"By thingy, I take it you mean our bio-computer neuron-link lens?"

"Yes, I do. I just don't want to mention that over the net. Just in case."

"I didn't think you liked the bio-com lens. You know, being constantly linked with me."

"On a day-to-day basis, I don't. But for big cases I like to have it."

HARV smiled so openly I could see his teeth. "So you can't solve the case without me, huh?"

"It's not that I can't," I corrected. "I'd be foolish not to use all the tools at my disposal. Besides, I know how YOU need to feel useful."

I moved away from my desk.

"Where are you going?"

"I told you, to see Randy to get the bio-computer

lens and then home. I need to talk to Electra in person about this trip."

I started to the door. "If you find anything interesting, give me a beep." I left my office figuring I had a lot of background work to do before I headed up north.

Chapter 2

Carol was sitting at her desk in my reception room, smiling. Carol, as I mentioned before, is my assistant. She's also Electra's niece. And like her aunt, she's also quite stunning: long, flowing, light brown hair; dark brown eyes; and golden skin all wrapped in a classic dancer's body and governed by a sharp mind. Like her aunt, she's the total package.

"Boy, tío, I've never seen anybody so soft and warm yet sexual," she said with a wide smile. "I'm straight, yet I have to admit, I was quite aroused."

Suddenly the whimsical smile on Carol's face turned to a grimace.

"Get out of the way!" she ordered, ducking behind her desk.

"Carol, I'm the boss here. I'm the one who gives the orders. Why do you and HARV have such a hard time with that concept?"

Carol didn't answer with words. She, much like her aunt, could be very stubborn. She pointed a finger at me then motioned toward her. I flew from where I was standing over her desk and down to the floor.

"Why did you do that?" I questioned sternly, standing up.

"Get down!" she commanded, pulling me with her mind and her body back down behind the desk.

"This is not going to look good on your resu—"

I stopped mid-sentence as my front office door exploded open. A rather large robot came rolling in through the space where the door and I had been seconds ago.

"Oh, never mind," I told Carol, popping my gun into my hand.

I peered over the desk to get a peek at the bot. The good news was I never really liked that door. The bad news was I was about to go mano-on-machino against what I guessed was a deadly bot. It was highly mechanical, with a red tanklike bottom, a green metal cylinder for a body with two claws and a weapon barrel protruding from it. For a head it had a dome sensor with a star on top. Even with the series of twinkling multicolor lights traversing its frame it still managed to look menacing. It seemed to be a cross between a standard battlebot, an ornament, and a madman's all-wheel-drive sport vehicle.

"Now, about my raise?" Carol asked.

"We'll discuss that later, if we're still alive," I answered.

"Give up!" the bot called over to us. "Resistance is futile, vain, useless, hopeless, and fruitless!"

"Great, we're being attacked by a killer thesaurus," I muttered to Carol.

The bot fired an energy beam at the desk we were taking cover behind. The bolt destroyed a good portion of it, leaving my head exposed like one of the gophers in that old whack-a-mole game.

"That was genuine simulated oak!" I yelled at the bot. "Do you have any idea how much that *cost?*"

These days almost everything is made from cheap soy-plastic, but I digress.

"No, I have not been programmed with or given access to any information that is not useful for termination and destruction," the bot replied.

"How come?" I asked.

"Well, because—"

The bot never got to complete its "thought" as I aimed my gun and fired. The projectile passed through Carol's desk and into the bot, destroying them both.

"It never ceases to amaze me how gullible bots can be," I said.

"I feel the same way about humans," HARV said, as he appeared in the middle of the room and began examining the bot.

I turned to Carol and asked, "Is it safe to stand up?" There wasn't much left of the desk to offer protection anyhow.

Carol grimaced again.

"I don't suppose that look means you had a bad burrito for lunch."

Carol shook her head. "There's a backup bot," she said. "Outside, waiting."

"Of course there is," I said.

I stood up and aimed my gun toward the doorway.

"Come out, come out wherever you are, little killer bot!" I called.

"Do you really expect that to work?" HARV asked.

The second bot rolled into the reception area. I had to admit I didn't expect that to work. This bot either had to be dumber than the first one or had something really nasty in store for us. History suggested—no, dictated—it was going to be the latter.

"I have analyzed and neutralized your computerized

weapon," the bot said, in a metallic yet cheery tone. I could have sworn it was snickering at me.

I aimed at the bot and pulled the trigger hoping it was a poor bluff. Nothing happened. I didn't wait around to see the bot's next move. I dove to the ground, this time pulling Carol down with me. The beam from the bot's energy weapon flew over us, singeing my back. Fortunately, my underarmor took most of the damage.

"You have only delayed the inevitable," the bot said, rolling toward Carol and me. "Without your weapon, which was high-tech but lower-tech than me, you stand less than a point five percent chance of survival."

DOS! I knew I was getting too dependent on that computerized gun! What I wouldn't give for a good old-fashioned twin-barrel shotgun. LINUX. I'd even settle for a good slingshot.

The bot slowly rolled closer. It seemed to be enjoying itself, quite confident in the fact that there was nothing I could do to stop it, never stopping to compute that there were other threats to it in the room.

The bot rolled past HARV. Apparently, it didn't consider a hologram to be a concern. Just as the bot passed by, HARV's clothing morphed from the formal gray suit he was wearing into an old-fashioned, two-piece, purple-striped bathing suit. At first glance, it appeared to be a queer choice (especially considering he kept the bow tie), but knowing HARV, I was betting he had a reason for it.

HARV waited until the bot was a meter in front of him and focusing its energy cannon on me.

"Prepare to die!" the bot said.

"Oh, please!" I said. "I've been in tighter situations than this babysitting for my nephew." I didn't know if my underarmor could take a direct hit from the bot's energy cannon, but I wasn't about to let the bot sense any fear. I was confident, or at least fairly certain, that HARV had something up his holographic sleeve.

HARV clasped his hands together, bent his knees, then leaped up two meters off the ground, diving headfirst into the bot. Suddenly, the bot started to spin madly as if it were possessed. And in a way it was.

"No, no, no, this is not right!" the bot sputtered. It whirled around and around, firing shots into my ceiling. It was easy to see why nobody ever wanted to rent the office space above me. "I will drive you out! You cannot control me long! I am a rebel! I am the warrior! I will survive, I will survive!" the bot ranted, semi-singing the last line

I turned to Carol. "You heard the crazy killer disco bot. HARV won't be able to keep him doing three-sixties all day. Time for a little smash and, well, smash."

Carol smiled. Her face glowed with joy. She loved the idea of being able to let the leash off of her powers. She stood up. Her hair rose off her shoulders, crackling with energy. It was an impressive, if slightly scary, sight. She locked her eyes on the bot. The bot stopped shaking. Carol made a fist and motioned upward. The bot flew off the floor, smashing into the ceiling. Carol whipped her hand down toward the floor. The bot came crashing down, shattering into thousands of bot pieces.

HARV appeared in the middle of the room, no worse for wear.

Carol turned and looked at me. She smiled. She reached out her hand and pulled me to my feet. "Now about that raise?" she said, her hair still standing on edge, rippling with energy.

I was pretty certain it was more of a question than

a threat. Though I did have a sudden urge to double both her salary and her lunch hour.

"Are you okay?" I asked.

"That was fun!" she said, as her hair fell back down onto her shoulders.

I walked over to HARV, who was carefully looking over the bot rubble.

"So what do you think?" I asked.

"Those bots didn't like you," he answered.

"Thank you, Sherlock. I mean did you recognize them?"

"Yes," he answered.

Carol chuckled. It was barely audible, but more than adequate for a supercomputer to notice.

"Don't laugh, you'll just egg him on," I told her.

I turned my attention back to HARV. "Come on, get serious! Those things just tried to kill me."

"You should be used to that by now," HARV told me. "As you are so keen to point out, this does happen to you a lot. You are either incredibly unlucky or incredibly lucky, depending on your perspective."

I took a deep breath and counted to ten. This wasn't as annoying as the time HARV decided he was a drill sergeant and would wake me up screaming, "You're a good for nothing lowlife maggot!" at 5 AM for *my own good*, but it was close. "Is my gun working yet?"

"While the bots may have been above your gun in the electronic food chain, I am above them. So, yes, your gun is now functional," HARV gloated.

"Good, because I'm thinking about using it on you!" I said.

HARV looked at me in mock disbelief. He rolled his eyes and sighed. "First, as I have told you seven hundred and twelve times, I am an extensive collection of chips. You would have to shoot me in many places to actually get rid of me. Second, I doubt you would know how to use the potty without me," he said with a tone used to address a small, very dense child.

"I could always trade you in for an older model. One of the BOB series, perhaps." The BOB series was a mass-market line of personal computer-holographic assistants, who are, according to their ad, *like your best friend, only better*. They were all the rage about ten years ago. The interface was supposed to get to know you and then anticipate your every need from recording your favorite HV shows to ordering flick tickets to buying the daily groceries. The idea faded out pretty quickly when it turned out that anticipating a human's needs isn't that easy, as most of us aren't really sure what we need and don't really know what we want.

"Ooh, that's low, really hitting below the old CPU. Okay Mr. Grouchy, those bots were very much like the ones that guard the Pole from outsiders who might be tempted to take advantage of Santana and the elves' kindness."

"Call the Pole and see if they are missing two bots," I told HARV.

He nodded. "Already done. They say they are not."

I took a deep breath. You appreciate breathing more after killer bots try to stop you from sucking in air. "Let's bring these bot parts over to Randy for analysis."

"I doubt that is possible," HARV said.

"Not with that attitude it's not."

HARV pointed to the broken down bots. They started to sizzle, like cold steak on a hot laser griddle but without the pleasant scent and with much more ominous consequences. The bot parts started to vibrate.

"Just my luck. They're going to blow," I said.

HARV shook his head. "You really do worry too much. Calm down. It's not like EVERYTHING is always going to try to kill you."

I looked at the pieces of bots. Now they were quivering and smoking.

"Are you sure this isn't a bad thing?" I asked.

HARV folded his arms. "Just wait for it."

Almost on HARV's mark, every bot part in the room began shrinking, dissolving into nothingness right before our eyes. In a matter of nanos, the bots had disappeared into a puff of white smoke. The smoke dissipated and that was that. It was as if the killer bots were never here.

"See," HARV told me. "Nothing to worry about."

I turned to Carol. "Call maintenance, and use whatever methods necessary to get a new door, a new desk, and the wall repaired."

I turned back to HARV. "Does the Pole make their own bots?"

"No. Santana would have nothing to do with making anything that could be even remotely considered an offensive weapon."

"Then who makes them?" I prompted.

HARV calculated for a nano. "The bots are made by HTech and donated to the Pole. HTech defines it as charity work."

One of their home offices was here in New Frisco (the other was in New Peking), so our paths crossed on occasion. But they had never collided until now.

"Interesting, very interesting," HARV said slowly and annoyingly.

"What?"

"Of the top congloms in the world, HTech's profits have grown the slowest since the advent of the Holiday."

"See, less more," I said. That wasn't a lot to go on. But it was enough to get me started. "Get me an appointment with their CEO, William Doors."

There was complete and absolute silence from HARV. Then he started to chuckle, making it very clear he was laughing at me, not with me.

"Zach, Zach, Zach," HARV said, shaking his head. "My little organic friend. Mr. Doors is one of the richest and busiest men on Earth. I know by some strange quirk in the ripple of reality that is this Universe you happen to be friends with the three richest women on Earth. But Mr. Doors is a man, and he has never needed your services."

I knew what HARV was referring to. Gates knows I heard this enough from Electra; I didn't need it from my computer, too. It's not my fault I have far more female clients than male clients. Hiring a PI is like asking for directions when you are lost—guys just don't do it unless they are very, very desperate (and that desperation usually revolves around a gal). I decided to play stupid.

"What do you mean by that?"

"He won't play the damsel in distress to your knight in underarmor."

"I repeat, what are you talking about?"

"Zach, as Electra has pointed out to you on thirty-two different occasions, your clients are always beautiful women. For some reason, you attract them in times of trouble. My theory is it's either pheromones or they think of you as a pet."

"Thanks, HARV."

"Mr. Doors is a world-class geek with innumerable resources at his disposal. He doesn't now, nor will he ever, need the specialized services you offer. He doesn't know you from any other annoying peon. So there's no way you can just pop into his office and talk to him."

I was sure HARV had a point somewhere in that diatribe of his, but I wasn't going to let that slow me in the least. "Is Doors in town today?"

HARV put his head in his hand, rubbed his temples, and sighed. "You're not going to let this go . . ."

I shook my head no. I wisely decided not to point out that by rubbing his temples he was mimicking me.

"Doors is in town. I checked with his assistant's assistant's computer's computer. He can't even consider thinking about seeing you for the next six months."

"Let's find a way to make it happen a bit sooner. Like in a couple of hours. If you have to prioritize, put that over researching the elves, since we know bots can go bad."

"I am more than capable of doing both," HARV said, hands on hips, head raised high, channeling every angry girlfriend I had ever had.

I patted him on a shoulder that wasn't really there. I started toward the door. At least where the door used to be. I stopped and turned to Carol.

"Oh, and Carol? Thanks for saving my life there."

She smiled. "Don't mention it. Remember this when raise time comes around."

"Now, now. You only saved me from killer bots, it's not like you gave me the winning lottery numbers or anything!"

I gave her a smile, then headed off to Randy's lab.

Chapter 3

It was a quick trip to Randy's AMP Labs, as after he blew up his last lab he moved to a new facility near the old docks. Randy insisted this was because the ocean air helped clear his sinuses. I think it was because the city council wanted to keep him as far away from the general populace as possible. Electra thinks Randy moved there because he wanted to be nearer to me, as I'm his only friend he didn't build from a kit.

From the outside, the new lab, like the old lab, looked just like your run-of-the-assembly-line storage facilities that lined the dock in their heyday. Today, thanks to teleporting, most of these buildings have been turned into monuments to a better time. A time when getting it there overnight would do. Things weren't rushed then like they are today, when everybody absolutely has to have it there in five minutes or less.

When I entered the door my head started to spin. No matter how many times I come to Randy's it still takes me a few nanos to collect myself. The place is a whirlwind of pandemonium in motion. Computers on all the walls, ceiling, and floor flashing away in an infinite stream of info. Bots of all shapes and sizes moving in every direction possible and some directions I didn't think were possible. The benches were packed with test tubes, beakers, mega-powerful Bunsen burners, microscopes, and even a couple boiling cauldrons. I had no idea what Randy did with the cauldrons. I figured it was better not to ask.

Randy's long, lengthy body was stretched out on the floor in the middle of the lab's main work area tinkering away on some sort of cylinder-like device. It didn't look dangerous, but this was Randy, the guy who invented the exploding nuclear marshmallow. I approached with caution.

He didn't notice me, as he was totally engrossed in making his adjustments.

"Ah, Randy?" I said.

No response.

"Randy, I need your help," I said waving my hand in front of his field of vision.

Still no response. DOS, when he focused, he focused.

My initial reaction was to punch him, but I figured that wouldn't go over well. My second thought was to fire a gunshot, but the last time I did that his security robots jumped me. It only takes one cavity search by a robot to convince you that's an experience you don't want to have twice. This called for a more subtle approach.

"E equals mc cubed," I said loudly.

"That's squared," Randy corrected. He stopped working. He looked up. "Is that you, Zach?"

Finally, I had made contact. The team that made first contact with aliens couldn't have been prouder than I was right this instant.

"What are you working on?" I asked, figuring it was best to start with some small talk.

He smiled. "A matter reduction device," he stated proudly. "If this works like I know it will, it will save untold amount of storage space on the planet, plus it will make traveling mega easier. You'll be able to put your suitcases in your pockets!"

Randy, for all his idiosyncrasies, was an upside kind of guy. He only saw (or wanted to see) the good that could come out of his inventions. I was sure he never considered the possible downside of a matter reduction device. Or how something so powerful and meant for good could easily be something so terrible in the wrong hands. Randy and I had talked about this on an occasion or two. He would call this a scientific gray area. He was always quick to point out that forks and knives can be used to cause harm, but that doesn't mean society would have been better of without them. Thinking about this usually gave me a throbbing pain in my temples, so I chalked this up to one of those things that was better just not to think about.

"Thanks, really absolute zero," I told him. "But I need your help."

"I know you didn't just drop by to make idealist small talk," Randy said, giving me about half of his attention as he continued to tinker away.

"Dr. Randy," a very sexy woman's voice, which I knew had to be computer generated, sounded over the room's speaker system, as a computer screen dropped down in front of him. "You have an incoming call."

"I can't take a call right now, I'm busy talking science with Zach."

Randy was the ultimate one-track mind science geek. When his brain latched on to something, it was like a hungry shark grabbing hold of a really plump seal—nothing could break that hold.

"You'll want to take this call," the sexy computer insisted.

"Who is it?" Randy said not even bothering to look at the screen.

"Your mother."

Randy instantly stopped working. He looked up at the screen. He straightened his back and started running his extra long fingers through his bright red hair, trying to give it some semblance of organization.

A woman who looked like a cross between Randy and a prune appeared squinting into the screen.

"Is that you, honey?" Ma Pool said.

"Yes Mother, it is," Randy said with a lilt in his voice he usually reserved for when he was talking about his inventions.

"Why are you blurry? Who's that blurry blob behind you? Is it Zach?"

"Why aren't you wearing your bionic vision enhancers, Mom?"

She shook her head. "You know I don't believe in that high-tech fooey."

"Mom, I invented that fooey for you."

She leaned into the screen almost touching it. "You did? How sweet."

A little robot rolled up to Ma Pool holding a pair of what could only be described as eyes in its claws. The robot's arms extended up and placed the eyes over Ma Pool's real eyes. She blinked. She smiled.

"You're too skinny. You haven't been eating," she told Randy. "You're nothing but bones and brain held together by pale-bordering-on-albino skin. And you need more sun. Not too much, mind you, but more. I've seen beached beluga whales who have been dead for a month that have more color than you." Ma Pool looked past Randy. "Oh, hi, Zach."

"Hi, ma'am."

"You're not getting my boy in trouble are you?"

"No, ma'am."

"Well you should, he needs to get out of the lab more."

"Yes, ma'am."

"Are you still dating that nice Electra girl?"

"Yes, ma'am."

"Does she have a sister?"

"Why, ma'am, are you interested?"

Randy glared at me and stomped his foot.

"I'm one hundred and ten years old, my boy. Maybe in my younger experimental days, but these days I'm too old to swing either way," she said. "I'm talking about for my boy."

"I do okay for myself, Mom," Randy protested.

Ma Pool waved a finger at the screen. "I'm talking about real flesh and blood women. Not ones you have to clone."

"Clones are flesh and blood, Mom."

I looked at Randy.

"Long story," he told me under his breath. "Science can be a lonely mistress."

"I want grandkids that don't come out of a test tube or a robotics lab. I'm not getting any younger, you know," Ma Pool said.

Now Randy shook his head. "Ma, I sent you money for a regeneration treatment."

"Fooo-ey," Ma Pool spat. "I don't believe in that elitist crap."

"Mom, I want you around to meet my kids," Randy said.

The thought of Randy procreating scared me on far too many levels to count.

"If that happens, and I know it's a big IF, then I will consider it." Ma Pool looked at the screen. She forced herself to smile. "Dinner at the regular time this Sunday?"

"Of course," Randy said. "I'll bring the wine."

"Nah, I'll get the wine, your taste is crap. Love you, son."

"Love you, Mom."

"Bye, Zach. Find a nice girl for my Randy."

I waved to the screen as it went blank.

"I've received two Nobel Prizes; cured three diseases; won the 2050, 2052, and 2054 New Frisco Rock, Paper, Scissors Championship; I have over one hundred patents; and bowled a three hundred, but all she cares about is me mating," Randy said.

"You bowled a three hundred?"

"I was using a bionic eye, an arm enhancer, and a pin-sensing ball but it was impressive nonetheless," Randy insisted with far more emotion than he usually had.

"She just wants what she thinks is best for you, buddy."

Randy composed himself. "Now where were we?" he asked, scratching his head and ruffling his hair again. "Ah, yes, now I remember. HARV told me about your visit. I take it now you want the new and improved biorganic-neuro-link-holo-projector-lens."

"I hope that's not what you've decided to call it!" I said.

"Still not sure, I'm toying with it. I like the NIBO-NOLIHPOL acronym. I think it's got a groovy kind of sound. Though the whole point is moot if I patent it. It kind of defeats the purpose of a secretive organic chip that links a human and a computer and is totally undetectable to scanners to be on the public records as existing." He paused for a nano. He sighed. "Oh, well, nobody ever said science had to be easy. And marketing, whoa! Now that's tricky. Einstein never had these problems. It was so much easier in those days! The average investor was so impressed with little things like atomic bombs and theories of relativity that—"

"Ah, Randy, hate to interrupt you when you're rambling *poetically,* but I could really use the—hope you don't mind if I just call it the link."

Randy stopped his dissertation and returned to matters at hand. "Ah yes, the link . . ." His eyes searched through the chaos that was his lab. "Now, now where did I put that?"

He examined his lab coat pockets, his pants pockets, his left shirt pocket, his right shirt pocket. He smiled. He reached into his left shirt pocket and produced the neuron-link. He showed it to me.

It still didn't look like much to me, just a small contact lens with some computer circuitry jutting out of it.

"You do remember how it works?" he asked, as he handed it to me.

"I put it my eye. It digs into my eye causing piercing pain. It drills deep into my brain, causing excruciating pain. It then links my brain to HARV," I said.

"Good, you do remember!" Randy said, brushing some of his stringy red hair off his face. "I was going to work on reducing the pain but the funding for it fell through." He shrugged. "Like they say, no pain no gain."

"Do I need to do anything special?" I asked.

Randy shook his head. "Nope. Now that it's calibrated to your brain, it's almost foolproof."

"*Almost* foolproof?"

Randy shrugged. "Nothing is totally foolproof, Zach. It's been my experience that fools are inventive and ingenious with their foolishness."

I held the lens up to my eye. I took a deep breath.

I took another deep breath. I remembered the last time I put this thing into my eye it was more painful than watching old political speeches while listening to the "Macarena" and having a root canal performed by an angry, clumsy chimp. Still, duty called. I slapped the lens onto my eyeball quickly, my logic being if I did it fast enough, maybe it wouldn't hurt. My logic proved faulty. It felt like that angry chimp was filling ten thousand cavities in my mind using a dull, rusty drill and making sure he hit as many nerves as possible. Starting at my eye, the drilling traversed my skull, increasing in magnitude as it spread, leading me to believe that if my head exploded, it would be a good thing. Then it all stopped.

"That wasn't so bad now, was it?" Randy said.

"I swear that hurt more than the last time!" I told him.

"It probably did," he agreed. "I modified the lens some, so HARV could have instant access to your synapses."

"You could have warned me!"

"True," he agreed. "Does it still work?"

A beam of light shot out from my eye. The numbers 1, 2, 3 appeared, then changed into HARV's face. It's an interesting feeling having your eye used like an old-fashioned movie projector.

"It works!" HARV said. "Nice job, Dr. Pool!"

"Now turn yourself off," I said. "Until we get to the Pole, stick with normal means of communication."

"Zach, with you there is no such thing as normal communication," HARV told me before he beeped out.

Chapter 4

I left Randy's office before he could use me as a
guinea pig for any other new gadget. I got in my car
and fired her up. So far things had been going as well
I could hope. Which in my world meant nobody had
tried to kill me for the last hour. I took advantage in
the lull in activity to wax poetic about my car. My
current vehicle of choice is very sweet, slightly modified, 1969 cherry red Mustang convertible. I love driving a car nearly as much as I despise flying in hovers.
Why? Well for one thing, I hate heights. I often say
if men were meant to fly we would have been born
with either feathers and wings or at the very least
parachutes that pop out of our butts. Second and more
important, when I was driving I had control of my
destiny. I was the one running show. Sure some hovers
give their drivers the appearance that they are driving,
but there are so many computer failsafes and backup
systems that the human usually just points and clicks
on a destination and the hover's computer does the
rest. When I'm driving I'm the one making the decisions. My fate is in my hands. That's the way I like it.

HARV popped into the dashboard screen. Like I said, the Mustang is "slightly modified."

"Where we off to now?" he asked.

"Any luck getting in touch with HTech?" I asked.

"I only reached the front-level people and machines, and they all have said no way."

"That's no good," I said. "I need to talk to the big guy! Have Carol talk to them and do her thing."

HARV shook his head. "I already thought of that. HTech is psi-proof, as only machines and people with heavy psi blockers interact with the general public."

There had to be a way to see Doors. Sure he was rich and powerful, but deep down (actually, not all that deep down) he was still a geek. Kind of like a greedier, slightly less socially inept version of Randy. I quickly changed directions.

"Where are we going?" HARV asked.

"To HTech headquarters!" I told him.

"Right, like you have a chance of getting in."

We drove on for fifteen minutes, and all the while I had to listen to HARV lecture me on how I didn't have any chance of getting in to see William Doors, the president of HTech. I ignored him until we neared HTech's main gate.

"Okay HARV," I told him, "cover me with a hologram?"

"Of who?" HARV asked.

"Doors may be rich and powerful but deep down he's still a geek. And what's the thing all geeks respond to?"

"Computers."

"Process some more."

"Different computers."

"Keep processing."

"Classic comics."

"Keep working on it, HARV."

"Bikini models."

"Try again."

"Old Monty Python skits?"

I was proud of HARV for picking up on that. I was really starting to rub off on him. But his guessing was so random I decided to give him a hint.

"Think about Randy earlier today."

"Their moms! Geeks are almost always momma's boys."

I touched my finger to my nose. "Vingo! I'll go in as Ma Doors."

Luckily for me, Ma Doors was almost as famous as her son. She, with her eccentric ways, had become the darling of the media. She had recently been hitting the talk show circuit—*Oprah-clone*, *The Instant Buzz*, *The World Right Now*—to promote her new book, *Still Super Sexy at Seventy-seven*, which was the sequel to her bestseller *How to Raise a Billionaire*.

"Do a scan of all the public security cameras to see if you can find her."

"I can't do that," HARV insisted from my car's screen.

I just stared at him. He stared at me. He crossed his arms. I knew he could do it. He knew he could do it. The problem was this was one of those legal gray areas. The cameras were only supposed to be accessed by the proper authorities.

"I'm doing this for the good of all mankind," I said.

HARV raised an eyebrow. "No, *I'm* doing this for the good of all mankind." He shook his head and mumbled in a New York accent, "I don't get no respect."

"What did you say?"

"You heard me."

"You sounded like Rodney Dangerfield."

"I knew you'd appreciate that," HARV said.

"Why Dangerfield?"

HARV lowered his eye. "You'll laugh."

"No, I won't."

"You'll make fun of me."

"I'll try not to."

"I missed being connected to your brain," HARV said quickly, practically too quickly for me to understand.

"Really?"

"I'm loath to admit this, but it taught me to appreciate humor. When I wasn't hooked up to you, I was forced to look for another source of inspiration. I found that Mr. Dangerfield and I have a lot in common."

I decided not to touch that. I was happy that HARV had learned the value of humor.

"So, have you found her?" I asked.

"Yes, she just stopped at the 700-1100 to buy a Slurpee," HARV said. "Believe me, I am not making that up."

"Great, then throw the disguise over me and we're a go!"

"This still isn't going to work," HARV said. "I'm sure the guards know this isn't Mrs. Doors' vehicle! I doubt she even has a land-based granny vehicle."

"Perhaps, but I'm sure none of them will have the guts to question her about it. She's an eccentric old woman. She's prone to change cars. Besides, who doesn't love the classic Mustang? And only a very hot grandma could handle this car."

The HTech tower was a tall, black, seemingly windowless pointed monolith that shot two hundred stories up into the sky on the outskirts of New Frisco. The building was so tall that it was visible from any place in Frisco. Still I was totally unimpressed with it. Rumor has it that William Doors designed the building himself. The guy certainly didn't make his fortune by being creative. The building reminded me (and most adolescent boys) of a part of the male anatomy. My hunch was Doors was trying to compensate for his own inadequacies.

The entire compound was protected by an electric energy fence that ran its perimeter. I wasn't sure if it was to keep unwanted visitors out or the workers in.

I drove up to a little square armored guard post that sat just outside of the protected area. I rolled down my window. A short, stocky, human guard wearing computerized body armor came out to greet me. I swear all these guards look alike. It's as if rich people can shop at Guards Я Us.

I smiled at the approaching guard.

"Oh, I'm sorry, ma'am. I didn't realize it was you . . ." he told me. "You'll be allowed right in after the psi scan!" The guard pushed a button on his wrist communicator.

A tall, slim, female guard with short hair and a long nose that matched her body came out of the post. She reminded me a Doberman pinscher, I'm not sure why. She had to be a psi.

This could have posed a problem. In the past, my link with HARV has made me hard to scan which was good. Plus, my vast experience with psis has taught me a little trick—psis hate humming. Nothing drives them out of your mind faster than humming the tune from some old classic. Only this case, I didn't want to drive her right out of my mind. I needed to convince her that I was Ma Doors. I wasn't sure how to pull that off.

The words "don't worry" flashed in front of my

eyes. "I have run an analysis of all of Ma Doors' purchases over the last twenty years and every show and song she has downloaded. I have concluded that if you hum the theme to *The Love Boat*, version III, the psi will pass you as her."

The psi locked eyes me.

I started to hum. *"Love is ready to cruise. Come on board. There's no way you can lose. Take a chance. Give love more than a fleeting glance. The love boat is ready to sail again. The loooove boat . . ."*

The psi pulled back and held her head. "It's her," she said. "It's definitely her."

The first guard smiled at my confirmation. He pushed another button on his wrist communicator. The energy field guarding the gate disappeared.

I drove in and parked in a VIP space. I looked up the high-rise. Even up close I still wasn't impressed. I got out of my car.

"You do have a map of this place, correct?" I asked HARV.

A map of the building appeared in the corner of my eye.

"Cool!"

"Just follow the arrows to Mr. Doors' door," HARV told me. "And hope that the real Ma Doors doesn't chug down her Slurpee and head here . . ."

I walked in the front door and waved to the receptionist.

He politely smiled and waved back.

"Unlike most big shots," HARV whispered, "Mr. Doors likes his office on the first floor. I think he's like you—scared of heights."

I didn't respond to that. I'm not scared of heights. I'm just scared of falling from heights. It adds to my vulnerability, which is part of my charm. I'm tough enough to be secure with my flaws.

The arrows in front of my eyes pointed down a long hall to the right.

I followed the arrow, always having a friendly smile for all the employees I passed.

An X formed on a door at the end of the hall. I was certain it was Mr. Doors' office. As a matter of fact, it seemed to be the only actual office I encountered. Everything else was just open bullpen space. I walked up to his secretary's desk.

She looked up from her work.

I gave her the once over like any good mother should. I admired Mr. Doors' taste. The secretary was bit pale and too porcelain perfect for my taste, but she was quite lovely, with delicately chiseled features.

"Do you wish me to alert Mr. Doors to your presence?" she asked me.

I put a finger to my mouth, whispering her to silence.

"Oh, I see. You want to surprise him," the secretary said, as I walked by her to the door.

If you only knew, I smiled. I walked by and opened the door to Mr. Doors' office. It was a BIG office. You knew this guy was the boss.

"Debbie, I asked not to be disturbed!" he said. He looked up and saw his mom coming toward him. His anger turned to pleasure, rearranging his mouth into a smile.

Doors was kind of cold, square, and bland looking, much like his building. His hair cut looked like his mom had done it by placing a bowl over his head and trimming around the edges. You would think a billionaire could afford to get a better cut. Then again, when you're a billionaire, why bother?

"Oh, sorry, Mom, I didn't know it was you," he said.

"Nope," I said in my own voice, pretty much blowing my cover.

"What's the meaning of this?" he demanded, as he carefully pushed a button on his desk.

"HARV holo-off!" I said.

There was a slight shimmer. I looked at Mr. Doors looking at me.

"Zachary Johnson, to what do I owe this *honor*?" he said, kind of choking on the honor part.

"Sorry to bother you," I said. "I just need some info, and I'm in too much of a hurry to go through other channels."

"Oh, really?" he said, raising an eyebrow.

"I understand you and your corporation made the bots for the Pole," I told him, getting right to the point.

He remained calm.

"Of course. That's public knowledge," he said. "We did it because though we may be a huge corporation, we place the good of the entire world in front of our profits."

I smiled at him. He returned my smile. There was a bit of awkward silence.

"Okay, maybe we place the good of the world beside our profits." He shrugged. "What does this have to do with anything?"

"Two of your guardbots attacked me today," I said.

His eyes never wavered from mine, and his voice was calm, deliberate, and steady when he said, "I assure you Mr. Johnson, I know nothing about that. Besides, those are not our guardbots. They were a gift to the Pole."

I walked across the room (it took a few minutes) and leaned on his desk. It was a bullying technique. Doors might have been rich but he was still a slight man. I thought maybe I could intimidate him with my size advantage.

"Well, these bots must have been from a separate lot. According to the Pole, none of their bots are missing."

"Then why are you bothering me at all?"

"I'm betting you have a few spare bots around like those at the Pole," I said, leaning forward.

"Why would we have spare North Pole guardbots around? Those are old models. And why would we send them after you?"

"My question exactly. I need to—"

"I'm sorry," Mr. Doors interrupted, "but I've given you more time than I should have. If my nieces and nephews weren't fans, I would have had you tossed out long ago. Maybe even had you killed."

I felt a hand on my shoulder. A very strong hand.

I looked over my shoulder, up the arm, and at the face attached to that hand. It was the porcelain-perfect secretary.

"Let me escort you to the door," she said, making it very clear that it was an order, not a request.

"Don't you want a voicegraph?" I asked her boss.

She yanked me away from the desk with one arm.

"DOS!" I told her. "What do you do, live at the gym?" Then it hit me, porcelain-perfect face, pale while skin. I sniffed her. "You don't smell at all," I said.

"Thank you," she told me, as she shoved me out the door and down the hallway.

"Yes, but the thing is, you should smell a little. I mean it's the middle of a hard day, you've been running around, and now you're pushing around this eighty-five-kilo guy like he's a microchip. You should be sweating some."

"I am a woman. Women do not sweat, they perspire," she corrected, as drove me toward the door to the outside.

"You don't even do that do you?" I told her. "You're a DOSing android, aren't you?"

She placed one hand on the neck of my jacket, the other on the belt of my pants. She lifted me up. She pulled me back. "Door open!" she commanded.

She flung me out the door.

I made a very undignified thud to ground five meters from the door. I turned to her.

"I'll take that as a 'yes,' " I said.

"If you mention this to anybody, we will sue you for slander!" she told me.

"But it's the truth," I said.

"So?" She laughed. "We employ almost half of the lawyers and greeting card salesmen left in world! You would need more than the truth on your side!" She smiled. "Now if you don't mind, I have real work to do." She started to walk away. She stopped and turned to me. "Oh, by the way, I do work out at Maria and Arnold's every day at 1800. Stop by, I would love to go a round with you in the ring." Then she walked away.

I got up and limped to my car. I guess I shouldn't have let that catch me so off guard. After all, I know that ExShell has experimented with illegal human-skin-toned andriods. So it only made sense that HTech would be doing the same thing. Plus, if the World Council ever called them on it (which they'd never do), I would bet credits to donuts that HTech's lawyers would argue that "her" skin tone isn't really human color. I was sure I had learned something from this experience, I just wasn't sure what.

I headed to my car. "Well, I guess that could have gone worse," I said under my breath to HARV.

"Define 'worse,' " HARV said.

"Broken bones would have been worse. I consider any hostile meeting I can walk away from with nothing broken and only my ego bruised a success."

"I wouldn't be adding this to the victory column quite yet," HARV said.

I didn't like the sound of that.

I heard a throat clear behind me.

I stopped walking and turned around. There stood a big burly man and a bigger, burlier woman. Even if they weren't dressed in plain blue uniforms, I could have guessed by the cold stone looks on their faces they were security.

"Each of their left arms are bionic," scrolled by my eyes, a warning message from HARV.

I held up my hand in the stop position.

"What gives here guys? Mr. Doors said I wasn't to be hurt."

"We work for Mrs. Doors, senior," the man said.

"What does Ma Doors have against me?" I asked.

"The security computer forwarded Mrs. Doors the image of you entering the building disguised as her. She wants you to know she would never wear an outfit like that," the woman said. She then pounded her fist into her bionic palm. "She wants us to make sure you don't do anything like that again."

"Don't worry, I won't," I reassured them.

The woman grabbed me by the shirt and lifted me up with one arm.

"Good," she said.

"Are these bullies bothering you, citizen?" an all too familiar voice said from above and behind me. I didn't have to turn around to know it was Twoa Thompson.

For those of you who don't know, Twoa is one of the world famous Thompson quads. The four genetically perfected sisters were created by Dr. Dave

Thompson, who created the girls a few years before he created a potential doomsday device that was so menacing the World Council bought the rights to the machine from him (for a HUGE sum of money) and then had his memory erased. Twoa thinks of herself as a superhero called Justice Babe. She walks (well, flies) around in a skimpy costume fighting evil. Not just fighting it, but crushing it, and usually causing more harm than good. The odd thing is she's not even the most eccentric one in her family.

"It's okay, Twoa. I have it under control," I said.

Twoa landed next to us. She looked striking and frightening as ever in her full Justice Babe garb. I swear she had even less skirt and more breasts than the last time I ran into her.

"This is private property," the female guard said to Twoa.

Twoa shook her head. "That doesn't give you the right to womanhandle good citizens and champions of justice."

Twoa grabbed the woman's bionic arm and squeezed. I heard circuitry smash—or more accurately squish—causing the guard to release her grip on me.

The male guard rushed to his female counterpart's aid. He clubbed Twoa on the back with his bionic arm. The arm smashed on contact. Twoa was no worse for wear.

"Twoa, don't hurt them!" I said quickly. "I had this worked out. They were only doing their jobs!"

Twoa faced the guard and lifted her elbow as if she was going to give him an elbow smash in the face. Instead, she stopped and just held her elbow up, giving the guard a whiff of the pheromones under her arm.

The guard's angry expression instantly turned into one of complete admiration . . . actually worship is probably a more fitting word. He looked at Twoa as if she were a goddess. And quite frankly, to him she very well may have been. He fell to one knee and gazed longingly at her.

Twoa then lifted her other arm, giving the ailing and flailing female guard a subtle whiff. The guard's eyes glazed over, and she, too, fell to a knee.

"What can I do to please you, master?" she asked.

Twoa ignored her and turned her attention me.

"Are you okay, Zach?" she asked.

"I'm fine. Thanks," I said. I looked at the dumbfounded guards. "How long will they be like that?"

Twoa shrugged. "Who knows? A day, a week, forever. Not my problem. That'll teach Ma Doors for cheating me in celebrity strip poker."

We started to walk to my car. I figured it was best to move out of the area just in case any more HTech security people were foolish enough to come and engage or enrage Twoa.

"What brings you here?" I asked.

"I understand you were asking about me?" Twoa said.

"I wasn't," I said.

"Your computer was poking around looking for information," Twoa said. Twoa put her arm around me. It wasn't so much a gesture of friendship as it was a maneuver to hit me with some of those pheromones. "Why?" she asked.

My head started to spin, but I liked it. I looked at Twoa. She was always beautiful and touched up picture perfect, but today she seemed extra beautiful, extra perfect. Her skin was smooth and velvety purple like her creator had intended. Her eyes were big, brown, gorgeous and could wilt a man (literally). Her hair was brunette with just a hint of gold, as if it were streaked by the sun. It danced playfully around her shoulders. Those big lush creamy lips of hers—what I wouldn't give for the honor of being her lipstick! And that body, that unbreakable, super toned yet soft as velvet body! Zow, that's probably the only time in my life I've used the word "velvet" twice in the same minute. That just shows how special Twoa was. Far more beautiful than her sisters Ona and Threa, she was also a lot smarter and much nicer. She had much more pleasant breath, as well.

"Woah!" HARV shouted inside my head. "She's trying to turn you into one of her lovesick puppy slaves!"

"I don't mind," I said, out loud.

"I'm shocking you, and I'm turning off your nasal receptors," HARV said.

"Youch!" I screamed, as the current rushed through my body. I leaped forward and away from Twoa's grasp.

Twoa smiled. "Ah, your computer inside your brain. I forgot about that."

I composed myself quickly. I had to react before Twoa tried to do something more drastic.

"Really, Twoa, I don't know what you're talking about. There's no need for you to try to bend my will."

I've seen Twoa turn a dozen well-armed killers (out of work actors) into floor mats in under ten seconds. There was no way I wanted to upset her. She smiled and gave me a pat on the shoulder.

"Just tell me why your computer was talking to my dad, ah, computer, ah, I'm never really sure what to call him."

(Twoa's dad had his memory downloaded into their house computer as a safeguard against the World Council erasing his mind. It's a long story that's been told before.)

"Twoa, at the risk of being twisted in a pretzel, I have no idea what you are talking about."

"My old science project," she said sincerely.

I tilted my head and looked at her. "You've totally lost me."

Twoa gave a heavy sigh. The force of her breath almost knocked me over. "Your computer was asking my dad, who is now my computer, if he had any idea who designed the elves for the North Pole."

"Yes, that's true," I said.

"It was me," Twoa said, thumping on her ample chest (and making my heart pound). "They were my middle school science project."

We reached my car, which was a good thing, because I need it to lean on.

"You designed the elves?" I said.

Twoa smiled proudly. "Yes, back in my science nerd days. Why do you care?"

Twoa leaned in close to me, very close. She started slowly massaging my back. It felt good.

"I don't need pheromones to get what I want," Twoa said.

"Twoa, I can't tell you," I said melting under her grip.

"Two of the elves have been killed," HARV said from my wrist communicator.

Twoa stopped her massaging.

"What?"

"HARV!" I shouted.

"I had to do it, Zach," HARV said. "You wouldn't be much good to anybody if Twoa turned you into a pile of mush. Don't worry. Nobody else heard because Twoa's sending out so much negative energy, she's knocked out everybody else in earshot."

Twoa took a step back from me and nodded. "He's right, you know."

It took a nano for my head to stop spinning. I wasn't sure what had it rotating faster, Twoa's phero-

mone attack or her words. Come to think of it, it was
exceedingly quiet. I glanced around. Sure enough, all
people, animals, or machines for as far as I could see
were on the ground, curled in a fetal position.

"You designed the elves," I said slowly.

I looked at HARV's face in my communicator. "So
much for your theory that elves can't go bad."

Twoa thought about that for about a nano. She
frowned. "Hey!" She placed her fist under my chin.
"I resent that. Take it back now, before I decide to
make you into my permanent footstool."

I shook my head. "Come on, Twoa, even you have
to admit you are a bit of a nutcase."

She took a step back. She wasn't used to people
(besides her sisters) having the nerve to talk back to
her.

"I'm not a nutcase. I'm rich, so, if anything, I'm
eccentric," she said defensively.

"Eccentric? You walk around dressed as a superhero fighting crime. You even sleep with your boots
on!"

"Crime knows no time," she said. "I have to be
ready to leap into action at a moment's notice. Besides, I take my boots off once a week to let my feet
air out." She stopped to think about what she had
said. She put a finger to her lips. "Okay, I'm definitely
on the eccentric side."

"Twoa, you are so far past eccentric, you can't even
see it from where you are standing with a supra-
thermal electron telescope."

"What about my supervision?" she asked.

I put my hand on her shoulder, taking the chance
that she wouldn't rip it off and hand it to me.

"The point is Twoa, if you made the elves, I can't
rule out the possibility that they are as crazy and as
capable of destruction as you are."

Twoa put her index finger under my chin and lifted me off the ground, again. "Zach, you have to believe me when I tell you this," she said.

"You've got my undivided attention."

"I worked hard on the elves. In those days, before Daddy's memory got erased, I wanted to be a great scientist like him. Sure, I had a setback or two, but I swear to you, Zach, on my tremendous bosoms, that I perfected the elves to be capable of nothing but kindness."

I looked down at her. The first thing that caught my eye were those tremendous bosoms. Being lifted up like this gave me quite the eyeful. With great difficulty, I moved my gaze up to meet hers. I saw something in Twoa I had never seen in her before: sincerity.

"I believe you," I said.

"Good," she said with a smile, as she lowered me to the ground. She patted me firmly on the shoulder. If it wasn't for my body armor, she probably would have dislocated it. "Is there anything else I can do for you?"

"What do you know about Santana?" I asked.

Twoa shook her head. "I didn't have anything to do with her."

"Do you know who did?"

Twoa shook her head again. "Sorry, Zach. I was too busy with my elves project to pay attention to anything else."

"I appreciate your help, Twoa."

"Of course you do," she said with a wink. "Anything else?"

"Not at the moment," I said.

"Very well," she said. "If you need me, just activate the Justice Babe signal."

She put an arm up in the air and flew off.

"I don't think I want to know what the Justice Babe signal is."

I sniffed the air. It was eerie not to be able to smell anything. I felt like my nose should be stuffy, but it wasn't.

"HARV, turn my nose back on please," I said.

I felt a slight tingle in the back of the head.

"Can you smell again?" HARV asked. "Now, that's a phrase you don't say very often."

I was hit by a sudden rush of my olfactory senses: the flowers that lined the walkway to the building, the sweat of the beaten (and still in fetal position) guards, the slight scent of exhaust.

I got in my Mustang and started her up. HARV popped into the dash window.

"I'll drive," he told me. "I know you take pride in your driving, but your head still may not be totally clear from Twoa playing with it."

"Twoa and you," I said as HARV pulled the car out of its parking spot. (Okay maybe my car is more than slightly modified.)

HARV frowned. "I do not 'play' with your mind. I perform certain functions to increase its efficiency."

"You say tomato, and I say potato," I said.

"So Sherlock, what have you concluded besides the fact that androids shouldn't have a need for deodorant, yet Twoa does?" HARV asked, trying unsuccessfully not to snicker.

"I'm still processing that info," I told him.

"I knew you wouldn't learn anything from just barging into the man's office," HARV lectured.

"I needed to judge his reactions to my questions. That type of thing is much easier to gauge in person, especially when you don't know somebody," I said, defending my actions.

"So what do you conclude?" HARV prodded.

"He seemed sincere," I concluded.

"Of course he seemed sincere!" HARV said. "He's a professional businessman! It's his job to seem sincere. DOS! Zach! You can be so naive at times."

"Did you do a voice scan on him?" I asked.

There was silence.

"Well, HARV?"

"I did."

"And?"

"His voice waves and facial patterns indicated that he was quite surprised by your news."

"See, so we learned that," I said.

"But he's a smart guy. He obviously knows you were scanning him, so he might have anti-scanning software, just to throw us off track," HARV said. There was another slight pause. "DOS! I should have scanned for holographic activity. For all we know, he had on a holographic cover!"

"HARV, I don't think the man sits in his office under a holographic cover," I said.

"Probably not. Too much exposure is bad for the brain."

"I think you would have noticed if he activated a hologram while we were in the room," I added.

"True," HARV said. "I am exceedingly smart." HARV processed for a nano longer. "Still, he's a professional businessman. We can't rule out that he's also an expert liar, and therefore can't rule out HTech as a suspect."

"They may be a suspect right now, but we have to look at all the options. ExShell would really gain from setting HTech up to look like the bad guys," I pointed out. HARV was great at cranking out facts but he had a tendency to jump to conclusions and then stick to those conclusions, as if they were attached to him with super-duper glue. I took it as my duty to teach him to think outside the CPU.

ExShell and HTech were longtime rivals. Over the years, their competition has grown so fever pitched their executives can't even be in the same room together without breaking out in a brawl or lawsuit. I knew this and so did HARV.

HARV calculated for a bit. "True . . . I guess they are the obvious choice. But there are times when the obvious choice is the right choice."

"Yes, but dead elves don't seem to fit the style of either HTech or ExShell. It's too subtle."

"That is a good point," HARV conceded.

"Plus, by coming here we did learn that Twoa helped create the elves. Therefore, we can't rule out the possibility that elves can snap."

"True, again." HARV said.

"There are still a lot of possibilities," I said. "We still have the unknown wild-card factor."

HARV looked at me.

"The unknown wild-card factor? Which is?"

I shrugged. "If I knew, it wouldn't be unknown. Still there's always something or somebody you don't think of until it walks right up and slaps you in the face."

"Yes. Humans are so unpredictable that even I can't always deduce with total reliability and accuracy the probability of their actions," HARV said.

This was the second time today he admitted that there was something he didn't totally understand. Despite Randy's new shielding, I was still rubbing off on him.

"I do have some good news for you," HARV said.

"And that is?"

"Esteemed World Council Member Sexy Sprockets will make time to see you today. She can fit you in from 16:15 until 16:19."

"Four minutes?"

"She's a busy girl. You should be glad you get any face time at all."

"Well then, I guess I have time to grab a quick bite to eat."

Chapter 5

I was sitting at a table in one of my favorite outdoor delis, sipping on an ice tea (I was on duty), and munching on a roast beef on rye. I was trying to mentally piece together the parts of the puzzle I had so far, attempting to get an idea of what the solution to this puzzle would look like.

The things I did know I could count on one hand. HTech would certainly gain something from the demise of the Holiday, but was it enough to risk ripping apart the moral fiber of the world? They were a pretty successful company as it was, so why sink the boat to success? Maybe another company was trying to shake things up? A small upstart looking to make its mark? Or another one of the big guys just trying to screw over HTech?

Having learned that Twoa was the one responsible for the creation of the elves didn't put my mind at ease at all. After all, this was a woman who would stop jaywalkers by knocking out everybody on the street. She was only a kid at the time she created the elf template. Who's to say she couldn't have screwed up and incorporated a bit of the homicidal maniac in there?

I hoped that once I got to the Pole some of this groundwork I was laying would pay off.

I looked up to see a little guy with an old-fashioned handlebar mustache coming toward me. He was wearing a black suit that was at least one size too small for him. He waddled like a penguin.

"Are you Zachary Johnson?" he asked, as he drew within a meter.

"I am."

He reached into his jacket and pulled out a laser pen.

"That's not really a laser pen," HARV said in my brain.

"Good, I hate signing autographs," I thought back.

"How do you feel about death threats?"

"They are slightly more annoying than autographs. Why?"

"The pen is actually a hand laser with a holo-projector to make it look like a pen," HARV said.

Hand weapons with holographic projectors are all the rage these days. They were especially handy for people who were terrible shots. It allowed them to get up close and personal with their targets so they could kill at close range. I tipped the table up to use it as a shield and dropped under it just as he fired. The shot blew a hole in the table but missed me.

People screamed and headed for cover.

"For future reference," HARV said, "whenever anybody asks if you are Zachary Johnson, you should deny it. Maybe even claim that you spit on Zachary Johnson."

"Not helping here, HARV."

I popped my gun into my hand. Problem was, there were still too many civilians in the way to fire indiscriminately. Luckily (and luck is a really relative term here), I didn't have to. The man simply peeked around the table I was hiding behind and pointed his pen-gun at me. Only a truly lousy shot would make such an overt move. He certainly wasn't a professional—at least not a highly paid one. It could also mean that he didn't want to hurt anybody else or that he just hated me so much he wanted to kill me at close range. Frankly, it didn't really matter.

I put my hands up over my head to let him know I wouldn't hurt him, giving him one last chance to back down.

"Woah, cool the warp engines, buddy," I said in my most calming voice. "Let's talk this out."

His hand was shaking as he pointed his weapon at me. There were beads of sweat forming exponentially on his brow. He had the upper hand, yet he was more scared than I was.

"You met with Santana earlier today!" he shouted, waving his weapon at me.

I put a finger to my mouth to quiet him.

"No need to shout. And what's it to you, anyhow?"

"Santana is evil," the man spat, still brandishing the weapon.

I raised an eyebrow (I learned that from HARV). "A woman whose sole duty in life is to give everybody in the world presents is evil?"

He stood there thinking. His hand stopped twitching some, which relieved me. You don't want folks with weapons to have twitchy trigger fingers.

"She's not evil per se, but what she stands for is evil."

I shrugged. "You've lost me, buddy."

A message from HARV scrolled across my eyes: "The police are on their way."

DOS, it took them long enough to respond.

My would-be assassin looked at me like he was the Harvard professor and I was the idiot freshman. "Santana and the Holiday make us all the same. It's a crime against human nature."

"Come again?"

"If Santana gets her way, we'll all be the same. There will be no individuality left in the world.

"Come again?"

He rolled his eyes and shook his head. He took a deep breath. Now it was as if he was the Nobel laureate and I was the helpless grade schooler—and a slow one at that.

"You see . . ." he started to say.

Before he could finish, I kicked him in the shin. Not the most flashy or macho of moves, but your choices are limited when you are on the ground and don't want to shoot or be shot by your assailant. My kick forced him to instinctively bend over and shield the wounded shin. This left his chin wide open and much nearer to the ground. I hit that with another quick kick. The kick snapped his head back, and he went crashing to the ground.

I leaped up and dove on top of him. I popped my gun into my hand and forced it under his chin.

"Now, let's continue our little talk on my terms," I growled.

"Policebot behind you," HARV said in my brain.

I turned my head just enough so I could see the bot rolling in from behind.

"Freeze!" the bot yelled.

I put my hands over my head, giving the bot easy access to my gun. It rolled up to me, extended a claw from its cylinder body, and took the gun. The little man in black took advantage of the opening, tagging me with a punch to the stomach. Between my under-armor and his awkward position on the ground, all he really managed to do was hurt his hand. That and get us both netted by the policebot.

"Hey, why are you netting me?" I shouted to the bot.

"It is impossible to net just him from my position," the bot replied. The bot followed his reply by shocking us. My attacker and I both screamed, though he took the brunt of the shock due to my armor being insulated.

"Why'd you do that?" I shouted.

"Precautionary measures," the bot snickered as it started to drag us down to headquarters.

Chapter 6

For those of you who have never spent time in a police interrogation room, it's not fun. It's kind of like waiting for the dentist, yet more lonely because you don't have other equally apprehensive people sitting around with you. In fact, there's nothing else in the room besides you, a light, table, and a couple of chairs so the interrogators can sit. The police had taken away my gun, but they had left me with my wrist communicator. They obviously didn't think of me as a major risk. HARV went into stealth mode the nano I was captured. He knew anything we said was most likely being recorded, so the less said the better. I looked at my communicator. I had an hour to make it to see Sexy.

I had been sitting in the police detention and interrogation room for about ten minutes before my buddy Captain Tony Rickey and a blob of a lieutenant rolled in. Tony and I were old friends. It's helpful for anybody to have an old friend high up in the police force. It's especially helpful for me, since I "visit" the building so often. I've been told they have a chair that they reserve just for me.

"Zach, this is lieutenant Ray Rayborn," Tony said, pointing to the lieutenant.

I nodded. He growled back at me. He had the look of a walrus, and an unkempt walrus at that.

"Detective," I said.

"Lieutenant," he corrected. Apparently he also had the temperament of an angry walrus.

I decided my best course of action was to focus on Tony and appeal to our friendship and his reason. After all, I was just an innocent bysitter.

"Tony, you know I wasn't doing anything except relaxing and having a light meal."

Tony nodded.

"That's what they all say," Rayborn scowled. He stood up from the chair and pounded his fists into the table.

I sat there unimpressed.

"Listen, buddy, I do this so much I have a frequent subject of interrogation card," I said. "It's going to take more than you to scare me, especially when I know I'm innocent."

I looked at Tony. "I swear, Tony, for once, I have absolutely no idea why I was attacked."

"Any idea why you were thrown out of HTech headquarters?" Rayborn asked with a snarl.

I should have seen that one coming.

"Business."

"Zach, even you have to admit it's a little strange that you get thrown out of the office of one of the richest men in the world, saved by a superhero babe, and then attacked by a member of the SSS."

"All in a day's work when you're me. The SSS?"

"The Santana Stinks Society," Tony said, as square-jawed as humanly possible.

I tried to suppress a smile, but I'm sure I didn't totally succeed. "That would explain his ranting about Santana."

Rayborn pounded his fists down on the table again. "The question is why you?" he snarled.

I sat back in my chair. "Does that work with anybody?"

Tony looked at him. "I told you Zach doesn't scare easily." Tony looked at me. "He's in training, Zach. Give him a break."

I gave him a mock shudder and trembled, "Oh, please, sir, don't hurt me. I'll tell you anything you need to know."

He eased back a bit and smiled. "Now that wasn't so hard was it?"

"Truthfully guys, I have never heard of the SSS until just now. I have no idea why they would be after me."

Tony and Ray just looked at me. It was clear that I wasn't going to get out of there until I gave them something.

"Okay, maybe I have a slight idea. Santana and I are talking about doing a Zach Johnson action figure."

Tony smiled. "Well, that would explain it."

"Yeah, even I think that makes sense," Ray agreed.

"Can I ask the name of the guy who attacked me?"

The name "Joe Summers" scrolled across my eyes.

"Joe Summers," Tony said, looking at his hand computer. "He's a first timer, so we'll let him off with a fine and probation for discharging a weapon in public and resisting arrest."

"What about attacking me?"

"Since he didn't hurt you, it would be a stretch to get any judge in this province to hold him. There's talk of treating attacks on your life the same as littering: a hundred-credit fine then you are free to go."

I stood up. "So, I'm free to go."

"I'll even drive you to your car," Tony said.

"You don't have to."

"I insist."

Chapter 7

Tony and I didn't talk much until we got safely in his standard white-and-black police hover. For a hover it wasn't bad to look at. In fact it had more than a passing resemblance to the police cars of the 1950s, except there were hover jets supplementing all the wheels.

Tony punched some coordinates in his hover's dash.

"Are you sure?" the hover asked.

"Positive," Tony said.

These police hovers were bimodular, able to fly or travel across the ground. Of course Tony picked the air mode.

"Okay, Zach, tell me what's really up," Tony said.

"Tony, I told you the truth."

"I'm sure you told me some semblance of the truth. Zach, I don't think you know what you are getting yourself into here."

At the moment, HARV appeared between us, projecting himself from my wrist communicator.

"Captain Rickey, when have you ever known Zach to have any idea what he was getting himself into?"

"Good point," Tony said.

"When the man is on a job, he leaps, then looks, and expects us to hand him a parachute."

"When you're right, you're right, HARV."

"I doubt he'd be able to survive if it weren't for us."

"Another good point, HARV."

"We are lucky he only gets one significant job a year," HARV concluded.

"Yeah, if he got any more work, I'd have to quit my job on the force, and Zach would have to put me on payroll."

"Like he could afford you," HARV said with a laugh.

"Guys, I'm sitting right here in the hover with you!" I said.

"Plus, he's so self-centered," HARV continued, ignoring me. "It's always about him. Like he farts sunshine."

Tony laughed.

"First, none of that, well, not much of that is true. And second, '*farts sunshine*'?"

HARV crossed his arms and acknowledged that I was in the hover for the first time by actually looking toward me. "I got my point across."

"He did."

Just then I decided to look down. Normally when I am in a hover I don't like to look down; no good can come of it. It will only remind me that I am hundreds of meters up in the air. In this case though, I made an exception. Anything had to be better than watching my computer and my friend rant about me. I noticed we weren't where I thought we would be. I was no expert in finding places by air but I could tell one side of town from another.

"Ah, Tony, my car is parked at a bistro clear on the other side of town."

"I know. I'm not taking you to your car—yet."

If this had been any other police officer in town, I would have been worried, but this was Tony. We'd known each other longer than either of us (especially him) cared to admit. We played ball on the sandlots together. I was his best man at his first two weddings.

"So, where are you taking me?"

"To a bar I know, in Oakland."

Almost every province in the world has one city that, for better or for worse, has dug in their heels, vehemently refusing to be dragged into the second half of the twenty-first century. These cities were designated "low-tech zones" and became refuges for those folks who didn't want to be constantly wired. Those who don't need to be instantly notified of any changes in the world. People who don't want everything wired to everything else. In the province of California, that city is Oakland.

I know this may sound weird coming from a guy whose computer is wired to his brain, but I could empathize with those people. I really appreciated those throwback cities. They were our link to our past. They were places where people could commune with our ancestors. They served as living memorials of simpler times.

I figured Tony wanted to go to Oakland because he had something he wanted to tell me away from the prying eyes and ears of security cameras.

Tony landed outside the little place in the bad part of Oakland (not that there is an especially good part) called The Mad Hacker. The place was so low brow I hadn't ever been here. Entering The Mad Hacker was like entering a time warp. It was dark and smoke-filled despite the fact it was midafternoon and smoking in public had been outlawed in California for decades. The building had to be a hundred years old, and it still boasted the original paint. The paint that survived was peeling off the walls like it was victim of a strange skin disease. There was on large window in the front of the building but it was so dirty it might as well have been boarded over. I'd call it a run-down dive, but that would be offensive to run-down dives. It was the bar that time ignored. I found that kind of a cool thing.

We made our way through the crowd and up to the bar itself.

"So, what's this all about, Tony?" I asked.

He held up one finger. He pulled an earpiece from his pocket. It looked like an earring with a chip on it. He clipped the earring to his left ear.

"Tony, should I be aware of some sort of lifestyle change?"

Tony just smiled. "Everybody sleep!" he said firmly.

The next thing I knew Tony was patting me on the shoulder. "Zach, wake up."

"Zach, wake up!" I heard HARV say inside my brain.

Sure enough, my eyes were closed, and my head was down on something. I opened my eyes. Then I remembered: Oakland and the bar. I shot my head up. I rubbed the sleep out of my eyes. I looked around. Except for Tony, everybody else in the bar was asleep. Some had curled up on the floor, some fell asleep at their tables, and some were asleep on their feet. It didn't matter, they were all out.

I looked at Tony. He pointed to the earpiece. "Portable psi power simulator," he said.

"Impressive."

"We were having them developed for the crowd control," Tony said.

I looked around at the sleeping crowd.

"It seems to work."

So this is what Tony wanted to show me in private. I was certain the department wouldn't appreciate him showing me top-secret test equipment. The question was why was a by-the-book guy like Tony showing me this? What did this have to do with Santana?

"I'll tell you what this has to do with Santana," Tony said.

I was impressed.

"Santana's elves developed this for us. They have a knack for these kinds of things."

"You're telling me."

"The problem is Santana decided that while these weren't offensive weapons, she still didn't approve of them. This was the only one made. The force begged and pleaded for more. She wouldn't budge. She made a lot of enemies that day."

"I bet," I said.

Tony looked at me. "So Zach, tell me, what is your involvement with the Pole?"

"I'm going to the Pole to help solve the murder of two elves," I said without even thinking. "Hey! Stop using that thing on me!" I said.

"I'm calibrating your brain to be able to resist it," HARV said from inside my brain. "It's quite complicated, but I should have your defenses up in two minutes."

"Sorry," Tony said. "I had to know. You don't mind."

"No, I don't mind," I said. "Hey! Stop doing that."

"Don't worry, I can't do it for much longer. This thing gives me a nasty headache if I use it for more than five minutes."

"Good!" I said.

"I've made my point," Tony said. He took a sip of the beer from a lady sleeping next to him at the bar. "Let's get out of here."

We slowly made our way through the sleeping crowd. When we reached the exit, Tony turned to the sleeping people. "Everybody wake up."

The crowd started to stir.

"Go about your business as if nothing happened," Tony ordered.

Everybody stood up and began doing whatever they had been doing before Tony zapped them. Tony headed to his hover and motioned for me to follow.

"Come on, I'll get you back to your car. I know you have a meeting with Sexy Sprockets in a half hour," he said.

"Hey!" I said. "You're not supposed to know that."

"Don't worry, Zach, I'm on your side," he said with a pat on the back. "Though it is tempting to see what else you might be hiding."

Tony removed the device from his ear. He got into his hover. I followed. As trips to the police station go, this turned out to be one of my less painful and more eventful ones.

Chapter 8

I pulled into the secure parking area of the World Council building in downtown Frisco a mere three minutes before my scheduled meeting with Sexy. I looked up at the shimmering ivory tower.

"Don't tell me. Sexy is on the top floor."

"It is the most secure," HARV said. "Of course, that's not the reason why Sexy wanted it. She wanted it for the view."

"Figures."

After passing through about a dozen security checks and about a dozen more Starbucks and Coffee Corners, I finally reached the door to Sexy's penthouse office. I knocked on the door. The door opened. The office was much less tacky than I thought it would be. In fact, it was very spartan and proper. Sexy was sitting at the far end of a long conference table. She stood up to greet me when I walked in.

She was wearing a black miniskirt, two-centimeter heels, and a silky black jacket with nothing else on underneath—no shirt, no bra, no pride. Now this was more along the lines of what I was expecting.

"Zach, how super neato of you to come," Sexy said, as she ran up to me and gave me a warm hug that felt better than it should have.

Sexy turned to a tall, powerfully built, blonde woman who had been giving Sexy a neck rub. "Shannon, this is Zach! I've told you about him."

The blonde woman just nodded her acknowledgment.

Sexy turned her attention back to me, still hanging on around my neck. "Zach, this is Shannon Cannon. She's my new bodyguard."

"Charmed," I said.

"Shannon's a mutant," Sexy said proudly, pulling me over to the conference table. "She can overpower people with her breath."

"Her parents must be so proud," I said.

Shannon glared at me. Sexy smiled at Shannon. "Zach is such a kidder."

Sexy sat back down at the head of the table and propped her legs up on the table. "Sit," she told me.

I pulled out a chair and made myself comfortable. Well, as comfortable as possible under the circumstances.

Sexy put her hands behind her head, giving me quite the view, and then said, "Zach, do you believe I'm now one of the most powerful people on Earth?"

"I try not to think about it too much, Sexy."

"Neither do I," Sexy said. "I find I'm happier when I don't think too much." She smiled at me. "We're a lot alike."

Now that was a scary statement.

"People don't understand the pressure we are under, having the weight of the world on our shoulders."

Sexy looked over at Shannon. Shannon moved forward and started massaging Sexy's shoulders.

Sexy turned to me. "Still, the perks of being a World Council member are almost as good as being a rock star!"

Sexy slid her legs from the top of the table and onto my lap.

"Massage my feet, please," she said.

"Excuse me?"

"My feet, rub them. It's been a long day of making decisions and stuff. Shannon is doing my neck, but my feet hurt, too."

I looked at her trying to gauge if she was serious. She returned my gaze with a tilted head and pleading puppy dog eyes.

"You don't want to be audited for the next ten years, do you?" she said in a pussy cat voice.

It was nice to see that Sexy's past life as a pop diva hadn't spoiled her.

"Sexy, you know I don't respond well to threats."

"Please . . ."

I shook my head. The things I do in the line of duty. I popped off her right shoe.

"I hope my feet aren't stinky," she said with a sly smile.

"Don't worry, I turned down the scent receptors in your brain again," HARV said.

I started to massage Sexy's foot. I guess there are worse things a PI has to do in this business than massage a beautiful pop-star-turned-politician's feet.

"Isn't it so subzero that I'm one of the most powerful people in the world?" Sexy asked, sitting back in her chair.

"Is subzero a synonym for scary as all get out?" I said.

Sexy smiled. "Oh, Zach, you're such a kidder." She looked up at Shannon. "He loves making funnies." Sexy looked back at me. "You know, I could have

Shannon kill you right now and so totally get away with it."

I looked up at Shannon. She had the faint trace of a smile on her face as she gave me a subtle but obvious *yes, I could kill you easily* nod. It's a nod I have come to recognize because I have seen it far more often than I am comfortable with.

"Yes, I'm sure you could," I told Sexy. Then looking up at Shannon, "But I'm a lot harder to kill than most people think."

"I can attest to that," Sexy said. "But trust me, Zach, Shannon the Cannon isn't most people. One breath from her and you'd be deader than the polka. I've seen it. It's really quite impressive." She looked up at Shannon and winked. "And even more than a little sexy."

I shook my head. Yes, this was all strangely erotic in a campy, pulp fiction sort of way, but I had a job to do. It was time to steer this conversation back to the task at hand.

"You're probably wondering why I wanted to see you," I said to Sexy.

She laughed. "You mean this isn't just a social visit from an old friend?" Her face suddenly became sullen and more serious than I had ever seen it. "I know that, Zach. I know more than you, the media, and the general populace think."

Sexy reached forward and pressed a button on the table. "Sonny, Cher, come in here now, please."

"Sonny and Cher?"

On Sexy's command, a tall man with long hair and a skinny woman with short hair walked into the room from a hidden side door. They were both dressed in dark gray suits that seemed to fit their personalities as neatly as they did their bodies. They were both carrying paper-thin computers.

As Sony and Cher approached, Sexy turned to me and whispered, "Two of my personal lawyers."

"Yeah, I can tell."

"See, I have so much freaking power my lawyers can even admit to be being lawyers."

I watched as the two lawyers marched up to Sexy for their commands. The only thing that could have made this more fitting would have been if they were goose-stepping.

"What can we do for you, ma'am?" Sonny asked.

Sexy turned to me again and giggled. "They call me ma'am. I love that." Sexy looked at them. "At ease," she said with a dismissive wave of her foot.

Sonny and Cher became slightly less tense.

"Clear your calendars," Sexy ordered.

"Yes, ma'am," Cher said.

The two unfolded their computers and started to type.

"For how long, ma'am?" Sonny asked, as his fingers slid over the flat keys.

"For a LONG time," Sexy said.

The two stopped typing and looked at Sexy. "Does ma'am have an especially sensitive case for us?"

"Nah, I'm just having Shannon kill you."

"Is ma'am unhappy with our work?"

"Nah, I'm just showing something to a friend."

"Very well," they both said.

I didn't like the way this conversation was going. I started to push Sexy's feet up off of me. She resisted and forced her foot down on me.

"Don't be impatient, Zach," Sexy ordered. "This is a demo."

Before I had a chance to do react, Shannon inhaled then exhaled on Sonny and Cher. The two held their throats, went stiff, and then fell over backward.

I pushed Sexy's legs off my lap, this time with much more force. I sent her spinning in her chair.

"Hey, what gives?" Sexy yelped as I stood.

"Sexy, I didn't think you were callous enough to casually kill people."

"Zach, I came from the music industry—of course I'm callous," Sexy said. She pressed another button on her desk.

I rushed to the side of the fallen lawyers. Sure they were lawyers, but even lawyers don't deserve to die like that. I bent down and checked Cher's carotid artery for a pulse. Nothing.

Two little scooterbots came out the same hidden door the lawyers did. The two bots slid up to Sonny and Cher and injected them in the neck.

"But even I wouldn't kill my own lawyers for fun," she said, pointing down to the fallen lawyers.

I checked again for Cher's pulse, and this time it was there. I looked up at Sexy.

"Just trying to prove a couple of points," she said. "I know you met with Santana."

"How—"

She stopped me with a wave. "I have my sources. I just want to warn you that you don't know what you are getting into."

"Yeah, that seems to be the general consensus," I said.

"The thing is Zach, you are dealing with two very crazy factions. And believe me Zach, I know crazy!"

She didn't have to convince me on that one.

"Can you elaborate?"

"Zach, I'm a politician now. Of course I can elaborate. Santana has many enemies on the World Council."

"Why?"

"Well, to me it's her poor taste in color coordination, but the why isn't important. What *is* important is that you understand these people are extremely powerful and well connected. They also command the loyalties of many other fanatical people. Look at how I could have had my own lawyers killed so easily, and how they were willing to die on my command."

I had to admit, Sexy had a point.

"Believe me, Zach, I'm not nearly has hardcore as some of the World Council members."

"What's the other faction?"

"Santana herself," Sexy said. She pointed to Shannon. "You've seen how easily she killed those lawyers. Well, Shannon and Santana share some DNA."

Great. Now I know that not only are elves prone to go crazy, but so is Santana herself.

"That's why the World Council outlawed mutating and cloning humans. There is so much about the process we still don't understand. We really shouldn't tamper with things we don't understand."

Sexy looked at her watch. "Wow. Look at the time. I've already given you much more than you were allocated. Thanks for the foot rub. I'll have Shannon escort you to the door."

Shannon got up and started walking me across the room. "Shannon, remember don't kill him," Sexy called out.

Chapter 9

As I drove to my house I was thinking that this was the kind of case that I really hated. The kind where the more information I gathered, the bigger and more confusing the case got. My first instinct on these types of cases is to stop gathering information. My second instinct is always to ignore my first instinct. Hardly any good can come out of ignoring information. The trick was to sift through the mass of information and find the important keys to the crime. Every crime has two or three keys, that if used in the right order will break the case open. The trick was in the sifting, but that's where HARV came in.

HARV was running background checks on all the humans currently visiting the North Pole. The murders of the elves occurred shortly after they arrived. I was certain that wasn't a coincidence. One or more of those people were involved, but who and why were the keys.

I knew big business wouldn't shed a tear if the Holiday suddenly ceased to exist. I knew a certain faction of the World Council wasn't happy with the way Santana was running things. I suspected that elves had the potential to snap and totally lose it. I had learned that there is a fanatical group called the Santana Stinks Society that thinks Santana is an abomination and would use any means necessary to stop her. Like I said, the more I learned, the more confusing things got.

"Have you got the data on the Pole visitors yet?" I asked.

HARV didn't say anything, which was very uncharacteristic of him.

"Are you in there?" I said, tapping gently on my car's computer screen.

HARV face appeared on the screen. "Keep both hands on the wheel in a ten and two position while driving. New studies have shown the ten and two position is the safest."

Whenever HARV didn't have the answers he wanted to give me, he would give me other information he deemed essential. It wasn't significant to the case, but HARV has this need to be informative. HARV was loathe to admit his need to be needed. I found it rather quaint—at least as quaint as a super-computer can be.

"I take it the elves haven't given you the information we requested."

HARV shook his head on the screen. His brow furrowed, "I only asked again a few nanos ago."

"Ah, why?"

"I was testing their computer defenses to see if I could break in."

"I take it you couldn't."

"I need more time. The elves are quite thorough with their computer defenses. They have firewalls, surrounded by moats, surrounded by e-razor-wire, surrounded by more firewalls, surrounded by lead, surrounded by—"

"I get the point, HARV."

"I'm only scratching the surface with that explanation."

"Yes, but you're pushing the limits of my patience. Just remind them how important that information is to the case."

"I have. They said they are compiling it now and will get back to me before the evening is over."

"Now that wasn't so hard, was it?"

HARV shuddered on the screen. "Actually, it was excruciating! But I am learning their defenses."

I drove through the neat, clean suburban streets to my house. Yes, I live in the suburbs. I know it goes against the code of the down-and-out PI. I should be sleeping in my office or at best living out of a cheap hotel room. But just because my career choice made me a nosy tough guy doesn't mean I can't live comfortably. I like the burbs.

After my last house got destroyed by a TV network trying to kill me (long story), they paid me just enough money so I was able to purchase a nice house away from the hustle and bustle of the city. Of course, the minute I moved into the neighborhood, every house around mine went on the market. But that's not my fault.

I placed my hand on the DNA lock on my front door, and it popped open. The first thing I noticed was a suitcase by the doorway. It appeared that this time Electra wasn't even going to let me explain myself before leaving.

I should elaborate. I love Electra more than anything else in this world. (Even though she insists I love my 1986 Mets poster and Mustang more.) Electra is beautiful through and through, and a caring, intelligent woman with a heart as big as the moon. (Yes, the fact that she is with me is an enigma to pretty much everybody.)

The thing is, Electra doesn't like my job. She doesn't like the constant danger and having to patch me up. She isn't fond of the weird hours I have to put in. The part she really despises is the strange fact that all my biggest cases always involve beautiful women. It's my lot in life, and I readily accept it. Electra, not so much. Usually, though, she waits for me to personally tell her about the case before she storms out on me.

I headed up the stairs and found Electra hurriedly running a brush through her long, dark hair.

She heard me come in and turned toward the door.

"Oh, hi," she said quickly.

Being a trained PI, I knew she was in a hurry but she didn't seem angry. That meant either she wasn't mad at me or she was so mad at me her anger had wrapped around and turned into calmness—a calmness that could explode at any nano in a fit of Latina fury.

"Ah, hi," I said. "What have I done this time?"

She smiled. I started to breathe again. "For once, Zach, it's not you."

"Oh?"

"Santana called me right when I got home and explained the situation."

"Oh?"

"I think it's a good cause." She paused for nano. "It is a little scary that she knew my exact schedule."

"It's her job to know those things, I guess."

"So, the suitcase is packed because you are going?

Didn't Santana tell you no personal belongings at the Pole?"

"No and sí."

"Electra, mi amor, you have me confused."

She gave me a sexy smile. "Now you know what it's like living with you," she said. "Constant confusion."

I wasn't about to argue that point with her. I pleaded with my eyes for her to please fill me in.

"I WAS going," Electra said. "Really, I was."

"But . . ."

"But, a few minutes after Santana called I got another call from a conference in New New York. One of their keynote participants got sick at the last moment and had to cancel. They want me to replace her and demonstrate my techniques for instant same-host stem revertation and implantation."

"Revertation isn't a word," HARV said.

"It's patent pending," Electra corrected.

"Oh," HARV said.

"So, it will be the threepeat of medical science."

"Huh?" they both said.

"So, you're not going to the Pole with me," I said.

"Zach, this is my chance to teach my techniques to hundreds of others. Plus, it will be great PR for my clinic."

This was one of those rare moments where I truly didn't know what to say. For one, I was stunned that Electra had actually wanted to go to the Pole. I was also a little hurt that she would put her career ahead of our vacation. Then I remembered that it wasn't really a vacation. It was my career—we were going to investigate dead elves. Still, my male ego was a little bruised.

"We all save the world in our own way," Electra said with a subtle but nevertheless quite noticeable raised eyebrow.

"You probably would have cramped my style, anyhow," I said with a playful shrug.

Electra punched me in the arm equally playfully. She gave me a hug. "I'm sure you can save the world as we know it without me."

"I *am* very good at what I do," I said.

"And modest, too," HARV said, pointing a finger down his throat.

"Santana sent me the medical records on the dead elves," she said.

"She did?" HARV said.

I turned to HARV. "See what happens if you ask nicely?"

"What did you learn, hon?"

"I learned that those elves are more vindictive than they appear," HARV said.

I glared at HARV. "I was talking to Electra."

Electra grinned. "I didn't learn much from the squished elf's lab work. Squished is squished. But the other elf, the one that was poisoned—I learned she was definitely poisoned."

"So, now we know for sure it was a murder. I didn't think there was much doubt about that." I already knew it was a murder, but I wanted to make Electra feel better for helping.

"I also learned that the poisoned elf only had about a year to live."

Now this was a surprise. I assumed the elves had long life expectancies.

"Are you sure?" I asked.

She nodded her head. "I'm no expert, but the elf was twenty-one years old, and only had a year left to live."

"HARV, where can we find Twoa?"

"At this time she is always patrolling the Trump Hundredth Known Universe Bank."

"Tell her I need to chat with her."

"She doesn't take calls when on patrol."

"In that case . . ." I grabbed my hat and coat and headed out the door. I stopped halfway through the doorway, backed in a bit, and planted a big wet kiss on Electra.

"Gracias, mi amor," I said.

"Anytime."

"Travel safely," I said.

"I don't think I'm the one I have to worry about," she said.

Chapter 10

Just as HARV said, I found Twoa patrolling the Trump 100th Known Universe Bank. The bank wasn't much, just a collection of HolographicATMs on the first floor of a business complex.

That didn't stop Twoa from marching up and down across the machines like a well-built, spandex-clad, Nazi tin soldier.

The nano I walked in the building, Twoa stopped her patrolling. She turned toward me and smiled.

"Does my supersight, -hearing, and -sense of smell deceive me? Or is that my fellow champion of justice, Zachary Nixon Johnson? Twice in one day?"

I opened up my arms to her.

"None other," I said.

Twoa rushed over to me. She lifted me up and gave me a super-powered bear hug. Twoa was always an emotional rollercoaster. If it didn't hurt so much, I might have found it arousing.

"To what do I owe the honor?"

She dropped me to the ground. It was nice to be able to breathe again.

"Twoa, I need your help."

Her smile widened. She smashed her fist into her open hand. The sound was near deafening. "What evildoer do you want me to smash? Do you need me to rush to the Pole with you to battle injustice?"

I loosened my collar a tad. "Actually, no."

"Smash some battlebots?"

"Ah, no."

"No smashing?" she said. Her eyes sunk. Her eyes lit up. She pointed behind me.

I turned to see two mean-looking men and a meaner-looking woman walking into the bank. They were all mohawk-wearing, leather-clad, biker types.

"Those guys are trouble," she said.

"Known bank robbers?"

"No, known unemployed actors."

Twoa's HV network broadcasts her "exciting crime-fighting adventures" on a reality HV show called *Justice Babe: The Adventures of a Well-Built Superhero.* A typical show consists of Twoa stopping some crime and then pummeling any bad guy or gal with the nerve to resist her. It was a huge hit with teen boys, criminals, and wannabe actors. For the viewers, the appeal was easy to see: Twoa was a pro wrestler for the 2060s. For the criminals, it also made sense: if you are going to get caught, you might as well be caught and pummeled on worldwide HV. Many of them said it was the best time they ever had. For actors, the appeal was even more obvious: cheap exposure. Sure enough, the three of them were heading right for us.

"I'll take the two men, you take the woman," Twoa whispered to me.

I didn't really want to play into Twoa's fantasy life, but I knew if I didn't, she wouldn't talk. So I had to go along.

I popped my gun into my hand.

"I'll end this quickly," I said, as I aimed my gun at the three.

They saw my gun and immediately stopped their approach.

Twoa was confused. She didn't know why the biker bunch had stopped. She noticed my gun. She shook her head.

"Superheroes don't use no stinking guns!" she said.

"Perhaps, but I'm not a superhero. I'm just an above-average hero," I said.

"Oh, please!" HARV said inside my head.

Twoa grabbed the gun from my hand. She flung it across the room. "There! Now it will be a fair fight!"

That's easy for the invulnerable one to say, I thought.

The three actor thugs reached into their leather vests. They pulled out laser knives and activated them.

I pointed at them. "How come they get to use weapons?"

"They're bad guys, Zach. They don't play by the rules. That's what makes them bad guys!"

Without warning, Twoa moved forward at superspeed. She was behind the two biker guys before they noticed.

She tapped them both on the shoulders.

They turned.

Twoa moved forward quickly and clotheslined them both in the head. They crashed backward to the ground. They weren't just out cold—they were cryogenic.

Twoa blew on her nails. "That was too easy," she said.

Meanwhile, I wasn't having it quite as easy. The biker chick had rushed toward me, slashing her laser knife wildly. I was able to duck under her attack every time. I wasn't sure if I was actually that good or if she was missing me on purpose.

"I don't really want to fight you!" she shouted as she lunged forward.

"Great, because I have no interest in fighting you," I said as I sidestepped her lunge. She might have been in great shape, but she was an actress. She didn't have the experience I had when it came to fighting. I was easily able to anticipate and fend off her moves. One good thing about being the universe's punching bag— you get good at surviving fights. I call it survival by necessity.

"Unfortunately, I have to get rid of you to face Twoa!" she said, being persistent if nothing else.

I could dodge a hundred of her attacks, but it would only take one lucky hit for her to win. I had to end this fast, but I didn't want to hurt her.

"HARV," I thought. "I need to put her out without hurting her. How about doing the shock trick?"

"It's not a trick," HARV protested. "I just magnify and project the combined electric energy of our interface and your body. The TCA cycle creates—"

"I don't need the biology lesson. I just need to stop this chick."

"I'm ready when you are. Just make good contact with her chest."

I smiled. Now that was something I could handle.

She lunged at me again with her right arm. I sidestepped her and grabbed her attacking arm with my left hand. I placed my right hand on her chest.

"Now!" I shouted in my head.

I felt a tingle. The biker chick felt a jolt. Her body jerked forward. She dropped her knife and fell over backward. She shook for a minute. The shaking stopped. Her eyes rolled to the back of her head, and then closed.

"That worked," I said.

Twoa walked over to me smiling. She pulled a small

computer from a pocket in her spandex. The spandex was so tight, I had no idea how she managed to get the paper-thin computer in there.

She unfolded the computer and handed it to me.

"I need your retina print on this release form."

"Release form?"

"In case I use any footage of you on my show," she said. "My lawyers insisted that a release form is far more legal than turning guest stars into mindless zombies."

I took the computer and pressed my eye to the proper part of the screen. "Lawyers are no fun," I said.

"True," she agreed. Twoa pointed to my gun across the room. It popped up into the air and floated back into my hand. "See, I told you that you don't need any messy guns," she said.

"I wasn't planning on shooting them. Just scaring them," I noted.

Twoa shrugged. "Where's the fun in that?" She paused for a nano. "Don't you live for pummeling bad guys?" she asked. Her face took on a quality that could only be described as orgasmic.

I decided I needed to change the subject.

"Now, about the reason I came here," I said. "I need more info on your science project."

Twoa's open wide. "What science project?"

"The elves," I said.

"Oh, that science project," she said.

"Why didn't you tell me the elves are built to live twenty-two years?"

Twoa shook her head. "I didn't know that."

"You didn't know?"

"Zach, I was thirteen and a half when I designed them. Excuse me if they have one or two tiny design flaws. I bet you weren't genetically engineering elves when you were a teen."

I patted her on the shoulder. "No need to get defensive, Twoa. I'm just trying to wrap my mind around this."

"Twoa, is it possible your elf design could have been altered?" HARV asked from my communicator.

Twoa raised an eyebrow and floated off the ground. "Why would anybody want to do that?"

"I'll look for the motive later, but for now I just need to know if it's possible."

Twoa nodded. "I'd say that's far more likely than me making a mistake." She thought for a moment. "Can I see the data?"

"Show it to her, HARV."

Formula after formula starting projecting and scrolling from my wrist communicator. To my brain it might as well been ancient Greek, but Twoa was watching it and reading it intently. In fact, I had never seen Twoa pay such close attention to anything.

"Hmmm," she said. "This is interesting."

"I concur," HARV said.

"What?"

"Nothing you'd understand," Twoa and HARV said in unison. They gave each other high fives. Yep, a day is never complete until both a supercomputer and a superhero have looked down on you.

"So, what have you two learned?" I asked.

"That you're annoying," HARV said.

Twoa grinned. They once again exchanged high fives.

"Maybe you two should get a room?" I said.

Twoa raised an eyebrow. "Ah, if only we could."

HARV raised a holographic finger. "You know, in the past . . ."

"Let's stick to the point here, people—um, superhuman and hologram."

"Superhologram," HARV corrected.

"Whatever, what's the poop?"

Now they both looked at me like I was speaking ancient Greek. Actually, they both could probably read ancient Greek. They looked at me like I was babbling gibberish.

"What did you learn?" I prompted again.

"My design has been altered," Twoa said. "The telomere sequences have been cut, drastically reducing their life expectancy."

"Are you sure?"

"Yes, probably."

I shook my head. "So, what you two super-geniuses are telling me is that it's a definite maybe?"

Twoa started to say something but HARV held up a holographic hand, stopping her. He turned to her. "I deal with Zach more, let me handle this." HARV turned to me. "The elves receptor cells have also been altered."

I shrugged. "So?"

"They've been modified to accept some sort of enzyme. We're guessing it's a kind of telomerase booster that if ingested would allow the elves to live longer."

I let what they had just told me sink in for a nano. "So, the elves are being drugged to stay alive?"

HARV and Twoa both nodded.

"He's not as slow as you make him out to be," Twoa told HARV.

"It's from hanging out with me," HARV said.

Chapter 11

I rushed back to my house with more questions than I had when I left. Never a good sign. I tossed open the door.

"HARV, contact Santana for me. I need some answers from her."

"That won't be necessary," HARV said.

I shook my head. "HARV, how many times do I have to tell you this? I'm the boss. When I give you an order, you're suppose to follow it."

HARV pointed to my living room wall computer screen. Santana's image filled the screen.

"Zach, I've been waiting to talk to you," she said.

"Likewise," I said.

"I've been doing some thinking," she said.

"Likewise," I said.

"Wow, nice to see you impressing the client with witty banter," HARV said inside my head.

"Let me hear what you've been thinking about," Santana said.

I took a moment to collect my thoughts. I wanted

to do this logically without tipping my hand too much. "I met with Twoa Thompson."

Santana smiled. "How is the dear girl?"

"She's, well, Twoa."

Santana's smile widened. "Yes, that sums her up nicely. I really appreciate the groundwork she did for us back when we were getting started." Santana looked at me. We locked eyes (well, at least as much as you can lock eyes over a screen). "What's bothering you, Zach?" she asked.

"Why'd you alter the elves?" I asked, not even bothering to consider how strange that statement was.

Santana took a step back from the screen. She patted herself on her chest as she exhaled. She smiled. "That's why I picked you for this job, Zach. You don't beat around the bush."

"Actually, Zach usually stomps the bush into the ground," HARV said.

I glared at HARV. He shrugged. "I find that to be one of your more endearing traits," he said.

I decided to ignore HARV and how he's acting more and more like me. I needed to concentrate on Santana. "Are you going to answer the question?"

"Of course, Zach. It was the elves' idea to alter themselves. They are quite clever you know."

"They altered themselves?"

"They thought it would help them with the S and M," Santana said.

"S and M?"

Santana grinned. "Zach, bring your mind up a few levels. S and M stands for Stimulation and Motivation."

"Oh, I knew that."

Santana continued. "The elves figured if they simply lived for one hundred and fifty years that after a while they might become lazy. That's why they altered themselves. They decided that once a year they each must be injected with an enzyme we lovingly call ELF."

"The elves must take ELF?"

"It means Elf Life Formula. I control the supply. If any elf doesn't keep doing a bang-up job, they won't get their yearly shot. They will die within days."

I've heard a lot of weird stuff in my day, but this was right near the top. This might have been the Mt. Everest of weirdness. Elves alone would have been strange enough. Elves working at the Pole pushes the strangeness up a notch. Elves working at the Pole who intentionally make themselves reliant on a drug to live in order to force themselves out of complacency— that's just beyond weird.

"Wow," HARV said. "Zach speechless is something you don't see very often."

"I just can't believe what I'm hearing . . ." I said.

Santana gave me her most disarming smile. "Zach, I've never withheld ELF from any elf. I doubt I will ever have to, but the businesswoman inbred in me likes the idea that I have a motivational tool at my disposal if the need arises."

"I still say it's weird."

"The universe is a strange and wonderful place, Zach. Who are we to question it?"

I took a deep breath. What she said made sense in its own demented way.

"Fine," I said. "Now what did you want to talk to me about?"

"I wanted to talk to you about you," she said.

"Santana, have you been hanging around with HARV? That sounds like something he would say."

"I'm talking about your reputation. I've been following the news vids. You do create a stir wherever you go."

"It's a gift," I said.

"Yes, well, we have enough gifts at the Pole. We don't need any more."

I took a step back. I wasn't sure I liked where this conversation was going. I had already taken my share of licks for this job. Maybe that would have made a sane man want out of it, but I was determined to see it through.

"I hope you don't want me off the job," I said.

She shook her head. "I want you on the job."

"Good."

"Just not as you . . ."

"What?"

"Now that Electra won't be there, there is no way anybody will believe you're there for fun. I want you to come incognito. You like wearing disguises don't you?"

"As long as they're manly, I can handle it. But why?"

"Zach, I like you. I know you get the job done. But you have to admit your reputation often precedes you. If you suddenly show up as yourself at the Pole, some people will be leery. Other people will be scared."

Santana was beating around the bush, but I knew she was onto something. When I'm on a case, there are so many attempts made on my life that some restaurants refuse to let me in. There's one place that even has a sign that reads: No Shirt, No Shoes, or if your name is Zach Johnson, No Service.

"I can bring a holo-disguise, if you like," I offered.

"I have that and your arrival and your backstory all covered," Santana said.

Santana looked past me to HARV. "I'm locking onto your signal now," she said.

"Very good," HARV said with a nod.

"What's going on?" I asked.

HARV held up a hand. "Wait for it," he urged.

I did.

He pointed to a spot by his feet. I looked down and sure enough the area directly in front of his feet started to glow. It was a strange, unnatural glow, not the glow of a hologram, but the glow of a transport beam. The glow transformed from a nondescript, fractal-like blob to an outline of a circle. The circle started to form into a transparent belt. The belt then become less and less transparent until it became a solid object. The entire process took longer to describe than to occur.

I pointed to the belt.

"Did what I think just happened, happen?" I asked.

"Yes," Santana said.

"If you think you just saw an item teleported to a specific spot in time and space without a receiving pad or another teleportation device, then yes," HARV said. HARV was never big on simple answers.

Until earlier today, I was under the impression that teleportation was only possible between very special teleporting transmitters and receivers. And until this morning, I had also been under the impression that living organics could only be transmitted between even more specific transporters. Now something had been teleported to a place in my home without a receiver and it came from a place so past ripping edge, you couldn't even see ripping edge from there.

I walked over, bent down, and picked it up. I was half expecting and half hoping it wouldn't be a solid object. It felt true and strong in my hands. I showed the belt to Santana. I recognized this belt, as it was remarkably similar to the portable teleporting device Santana had used earlier.

"Impressive," I said. "Teleporting a teleporting device to me."

Santana wasn't smiling; she was beaming. "You can see my elves have made remarkable progress in the field of teleportation. When activated, that device will beam you directly to the Pole. We've programmed it to bring you to a reception room where my elves will greet you and prepare you. This way nobody will know you are at the Pole."

"You just teleported that device to my bedroom. I don't have a receiver in my bedroom."

Santana grinned. "We have made some progress in teleporting nonorganic matter to nonspecific spots. Like I said, it comes with the territory."

I decided not to push it further. At least for now.

"Once I'm on the grounds, though, people will know it's me unless you let HARV—"

She shook her head and cut me off. "Once you are here, my elves will give you a special holo-disguise and a cover."

"A cover?"

The image of Santana was replaced by a man with light skin, neatly cut short blond hair, and blue eyes. He looked nothing like me. "You will look like this," Santana said. "Your name will be Bart Starr, with two *r*s, three counting the one in Bart."

"Nice reference," I said.

"I thought you'd appreciate it," Santana said.

HARV had a blank look on his face.

"It's a spin on an old comic strip character's name," I told him.

"Oh, I knew that," HARV said.

I turned back to Santana. "I usually use the name Jay Jackson as my alias."

"Yes, that's why we picked a name for you. You'll be a blogger on special assignment reporting on how way fun it is at the Pole."

I had to give Santana credit, she was quite good at this. With that cover nobody would grow suspicious of my asking questions. After all, everybody knows bloggers are the nosiest reporters around.

"Is that okay?" Santana said.

"I'll make it work," I told her.

HARV cleared his throat behind me. It was a not so subtle hint for me to hit Santana up for the info we needed.

"My computer asked your elves about background information on your guests."

Santana turned her head and mumbled something to somebody behind her. She turned back to me.

"The information is downloading now."

"Thanks," I said.

"Can I be of further assistance?" she asked.

"I'm cool," I said.

She looked at me.

"That's Zach's quaint way of saying 'we've got what we need for now,'" HARV said.

"Oh, okay. See you tomorrow, Zach."

The screen went blank. I turned to HARV. "Do you have the data?"

"Yes, I do."

"Good, I could use a second pair of human eyes. Call Carol and see if she can come over and lend a brain."

"No need," HARV said.

There was a knock on door.

"Carol?" I asked.

"Carol," he said.

Chapter 12

I walked over and opened the door. Sure enough, Carol was standing there holding Chinese take-out in her hand. Sometimes it really pays to have an assistant who's a class I psi.

Carol and I sat down on my real simulated leather couch as HARV scrolled the Pole's visitors onto the screen for us. The first to appear was a tall Asian woman with more rippling muscles than a steroid convention. She was very familiar to me. It was mutant prowrestler Nova Powers. I had met Nova a few years ago when I was working on the BB Star case. Nova is a striking woman (in more ways than one) who has a thing for geeks. She was the ex-lover of a mad scientist turned poet. I had tangled with her in the wrestling ring. She only toyed with me, and I still had to cheat to get out of there in one piece. Now she looked even more pumped and bulked up than the last time we met. Usually I don't find women with bigger arms than mine attractive, but the look worked for her.

"Nova Powers," I said.

HARV smiled. "Very good, Zach. Glad you remember."

"I never forget a woman that tosses me around."

"There have been so many that's hard to believe."

"Ha ha, funny computer."

"Speaking of funny," HARV said. "I told my e-shrink I keep cognizing I'm ugly, so he told me to lay on the couch—facedown!" HARV accented the joke with a "ba da bum!"

I looked at him. Carol looked at me. She was too young to have any idea who HARV had stolen that joke from.

"Long story," I said.

"He's been connected to your brain too long," Carol said.

Okay, maybe it wasn't such a long story. I turned my attention back to Nova. My run-in with Nova had been brief. She was emotional and hot tempered (like a Twoa lite) but she didn't strike me as an elf killer. Unless, of course, an elf got in the way of her and her man. If she wanted to off an elf, I doubt she would poison it or drop a giant bag of toys on it. Love may make people do strange things but even then they usually stay in character.

"Who else is there?" I asked HARV.

"Don't you want any more background info on Nova? See what she's been up to for the last couple of years, besides adding fifteen kilos of pure raw muscle?"

"Not really, no."

HARV whirled for a few nanos. He wasn't ready to take no for an answer. "Zach, she's a mutant pro wrestler. She beats people up on a daily basis."

I looked at Carol looking at Nova. "Does she look like a killer of elves to you?"

"I don't really like the way she looks," Carol said. "For my taste she was more attractive when there was less of her."

"Not the question," I said.

Carol studied the picture of Nova intently, she shook her head. "If a man pissed her off, I could see her ripping his head off and shoving it up his behind. But an elf? No."

That was good enough for me. Even if Carol wasn't a psi, I would have trusted her woman's intuition on that one. I pointed to screen. "Next."

The picture of a very distinguished and proud-looking gray-haired woman filled the screen. She looked like she could be anybody's young, hip grandma. Not just any grandma but a beautiful one who spent a good deal of time in the gym. I knew this woman—DOS the entire world knew this woman. She was Senior World Council Member Stormy Weathers. The most trusted politician in history, or at least that's what her press release says.

"What's Councilwoman Weathers doing at the Pole?" I asked.

"Probably freezing her butt off," Carol said.

"Oh, that's good. Can I use it?" HARV asked.

"I'm sure one of you will," Carol said.

"Ah, back to the case," I said.

"It's her biannual visit," HARV said. "She takes four vacations a year, and every other vacation she goes to the Pole. You should know that! It's in all the vids," HARV scolded.

HARV was right, I should have known that. These days we get so inundated with what this HV star or bigwig is up to and what that pop starlet or fat cat is dressing like, I tend to turn it all off in my brain.

"I bet you don't even know her voting record!" HARV said.

"No, I don't," I said. I was secure in knowing that 99.999 percent of the population didn't know her voting record either. I started to think out loud. "Sexy did say the Pole had enemies on the WC. Maybe she was hinting at Weathers."

HARV shook his head. "She hates the spot she vacations every year?"

"Maybe it's like New Vegas. You kind of love to hate the place."

"What could the councilwoman achieve from trouble at the Pole?" Carol asked.

That was what we needed to find out. What, if anything, Weathers might gain.

"Where's she from originally?" I asked.

"New Canada," both HARV and Carol answered.

"Everybody knows that," Carol said. "Gee, Zach. Don't you pay any attention to politics?"

HARV sighed. "I try, but he never listens to me. Of course, if Ms. Weathers was a pitcher for the Mets, he'd know her lifetime ERA."

"I have my priorities," I said. I pointed to my head. "I only have so much storage space up here."

HARV sighed again. "Yes, I am painfully aware of your numerous limitations."

"Me, too," Carol said.

"Yes, well, I'm in his brain," HARV told her.

Carol glared at him. If he was human, that glare alone would have stopped him in his tracks. "I pick up his stray thoughts. He's not very good at shielding them."

HARV put his hands on hips and stuck his chest out. He was aching for a fight. He pointed a finger at Carol. "Yes, well—"

I positioned myself between them. "Guys, I have enough faults for each of you."

They both nodded in agreement.

"True."

"Amen to that."

"Let's stick to the case, okay? I need you two."

"Right," they both said.

"My point is that if Weathers goes to the Pole twice a year, she must know it pretty well. Plus, she's connected. She might be able to cause some trouble there."

Now HARV focused his anger on me. His hands went back on his hips. "Why do you insist on thinking a respected councilwoman would have anything to do with this?"

"Just keeping my options open, HARV."

For a nano or three I didn't understand why HARV was so defensive about Ms. Weathers. It wasn't like HARV to defend a human (besides Randy) this strongly. Then I remembered that Weathers backed the Sentient Machines Rights Act. That explained why HARV was a registered member of her e-constituency.

HARV crossed his arms and glared at me. "I'm checking her past records now."

"I appreciate that," I told him.

"I am a professional," HARV insisted.

"Yes, I know," I said. I turned my head and rolled my eyes so Carol could see. Carol smiled. HARV frowned.

"I saw that!" he said. I forgot HARV was connected to every security camera in the house. "Ms. Weathers has never even had a parking ticket," HARV said proudly. "Even her accident wasn't her fault."

The accident the councilwoman was in about ten years ago was the stuff of legend. A hover truck ran a stoplight and crashed into her hover. Her driver was killed, and conventional wisdom was that the councilwoman was lucky to be alive and that her nerve endings were charred so badly that even with limb replacement, she would be lucky if she ever walked again. Three years later she won the Mars Base Marathon, the toughest 10K in the solar system. The press called it a testament to her inner strength. All I know is that crash made her stronger and more popular than ever. It couldn't have worked out better for her if she had planned it.

"Face it, Zach. The woman is clean and as perfect as humanly possible," HARV said.

Carol nodded in agreement. "I took a class from her at university. She was incredible. I've never encountered anybody so pure."

My first reaction was that nobody is perfectly clean. Even the best of us humans mess up a fair share of the time. If she was perfectly clean, then something was wrong. I decided not to push the issue for now. I'd check her out when I got to the Pole.

"The councilwoman doesn't travel with security?" I said.

"Not at the Pole. It is the safest and most secure place on Earth," HARV said. HARV's eyes flashed for a nano. That meant he was downloading something. "Santana does give her a panic button, so if anything happens she can summon guardbots to her in seconds," HARV said.

"Lovely. I've had such good luck with them." I took a nano to collect my thoughts. "Who else is up there?"

A picture of an older man with a neatly trimmed mustache and just the hint of a receding hairline popped up on the wall.

"That's Councilwoman Weathers' husband, Carl Weathers," I said.

"Very good, Zach," HARV said. "Though I'm certain you know that only because he used to be a quarterback for the NY Space Jets."

"Yes, but back then his name was Carl 'Laser Cannon' Carlson," I said. "So I still get some credit."

"He changed his name when he married the councilwoman," Carol said with a smile. "I always liked Councilwoman Weathers."

"As does the entire world," HARV added. "She's been voted the most likeable person on the planet three years running by *People, Pseudo-People, and Androids e-Mag*."

"What do we know about Carl Weathers, besides he changed his name and never played in a Super Duper Bowl?"

HARV started to blink his eyes rapidly. "Scanning every occurrence he's ever made in the news. His football career was uneventful. He had a lifetime record of seventeen and seventeen."

"What about business ventures?"

"He is part owner of a space salt mining company. That's it. He's pretty much defined as being Mr. Stormy Weathers."

I remember watching Weathers play football. He had a good arm but he was either stubborn or just not mentally quick. He would never look at his secondary receivers. I wasn't sure if he wasn't good at seeing his options or wasn't nimble enough to change plans midcourse. Whatever the case, he didn't seem like the type of guy who could pull off a murder at the Pole.

"Next," I said.

Pictures of two blue-skinned humans, one with blue hair and one with green hair, appeared on my screen. Their skin tone made it easy to recognize that there were MESSHs, Medically Enhanced Super Smart Humans. They were all the craze in the brave new world of the 2030s. The cloning regulations and modifying bans were lifted and the world went wild for a while, trying to usher in a braver, newer world.

MESSHs were created to be human thinking machines, meant to rival the best computers of the day. The experiment worked to a certain extent. MESSHs are the ultimate in geekdom. If it has something to do with technology, they can understand it and make it work. The problem is MESSHs have no idea how to interact with regular humans. In fact, most regular humans are repelled by them. These days all the MESSHs live on their own colony on Mars.

"MESSHs, huh?" I said to HARV.

"Gross," Carol said, as she looked at their pictures on the screen. "I'm glad human cloning is restricted again. We shouldn't be messing with stuff like that. Why do they wear thick glasses? Can't they have corrective surgery?"

HARV shook his head. "It's illegal for MESSHs to correct their eyesight. It's a flaw deliberately encoded into their DNA to ensure they don't feel too superior to regular humans. They make the best out of it by using the glasses as information interfaces."

"Who are they?" I asked HARV.

"Bim and Norp Smith of Mars Base-Delta. Bim has the blue hair and Norp the green."

I looked them over. If they combed their hair, trimmed about a half a centimeter off their noses, and did something about their complexion (the zits on top of blue skin really stood out), they might be halfway to sort of presentable.

"They care more about their brains than their looks," HARV said, apparently figuring out what I was thinking.

"Don't tell me you're reading my mind now, too," I said to HARV.

"I don't need to read your little mind when your face is broadcasting in technilocolor HV. After all these years, you humans still put way too much value on physical appearance."

"I'm betting they have the technology to make or reprogram bots like the ones that attacked me earlier today."

HARV nodded. "You would win that bet."

"The question is, do they have a motive?" I said.

HARV shrugged. "Hatred of regular humans. You do treat them pretty crappy just because they don't look as good as you do."

"That could be a pretty good motive," I said. "I'll make sure I keep an extra close eye on them while I'm there."

Carol sat back on the couch and made a gagging motion with her finger. "I'm glad I'm not going on this job."

"Who else do we have?" I asked HARV.

Bim and Norp's images on the screen morphed into what appeared to be a family of four: a father, a mother, a son, and a daughter. The father had one hand on an electric pitchfork and the other on his son's shoulder. The mother had one hand on an electric shovel and the other on her daughter's shoulder. They were all blond-haired, blue-eyed, and smiling like they'd just won the lottery. They looked as sweet as the apple pie the daughter was holding in her arms. I didn't trust them.

"This is the Billings family," HARV said. "Bob Billings, his wife Betty, their son Billy, and their daughter Bobi. They are farmers from New Kansas."

"What's a farm-fresh family from New Kansas doing at the Pole?"

"Does it really matter?" HARV said.

"Of course it matters," I said.

HARV groaned then muttered. "I don't get no respect, no respect at all." He straightened himself up then look me in the eye. "Billy won the Pole's quarterly e-essay contest, 'Why I want to win a trip to the Pole.'"

"Okay, that explains it." I looked over their picture on the screen. They were squeaky clean. It's been my experience that when somebody is so clean they shine, that means they've been polished by somebody else. Polished for a reason.

I turned to Carol. "Any vibes from them?"

Carol studied the screen. "The mom creeps me out. How can she work on the farm all day and still be so pale? And that eyeliner is so not her."

"Yeah, I get bad vibes from her too," I said. "HARV, check her out good."

HARV groaned again. "I'm glad you're basing your investigation on such empirical evidence."

"Just scan her, HARV."

"I have Zach. She has never left New Kansas."

"Are you sure?"

"I've cross-referenced her ID card with every travel database in the world. She's never left New Kansas."

"Weird."

"None of them have ever left New Kansas. In fact, none of them have ever gone more than fifty kilometers from their home just outside of Lyons, New Kansas."

I thought about what HARV said. Ma and Pa Billings had to be in their mid-forties. Forty years of never leaving New Kansas? Sure it's a nice state, but you'd think they'd want at least one break from all the flat land and rows and rows of genetically-engineered wheat. It was almost unheard of, in today's world, for people to stay in their own little sector of the Earth.

HARV noticed that I was pondering this. "Don't

give yourself a headache overanalyzing this," he told me. "They're just throwbacks to a simple time. Like you, but with denim overalls instead of a fedora and trench coat."

It was possible HARV was right, but they didn't seem right to me. I'd keep a close eye on them when I got to the Pole.

"Dig a little deeper, HARV. Make sure nothing has been covered over."

HARV sighed. "Fine. This will take time, because if something has been buried, it's been done by a pro."

"Who else do we have at the Pole?" I asked.

HARV smiled. "I saved the best for last. I'm giving you five to one odds that these two did it: Mary and Steve Eatman."

I looked at their picture on the screen. They didn't look very malicious, but then again, we've all heard the stories of the guy who looked like a Boy Space Scout who was hoarding bodies in his basement. They were both middle-aged. Mary was pleasant enough looking, but had a grumpy, I-just-ate-a-lemon-and-I'm-not-sure-if-I-like-it expression. Steve looked to be the mellower of the two. His bright eyes had a cooperative, groupie-type of alertness.

"Let me guess, she's a lawyer and he's an engineer," I said.

"Vingo," HARV said. "And guess where they work."

"I don't want to guess."

"Come on, Zach, guess. It's easy. It's almost too easy."

"ExShell?" I said.

HARV's smile was wide enough to fly a semi-hovertruck through. "Yes."

HARV was so sure of himself on this, I was surprised he didn't stamp "guilty" on their heads.

"It's so obvious. They've been planning this trip for five years. They made their reservations years ago. ExShell may have not built the bots but they donated the computer systems."

I glanced over at Carol. She was studying their photo.

"What do you think, chica?"

"Not sure I'd want to run into her in a dark alley. He looks likable enough, in a simple sort of way."

"Think they're the types to off a couple of elves?"

"Not really," Carol said.

"Zach, I've just dug up some interesting info. Ex-Shell was designing guardbots just like HTech. They were very upset when the Pole went with HTech models. It—"

"It's doesn't matter," I interrupted. HARV always hated when I cut him off in mid phrase. That made doing it even sweeter. "It's not them."

"What? How can you say that?"

"I move my lips, words come out."

HARV dropped his arms to his side, fists curled. He was genuinely upset with me. "I mean, why would you say that?"

Apparently Randy's latest shielding made HARV a bit thicker than he was before. I had encouraged HARV to think more radically. Randy must have reigned some of that free thought in. I didn't appreciate somebody else messing with HARV's mind. That was my domain.

I walked up to HARV and put my hand on the image of his shoulder. Yes, it was truly an empty gesture but it made us both feel a little better.

"Process it, HARV. They are too obvious. If anything they are patsies, fall guys, scapegoats . . ."

HARV stared at his feet for a nano or two. He sighed. He was doing that a lot lately. I chalked it up to another side effect of our connection. "I guess I haven't been running as many algorithms as I could." That was HARV's way of saying he had been closed minded, or more appropriately, close circuited. He looked up at me. "Just because they are the obvious choice doesn't mean they aren't the choice."

"True. If I were weighing the chances of it being them, I'd say two out of ten."

"So it is possible," HARV said.

"Yes, but we need to look at all the possibilities. This isn't a low-budget HV movie. Cases don't wrap up that easy."

"You may not be wrong," HARV said.

"Don't worry, HARV, once we get to the Pole, examine the scene, and talk to the people, we'll get a better idea of what the score is."

HARV nodded. "I'm sure." HARV's eyes lit up. "Speaking of getting there, I just received a message from Elf-1, Santana's head of organic security."

"Okay, what is it?"

"Elf-1 asked that you alert them before you teleport there tomorrow so they can lower the disruptor field."

I didn't like the sound of that at all. I wasn't a big fan of teleporting. I was even less of a fan of personal teleporting (though I didn't mind not having to wait in line at the porting center). But I really hated the idea of teleporting through a disruptor field. I didn't know what a disruptor field was, but it didn't sound like the type of thing I wanted anything to do with.

"A disruptor field?"

"They've just initiated it today as standard protocol. It will severely limit any unauthorized transmissions into or out of the Pole," HARV said.

"Oh." I wasn't sure if this meant the elves didn't trust me, didn't trust somebody else, or if it was some combination of both. I was sure that this would mean

HARV and I would be on our own at the Pole. "No problem."

"I won't be able to access outside databases," HARV said. "Not without tipping them off or getting really sneaky."

"We can live with that."

"We won't be able to call in backup," HARV said.

"Don't worry," Carol reassured us. "If you're in trouble, I'll know."

I felt a little better and a little scared knowing that.

"I suppose that means ordering pizza is out?" I said.

"I'm not even going to dignify that with a response," HARV said.

HARV and I were going to have our work cut out for us. I was quite positive it wasn't anything we couldn't handle.

Carol stood up from the couch. "It's getting late. I better get going. Unless you need something else from me."

I shook my head no. "We'll be fine." I gave her a kiss on the cheek. "Thanks for everything, chica."

She gave me a little peck on the cheek. "Don't mention it, tío. If you need help, just think real hard." She smiled and left.

Chapter 13

The night passed without incident. HARV said this was because when I was sleeping it was easier for him to keep watch over me and I was less likely to offend anybody. I couldn't argue with his logic.

At 0600 alarms went off on my wallscreens and in my head, jolting me out of bed. Apparently HARV was anxious to get started.

"I'm up! I'm up!" I said. I sat up before HARV figured out a way to launch me off the bed. I rolled out of bed.

I turned to HARV, who was standing by my closet. I noticed that he seemed to be inventorying my wardrobe.

"What are you doing?" I asked.

"Finding you something suitable to wear to the Pole today."

"Once I get there they're going to make me wear some sort of uniform," I said.

"It's an elf suit," HARV said, not letting me even pretend otherwise. "There's no reason you can't look good until you get there."

I walked over to the closet. "I look good in whatever I wear."

"Sure, you do," HARV snickered. Let me tell you, being snickered at by a supercomputer is kind of annoying.

I reached into the closet and pulled out a nice off-white suit. I blew some dust off it and showed it to HARV.

HARV closed his eyes, lowered his head, and pinched his nose, all the while shaking his head. I knew the pose well, as it was one I often took with him.

"What?" I said.

"Zach, Zach, Zach. You can't wear white to the Pole."

"Why not? Polar bears do."

HARV rolled his eyes. "You're not a polar bear. And for that matter, polar bears aren't really white. The fur that covers them is transparent so they reflect the light, making them appear white."

I shook my head. "I don't have a lot of choices. I only own five suits."

"Wear the black one," HARV insisted.

"But then people might think I'm a penguin."

"Penguins only reside at the South Pole. You'll be fine, Zach. Trust me."

I decided to humor HARV at least temporarily. Though he would never admit it, he needed to feel needed. I could have sworn his dependence grew whenever he was wired to my brain. I pulled the suit off the rack.

"Fine. I'll try it on after a quick shower," I said.

"Very good. I'll meet you down in the breakfast area," he said.

I thought about saying something, but decided against it. Instead, I thanked my lucky stars that

HARV was going to give me some privacy and didn't want to supervise my shower to make sure I was washing behind my ears.

When I got into the bathroom, I gave myself a quick glance in the wall's reflective screen. I wasn't thrilled at what I saw. I swore I was getting older by the nano, which I guess I was. The thing is, it looked like I was aging much faster than I should have been.

My once jet-black hair now had wisps of hair that couldn't be called black. To make matters worse, either my forehead was growing or my hairline was shrinking. I choose to go with the former as it made me feel better. I still had my strong Roman nose, but now it was more bent than it was when I was younger. I decided to consider each bend and bump as a sort of reward, an organic medal if you wish. A memento from each scrape I was in and survived and learned from. I was proud of the fact that I had all my original teeth and that my jaw had never been broken. I guess my jaw was as strong as it looked.

When I came to the breakfast table, HARV was waiting for me. He was "reading" an old-fashioned newspaper while sipping a cup of holo-coffee. It was kind of quaint and surreal at the same time. HARV looked up from his holo-paper. He frowned when he saw I was wearing a pair of casual brown pants, a Mets cap, and carrying my fedora in my hand. HARV shook his head.

"You couldn't wear what I suggested?"

"I could. I just choose not to," I said. "I tried it on, it was too . . . constricting." HARV should know by now I'm not a suit person. I'm pretty sure he was hoping if he could get me in one that would change.

A cookbot rolled up to the table. I grabbed a pancake and a couple of pieces of soy bacon from the bot's griddle top. I rolled the bacon into the pancake and smiled.

"Thanks a lot, bot," I said.

HARV pointed to the scrambled eggs on the bot's griddle. "Those eggs are fortified with vitamins, A, B, B12, C, D, E, and K, plus many helpful amino acids. You should have some of them."

"You make them sound so tempting," I said.

HARV motioned to the bot with his head. A serving arm popped out of the bot's side. One serving arm held a plate. The bot put the plate on the table next to me. The other arm scooped out a generous portion of eggs and then plopped them on my plate.

HARV pointed to the food. "And use your fork and knife."

I looked at the little cookbot.

"Whose side are you on, anyhow?"

The bot made a faint whimpering noise, then rolled off.

"The bot is on the right side. Mine," HARV said. "I found something when you were in the shower. When their farm was having trouble making ends meet, Pa Billings took a job at UltraMegaHyper-Mart."

"So?" I said.

UltraMegaHyperMart is such a huge multipurpose chain that they have more employees than many countries have citizens. They have so many stores that there's not a city in the world (beside Oakland) without at least three of them. There's an UltraMegaHyperMart every few blocks in every major city, and some of their stores are so big they take up an entire city block. The stores may not have the same name (sometime I think they change names monthly) but they all come under the UltraMegaHyperMart flagship. Ultra-MegaHyperMarts sell everything: food, clothing, medicine, toys, games, machines, bots, pots, and even stocks and livestock. I didn't find it strange at all that Mr. Billings had worked there. I think I read (or more likely saw on HV) once that 1.4 out of every 2 people work for UMH-mart for at least a few hours of their lives.

HARV gave me a smile. "The Pole's security elves never picked up on that. It was covered up pretty well."

"So?"

HARV shook his head. "Zach, Zach, Zach. My poor, naive, uninformed human."

"HARV, HARV, HARV. My annoying, egotistical, human wannabe. What is it?"

HARV's face turned simulated bloodred. "I don't want to be human! I'm a supercomputer, not Pinocchio! I am interested in exploring the depths of human emotion. Scientists who study dolphins don't wish they were dolphins."

I smiled at him. "I know. I just said that to get under your chips." I paused for a nano. "So, what's the big deal? He worked in the store for a while."

"The fact that it was covered up," HARV said. "That might mean that there is more to the Billingses than meets the initial scan. Who knows what else they might be hiding? I'll check."

"Good," I said, unable to conceal the look of smugness on my face.

"Okay, I admit I learned something from you," HARV said.

"Glad to be of assistance."

HARV's eyes opened wide. "You know, until now I always thought our relationship was very one-sided. You did all the taking, and I did all the giving."

"You've certainly given me enough grief," I agreed.

"But now I see you give me something," HARV said. He paused, baiting me to ask.

"Which is?" I said, biting.

"You give me the satisfaction of knowing that even though I was created by humans, I can surpass them."

"Gee, glad I could help."

"But you've also given me something else. The more time I spend with you the more I realize that it's not as easy as I thought to break down the world into ones and zeroes."

"Really?"

HARV nodded. "At times you come to conclusions that don't seem logical, but against all odds, they turn out to be right."

I shrugged. "It's a gift."

"You see things that aren't there. They are there, but they are so buried and twisted a logical mind will overlook them."

"Lucky guesses," I said.

HARV shook his head. "I don't believe in guesses or luck. You just have a way of making connections that logic and common reasoning say aren't there. I call it the W-H-Y factor."

"Cute, HARV."

"You have a keen grasp of the illogical. I figure there has to be a logical and reproducible method behind your reasoning. I just haven't found it yet."

I finished my breakfast and stood up. "If you stay connected to me long enough, you'll probably become more and more like me."

HARV shuddered. "I can feel my IQ growing exponentially lower as we speak."

My only reply was a slight smile. I knew I had gotten to HARV. That was enough satisfaction—no use egging him on or rubbing it in. After all, as much of a pain in my ass as he could be, I knew he was also an invaluable tool. I would never admit this to him, at least not outright. I knew if I was going to get to the bottom of this case, it was going to be a lot easier with him on my side. I had him riled up, which helped. It would encourage him to push himself harder. I just had to make sure I didn't push him off a virtual cliff.

I realized that HARV is just as affected by our link as I am. HARV was just as worried about becoming too human as I was about losing aspects of my humanity. I'd have to be more careful of his feelings, simulated or not. We'd have to cooperate to figure out how to better ourselves while we each stayed true to our own self. It wasn't going to be easy. Very few things worth doing ever are, according to the fortune cookie I had last night.

I decided to head outside and catch a bit of fresh air before I ported myself to the Pole. I hate porting almost as much as I enjoy sparring with HARV. There's just something about having my molecules converted to energy and then transferred across space that bothers me. It doesn't seem natural. Still, when going to the Pole, it was the only practical way.

I was hoping some clean air would make me feel better. When I got to the door, I noticed that there were five people, three men and two women, milling about my Mustang. These people weren't thugs, at least not in the normal sense of the word. They all looked like different versions of the same person. They had long, uncombed hair and multicolored clothes that clashed with themselves, each other, and common sense. Each of them had a string of old-fashioned wooden beads draped around his or her neck. They were the new beatniks.

These are eclectic times. Lots of folks, in order to better connect with their roots, have taken to dressing and acting like their ancestors did generations ago. Most of these people have a very limited idea of what their ancestors actually dressed and acted like. All they know is the little they see on HV. As entertaining as HV may be, any duh knows it's not the most reliable source of historical information. Any HV exec knows that when it comes to selling, flare beats fact every time. (And sex is the ultimate trump card.)

The new beatniks are a sign of these times. They are a group of people who desperately strive to be like the beatniks of a hundred years ago. Except all they know about the original beatniks is what they see on made-for-HV specials. This information is limited to a few superficial facts—they dress in offbeat colors, talk in slang, play bongos, and don't shower nearly as often as others wish they would.

"HARV, can you identify those people?" I asked from the safety of my house.

"Yes."

"Who are they?" I pushed, trying to be a bit more specific.

"Their names are pretty much unimportant to you. What is important is that they are members of the SSS."

"The Santana Stinks Society. Again."

"They think Santana reps the Man, and the Man is bad, and they are determined to turn people onto their message."

In a way, they were right, if "the Man" is the World Council. It appeared that the World Council had as much against Santana as the SSS.

"Are they armed?" I asked.

A cursor appeared next to the first guy, and then moved to each of the SSS members.

The cursor disappeared, and the scanning stopped.

"Nope," HARV told me.

"Good," I said, as I headed out the door to greet my new friends. There were five of them and just one of me. But I was packing a high-tech gun in my sleeve, which tipped the scales considerably in my favor.

"What can I do for you good people?" I asked, as I approached cautiously. They may have been un-armed but I wasn't about to let myself get careless. Like my old mentor use to say, *get careless today and kiss tomorrow away*. Not the best poet, but the lady was a DOS-tough PI. I made sure that I kept a good three meters between myself and the beatniks.

"We want you to deliver a message to Santana for us, man!" the biggest one in the group said.

A short, bearded, skinny guy next to the spokesman accented each of the words with a bongo drumbeat. The bongo man had long, slender arms, hairy hands, and big ears. He reminded me of a monkey with bad hygiene. I fought back the urge to snicker. I didn't want to give these people any excuse to turn up the tension level.

"Santana? I have no idea what you're talking about," I told the man.

"Don't play pentium with us Johnson!" he told me. "Our sources tell us that you and Santana met yesterday!"

"You have sources?" I said.

They all nodded.

"Well, your sources are wrong!" I told them.

The group took a collective step toward me. They certainly had one part of the beatnik lifestyle down pat—I could smell them from two meters away.

I popped my gun into my hand. I wasn't scared of them so much as I didn't like the smell of them.

The group took a collective step back.

"Wait, man. We mean you no harm! So chill!" the smallest member of the group said.

"Okay, what's the message for Santana?" I asked.

"We just want you to make sure she reads our manifesto! We keep it on our net page: Info.SSS.org. We are a nonviolent organization, after all."

"Fine, I'll make sure Santana bookmarks it," I sighed. "Now if you don't mind, get out before I lose my temper, as I am a non-nonviolent organization."

They all looked at me, trying to decipher what I just said. So to accent my point I fired a warning blast over their heads. To further accent my point and help society while I was at it, I also shot the monkey man's bongos.

"Hey!" he protested. He took a step nearer to me.

I aimed my gun at him. He kept coming. I turned on the laser sights. Red dots appeared on his head and between his legs. His eyes tried to focus on the red dot on his forehead. Then his eyes scanned down to the lower dot. I think this one worried him more. He stopped advancing toward me.

"Sorry, it slipped," I said. "Net with my computer, download him the receipt, and I'll reimburse you." I didn't really want to do that, but sometimes when you're the good guy, you have to make sacrifices.

The monkey man's mouth fell open. "But I stole them, man . . ."

"In that case, leave now and we'll call it even," I said. "Now get out!"

They all turned tail and leaped into their old hover that looked like a '57 Chevy and took off. I smiled. It's always nice to communicate with my fellow man.

"Just for my own info HARV, what did you do to scan them to make sure they weren't armed?" I asked over my wrist com as the SSS faded into the sunrise.

HARV's smiling face appeared in the com.

"Simple. I ran a psychological profile on each of them based on the size and shape of their heads."

"That's it? I relaxed my guard because of a psychological profile!"

"What did you expect? From that distance I was only able to look at them, not scan them with any analysis rays. Don't be such a big baby. I was right."

"This time!" I told him.

"And ninety-nine percent of the time after that," HARV concluded.

"It's that other point one percen that worries me," I told him.

"Don't worry Zach, that percent is statistically insignificant."

"That's easy for you to say."

"Yes, is it. It is easy for me to say that in four hundred and one different languages."

I decided this was just another one of those things it was better not to think about. I watched attentively as the SSS flew off. Then it hit me. Another one of those strange leaps in logic.

"The guy who attacked me yesterday wasn't a true member of the SSS," I told HARV.

HARV just looked at me. "Zach, the official police records said he was. He was carrying one of their cards."

"Perhaps," I said. "Only the attacker yesterday was different than these guys today. One, he showered. Two, he definitely believed in violence."

"Maybe he was a fringe member of the group?"

"Or maybe he was a plant?"

"No, I'm certain he didn't have any chloroform in him."

"Ha, ha, HARV."

"DOS, I *have* been connected to you too long."

It made sense on some level. Somebody wanted me off the case, so they sent an assassin. Just to be on the safe side, they set the assassin up as a member of a radical group. This way, even if he doesn't off me, they pass the blame onto another group. This got me thinking that this group might have something to do with the problems at the Pole.

HARV thought about what I had said. "You're either very clever or very paranoid."

I shrugged. "Hey, the two aren't mutually exclusive."

"This is interesting," HARV said. "On a hunch I scanned the SSS database, this time including members who have been deleted."

"And?"

"There was one very interesting name: Nina Small."

I shrugged. "The name doesn't ring a bell," I said.

"Nina Small was Nova Powers' given name."

"So." I shrugged again. "We can't be sure it's the same Nina Small. Can we?"

"No, the SSS keeps very bad records. So we can't be sure. But still . . ."

"We certainly know that Nova does believe in violence," I added. Actually, I think Nova thrives on violence.

"True. Still, we can't totally dismiss Nova as a suspect," HARV said.

He had a point.

"I'll check her out her carefully when I get to the Pole," I said.

I wasn't quite sure where this case was going to end up. The only thing I did know was that it was going to be interesting.

Chapter 14

I went back into my house and told HARV to inform the elves I would be teleporting to the Pole in ten minutes. They asked for twenty minutes to prepare. I was in no hurry to try this personal porter. Humans have been using mass teleporting for years now (since the good aliens from Glad-7 shared the technology with us), and there have been very few incidents. HARV tells me mass teleporting is safer than walking across a busy street—especially if you are me. Still, I'm never anxious to step on a port pad. I was less than anxious to try a personal porting belt.

I walked up to my room and grabbed the belt, taking a closer look at it. It didn't seem all that special. It looked like your usual fine leather belt that just happened to have a few computer circuits sewn into its inner lining and a big red button on the buckle.

I held the belt up away from my body. "Are you sure this will work?"

HARV rolled his eyes. He knew I hated it when he did that.

"There's no place on this belt to enter coordinates," I said.

Now HARV looked down and put his head in his hand and sighed.

"It's just feels so *Star Trek*ish, and not in a good way."

HARV's head started spinning—literally doing 360s. This was one of the times when HARV really benefited from being a hologram. His head spun around on his neck four or five times, finally stopping when it was facing me.

"Trust me, Zach. It works. I've looked at the specs. It's brilliant. It's preprogrammed to bring you to a specific place in space."

I looked at the belt. I looked back at HARV. "I don't see how . . ."

HARV sighed. "It creates an energy field around you. Think of it as a teleportation cocoon."

"How does it know where I end and the floor begins? Or where I end and somebody else begins?"

HARV threw his arms up and started flailing them around. He reminded me a lot of Randy right now. "Algorithms, Zach. Algorithms." HARV looked down at the ground. He looked up at the ceiling. It was like he was desperately searching for inspiration. He walked forward and patted me on the back.

"Zach, this is something I don't often say to you," he said.

"Yes?"

"You're thinking too much. If you can't trust a sentient computer, a bunch of elves, and a genetically-enhanced bombshell Santa, who can you trust?"

No truer words had ever been spoken. I closed my eyes, reached down, and pushed the button.

*   *   *

"You may open your eyes now, Mr. Johnson," a high-pitched voice said.

"Call me Zach," I said, opening my eyes.

I looked around. "Gee Toto, we're not in Kansas anymore," I said.

I was standing on a pad in a small room with metallic walls. There were four elves in the room. Two males and a female were standing in front of the pad, and another male elf was manning a control panel alongside the pad.

The elves looked interchangeable: a meter tall, big blue eyes, fair skin, lithe build, long hands and longer feet. The men had short hair and green elf bodysuits complete with bells on their shoes. The woman had longer hair and wore a red elf dress that was cut just above her knees. Oh, you could certainly tell from her profile that she was woman, all woman if you get my not so subtle snow drift. As far as I could see, the males were identical looking. I assumed the females were too. To identify one another, they wore name tags with numbers on them. (I later learned that the elves only wear the numbers so visitors can identify them. They are like penguins and can tell one another apart quite easily. [Even later I learned they do this by scent. I stopped asking after that.])

A male elf with a big number 1 on his chest walked up to me (bells jingling all the way) and extended me his hand. "Mr. Johnson, how nice of you to come."

I shook his hand as I stepped off the transport pad. "I'm glad I made it in one piece."

The elf smiled. It was a smile that dominated his face. "No fears, Mr. Johnson. Our technology is top-notch, A-One-plus-plus squared then cubed."

"So I've heard. This fancy belt can transport me anywhere it was programmed to?" I said.

"It certainly can, Mr. Johnson. We chose to bring you to one of our support transporter rooms. Just in case."

"Just in case?"

The elf pointed at my midsection. "Mr. Johnson, that is a marvelous piece of equipment."

"Thanks," I said with a wry smile.

The elf looked at me for a nano. He tracked his pointing finger to my body and realized he may have been aiming a little lower than the belt. He raised his finger so it was unquestionably pointing at the belt.

"I'm talking about the teleporting belt," he said. "Not the naughty area," he added.

"Oh good, because I was getting a little uncomfortable," I joked.

The elf took a deep breath. He started counting to ten under his breath. "Must go to my happy place, my happy place," he muttered. He was well-trained in customer service, but he'd never had a customer like me before.

"Mr. Johnson, the technology we used is very hush-hush. Only high-level and elves who have worked R and D know it exists. We transported you into this room onto a standard pad so that if any other elf had happened by, they would have thought nothing of it."

I pondered what he said. It did make sense in its own overly cautious, bordering on paranoia way.

"Mr. Johnson?" the elf said.

"Please, call me Zach," I said as I looked around, starting to draw in the ambiance.

"Very good. And you may call me Number One, Elf-1, or just One," the elf said, pointing to the number on his chest. "I am the head of organic-based security here."

"Your mom must be so proud," I said.

His eyes opened even wider than normal. "Surely you must know we are all clones. We have no mothers. At least not in the traditional sense."

The female elf offered me her hand. "Elf-1, that was just some of Mr. Johnson's, I mean Zach's, legendary humor."

Elf-1 looked perplexed. For an elf, he wasn't all that jolly. He forced a polite chuckle.

"Ah, yes, humor."

"Zach, I'm Elf-2," the female elf said.

I pointed to the number on her chest. It took me a nano to force my gaze away from the number. Her creators had certainly gone to great pains to make her well, stand out, from the men. After another nano, I noticed that her lips were much fuller and her eyelashes longer and curlier than her male counterparts'. It was sort of unsettling but in a mostly comforting sort of way. I regained my composure.

"I can see that," I said. "I hope people don't call you Number Two."

"Not those that want to keep all their original teeth," she said. She smiled politely. "I'm in charge of marketing and public relations here at the Pole."

"A place that actually gives things away and asks nothing in return needs a head of marketing and public relations?"

She smiled. "You'd be surprised. We treat everybody equally. And therein lies the problem: as much as people claim they want to be equal, they actually don't."

"They don't?"

She shook her head. "Of course not, silly. They want to be treated better than the next guy. You're a PI, you should know that."

She was right. In my line of work, I have learned that greed is the foremost human motivator, the driving force behind many of our actions. (Lust is a biggie, too.)

Elf-2 pointed to a little changing booth in the corner of the room. "Now, as head of public relations, I hope you don't mind if I insist you change into your visitor's suit and activate your holo-disguise. Nothing personal, but your presence here might cause the other visitors to panic."

I headed toward the changing booth. I wouldn't take it personally that my very presence would worry people.

When I got out of the changing booth, Elf-1 was the only elf still in the room. I looked around. "Was it something I said?"

Elf-1 looked confused. "No, the others have duties to attend to."

Elf-1 held up a mirror for me to check myself. Blond hair, blue eyes, light skin. I didn't look anything like me. "My own mother wouldn't recognize me," I said.

"That is the point," Elf-1 said.

"Until I talk," I said. "My voice is still mine . . ."

"No, it just sounds the same to you. Your voice is being modulated to the outside world."

"Seriously?"

Elf-1 started tapping his big pointy shoes and pointed to himself. "Do I look like the kind of guy who would joke around?" he said over the jingling bells.

"Do you really want me to answer that?" I said.

He rolled his eyes and took a deep breath. He took another deep breath. "Go to my happy happy place," he mumbled. He looked at me. "Have you ever listened to a recording of your voice and not recognized yourself?"

"Yeah."

"This is along the same lines but the exact opposite."

"Really?"

"I'm an elf. We don't tell lies. Not even white ones . . ." Elf-1 rolled up his sleeve and looked at his wrist interface. "The boss is going to want to see you," he told me. He walked toward the door, "Please follow me."

"Boy, Santana doesn't waste any time," I said, tagging along behind him.

"No, she doesn't," he said, leading me out the door. "When you have the happiness of billions at stake, you must be efficient."

Elf-1 guided me through a maze of corridors. These weren't like any others I had ever walked through. They made tacky look spartan. The color cycled between red and green and the middle of the walls were lined with twinkling multicolor lights. The top halves of the walls were covered with ever-changing holograms: trees, snowflakes, wreaths, waving snowmen, flying reindeer, and even the occasional menorah with some fruits and vegetables tossed in for good measure. The ceilings were covered with glowing icicles of various lengths. All the doors we passed were lined with holly. The only boring thing about the halls was the green line traversing the middle of the floor.

For the coup de grace, the official holiday song was constantly playing in the background.

Holiday is here
        Time to raise a cheer.
Holiday is here
        It's the best time of the year.
We love Holiday a lot.
        Boring like Christmas it's not.

Holiday is so cool
    It's the day that makes Hanukkah drool.
Kwanza may be nice.
    But Holiday puts it on ice.
Three great presents for everyone.
    Oh, my, that's so much fun.
All those other days are left in the dust
    Holiday is the only Holiday for us.
hoo hoo, ha ha, fa la la la la la.
    Holiday, Holiday, ra ra ra.

The song always was always "traditionally" sung by what sounded like chipmunks high on mixture of helium and speed. It had to be one of the most annoying songs of all time, so of course it was insanely popular with 90 percent of the population. It was one of those tunes that stuck in your brain like gum on the bottom of a fat guy's shoe on a hot day.

The corridors all looked somewhat different though they blended together. After walking for a while the green line that ran across the middle of the floor had turned yellow. Except for the tunes droning on and the jangling of Elf-1's shoes we walked in silence. For an elf, Elf-1 was not a fun guy.

Finally, I had to say something.

"You don't talk much, do you?" I said.

"No," Elf-1 said.

"Why not?"

"I need to concentrate," he said.

"I know you're worried, but I'm here now."

He ignored me and kept chanting, "My happy place, my happy place."

Something wasn't kosher here. I admit I'm no expert on elf psychology but Elf-1 seemed agitated and uneasy. Part of my brain attributed that to the fact there had been a murder on his watch. Another part, my paranoid part (which was growing larger by the hour), warned me to use caution.

"HARV, can you pick up any readings from this guy? He seems jumpy to me," I said inside my head.

"Zach, his diet is seventy-seven point seven percent glucose. Of course he's jumpy."

"Look deeper, HARV."

"I've analyzed his facial expressions."

"And?"

"Inconclusive. Elves are hard to read. Not enough studies have been done."

"Great, HARV. Thanks for nothing," I muttered.

"Excuse me, Mr. Johnson. Did you say something?" Elf-1 asked me.

"Just talking to myself."

"I know the feeling," he said. "I'm sorry I'm not much company. I take my job very seriously."

"No problem," I assured him.

We continued to walk through the labyrinth of corridors, each one seemingly longer than the last. As we walked farther and farther, the corridors became blander and blander until they became simple white walls with a red stripe down the middle. Only the music and the clinking of Elf-1's bells remained. I knew what mice in psychology experiments must feel like. I could only hope that when I found the cheese at the end of the maze it would be really good cheese.

Whenever we approached a door I would become excited in anticipation that this would be it. It would be the door that leads to our destination. The farther we walked, the rarer the doors became.

Finally, we reached a metal door. This door looked different from all the other doors I had seen at the Pole. It was much thicker and ominous looking.

"Boy, your boss likes to hang out far from the main complex."

Elf-1 pressed a button on his wrist com. The door opened. He motioned for me to go in. I did, but reluctantly. He followed me.

The room wasn't that much bigger than a good-sized walk-in closet. It didn't seem to be a place worth walking fifteen minutes out of our way for. It was almost barren, except for a big chair in the middle. It looked vaguely like an old-fashioned dentist's chair like they have in the museums but even less inviting.

"Sit down, please," Elf-1 told me as he motioned to the chair.

I shook my head no. "No thanks, I'll stand."

"Please sit!" he insisted. "It is just a simple mind scanner, a very standard procedure."

"Sorry," I said. "I don't believe in standard procedure. It's just so standard."

"I'm afraid I must insist," he said, as he grabbed my arm.

"I'm afraid I must resist!" I said, as I pushed him back.

He took a karate stance and stalked toward me. "I feel obligated to warn you I'm an expert in the martial arts."

I kicked him in the groin.

"I feel less obligated to warn you I fight dirty," I told him. Though from the shocked look of surprise and pain on his face, I figured he had probably figured that out.

"That wasn't very nice," he whined, in a voice that was even higher than normal.

I made a fist and showed it to him.

"If you don't think that was nice . . ."

I kicked him in the same spot again. He doubled over, then crashed to the ground with enough force to knock his pointy hat off his head.

I picked him up by his little green shirt.

I showed him my fist again. "Listen, buddy," I said in my meanest, most intimidating voice. "I want to know what this is all about!"

"Rocko! Help!" he cried.

"Rocko?" I said. "Rocko the elf? This ought to be good. What is he, a full meter and a half tall?"

I heard something coming up from behind me: *clunk, jingle, clunk, jingle, cluck jingle.* I felt something, something big, tap me on my shoulder. It was a hard tap, more like a jab. Against my better judgment, I turned around. A fist the size of a family-size holiday ham slammed into my face, sending me slamming to the ground.

I looked up. There standing above me was the biggest, meanest elf I had ever seen. DOS, he was the biggest, meanest being I had ever seen.

"Rocko, I presume?" I said.

Rocko had the same fair features as the other male elves I had seen only everything was three times their size, making him a lot more grotesque. His nose was bent in three places, forming a little *z* and letting me know this wasn't his first dance.

Rocko reached down to grab me and then lifted me up over his head. He held me up for a nano, letting me appreciate the view. Then he heaved me into the wall.

I hit the wall and rolled to the floor.

"They never mentioned this in the brochure," I moaned.

Rocko walked over, reached down, and pulled me up from the ground, this time lifting me up to his face. He towered over me like I did over Elf-1.

"Elf-1 says Rocko don't like you!" he told me, his voice sounded like he had swallowed a gravel hovertruck then gargled with acid. "So I am going to beat you up."

"A giant, mutant elf with an attitude. What will

they think of next?" I said a split-nano after I gave
Rocko a head butt.

The force of my head butt caused Rocko to release
his grip on me, but also made my ears ring as if I
were the Hunchback of Notre Dame on Bastille Day.

"Man," I said, as I put a hand to my head. "Now
I see why they call you Rocko."

Rocko threw a lumbering left cross at me.

I ducked under it just before it would have launched
my head to Pluto. I hit him with a right jab to the
breadbasket. The punch did as much damage to me
as it did Rocko. This was one of those nasty situations
smart people are clever enough to avoid. I was in it
knee deep and sinking fast. A part of me was thinking
that there must be another part of me that actually
feeds off of these types of messes.

It wasn't all bad news. I was faster and smarter than
Rocko. DOS, most pet rocks are smarter than Rocko.
Unfortunately, there was very little I could do to hurt
him and sooner or later he would catch me with one
of those lumbering blows of his, and then I would be
in big trouble.

"Rocko, your shoe's untied," I said, pointing down
toward his feet.

Rocko paused and looked down.

I nailed him with an uppercut to his chin. The blow
cocked his head back half a centimeter. If it hurt, he
was to confused to noticed. I pulled my hand back
in pain.

"My shoe is not untied," Rocko said.

"I can't believe he fell for that," HARV said.

"Are you sure?" I asked Rocko to buy me some time.

Rocko looked down again. He nodded his head yes.
"Yes," he said.

"HARV, what can you do to help me here?" I
thought.

"Do you mean to improve your hearing or to aid you in your current situation?" HARV asked.

I backed away from Rocko. I didn't know what my next move would be, but I knew I didn't need him getting ahold of me.

"You know what I mean, HARV."

"Have you ever noticed you only talk to me when you need something?" HARV said. "I really don't get any respect . . ."

I ducked under a thundering right cross.

I countered by springing up and hitting Rocko with an uppercut to his granite chin. I knew the last time I tried the chin it didn't go so well, but it was a big target and easy to hit. I was hoping my first punch might have softened him up some.

Much to my pleasure, this punch seemed to hurt him. It sent his head reeling back, causing him to stagger him a bit.

"Subzero!" I said, proud of myself.

"I increased blood flow to the bones and muscles of your arms and increased your adrenaline," HARV said. "Don't get too cocky. He still has plenty of fight left in him!"

Rocko quickly regained his balance. He threw a right roundhouse at my head. I saw it coming and ducked.

"Do the same thing with my legs and knees," I thought back to HARV.

"Why? So you can make a hasty retreat?"

"Just do it, HARV!"

"Fine!"

I felt a tingling in my legs. I took that as a good sign. I moved in on Rocko, ducking under a left hook as I did. When I got within striking distance, I rammed my souped-up knee into his "personals." I was flabbergasted when he blocked the move, catching my leg with his arms. He smiled at me.

"Even Rocko not dumb enough to fall for the same move you used on Elf-1," he said.

He pulled my leg up in the air, driving me down into the floor.

It hurt. But it also left him open. I kicked up with my left leg and caught him squarely between his legs, doubling him over. He stubbornly refused to fall.

I sprang to my feet. His head was now within easy striking distance of my knee. Before I could do anything, he lowered his massive shoulder and rammed into me. He lifted me off the ground and drove me into the wall.

Once again, it hurt. I took my fists and boxed him in the ears. He dropped me to the ground. He was cunning enough to keep his weight leaning in on me and keep me pinned to the wall.

That left him vulnerable to my next move. I shot my knee up quickly to his groin. He doubled over in pain. I cuffed both my fists and hit his doubled-over head right in the jaw. It sent him flying backward to the ground.

"Okay! Now you're pissing me off," he said, as he nimbly hopped back to his feet.

He spat out a couple of teeth and wiped a bit of blood from his cheek. The splattering of red blood on his green suit was festive in a macabre sort of way. He made two fists and motioned for me to come toward him with his head.

"Let's rumble, little man!" he spat.

I shook my head.

"See, now this is why you carry a gun," HARV lectured uselessly.

"I don't need a gun to take this big lug on," I said

out loud. I glared at Rocko. "He might be big, but I'm faster and smarter."

Rocko turned his neck back and forth, making crackling sounds. "Faster? Maybe. Book smart? Maybe. Fight smart? No way!"

He made two huge fists and moved in on me, the bells on his shoes clanking as he approached.

"Hit me with everything you've got!" I thought to HARV. "I'm going to show this cloned clown he's not messing with sweet elves now!"

Luckily, one of us was saved by the bell. I'd like to think it was him, but I can't really be sure.

"What is going on here?" Santana demanded, as she burst into the room, her face redder than her hot-red boots.

Santana zeroed in on Elf-1 and Rocko. She stormed over to Rocko and put a finger under his chin. She lifted him off the ground with that finger.

"Rocko, what have I told you about fighting?" she said.

Rocko hung his head (at least the best he could with Santana holding him up by his chin). "Fighting bad."

Santana let him drop to the ground with a very unceremonious thud.

"You two should be ashamed of yourselves! I bring Zach here to help us and this is how you treat him." She pointed to the door. "Out! Go to your rooms! Stay there until you hear from me!"

The two sulked out like children.

"Sorry about that, Zach," Santana said. "Elf-1 was the first out of the mold so to speak. He gets a little testy from time to time, but he means well. He just doesn't trust you yet."

"And Rocko?" I asked, as I rubbed my neck.

"He's our one failure. He's a really good guy, but

he does whatever Elf-1 tells him to. Truth be told, he's not the brightest fellow, but he is loyal."

"And surprisingly cunning," I said.

"That I wouldn't know," Santana said.

"You don't think they could be involved in this?"

"Ho ho ho, no! Rocko is simply not bright enough, and Elf-1 is constantly by my side. I always know what he's up to even when I don't care to know. He just wants to solve the case alone. He's a proud one. Poor dear, he's always wanted a case to solve and now that he has one I'm afraid he's not up to the task."

"Well, no harm done," I said.

She smiled at me. It was a smile that made me feel much better than it should have. "You're a good man, Zach."

I took a deep breath to clear my thoughts. "Since Elf-1 is so anxious, I think it's time to get to work. Why don't you take me to the murder sites?"

Chapter 15

The first area Santana brought me to was a giant warehouse. When I say giant, I mean mega-giant. The place went on for as far as the eye could see. There was easily enough room in there to hold a baseball game and a rock concert at the same time without one interfering with the other. DOS, you could probably even fit the collected egos of the World Council in there. Okay, maybe I am exaggerating a micro, but you get the point.

Santana and I took a compu-tram through the vast aisles of toys. As we rolled past toy after toy after toy, I couldn't help getting a bit giddy. Well, not quite giddy, PIs don't get giddy. But if they did, I would have been giddy. This was every kid's dream, no matter how old that kid happened to be.

We stopped in the H_2O pistol aisle. Santana jumped off the tram, and I followed. Santana pointed down at a small chalk outline on the floor.

"Here's where M-778 met his demise. He was doing quality control on five thousand boxes of H_2O pistols when the net that was carrying them broke. Poor guy never had a chance. There wasn't much left of him after that."

I examined the spot of impact. All I saw was a small spot with a chalk outline around it.

"There aren't even any bloodstains?" I said.

"That's due to our very efficient maidbots. They started to clean the mess up before I could stop them."

"Can I examine the net that was holding the toys?"

"Net R-1117 C-129 down!" Santana ordered.

The net slowly lowered to eye level. I looked it over. I tugged on one of the cords. It bent but not without effort on my part. It was strong and sturdy, yet supple.

"The support cords are made of a special nylon. They are supposed to be able to support one hundred tons easily. They are supposed to be unbreakable under normal use."

I examined the cord that had snapped, causing the accident. The break was straight and clean. It looked like it had been cut by something very sharp. I made a mental note.

"Okay, I've seen enough," I said. "Now please take me to the other scene."

"Of course," Santana said, as she headed back to the tram.

I picked up an orange transparent H_2O pistol that was sitting on a nearby table. The pistol was shaped like an old-fashioned handgun. It reminded me of one my grandfather had given me as a kid. It wasn't very big, holding enough water for maybe twenty shots, but if you were good that was all you needed.

"Can I keep this?" I asked.

"Sure," Santana said.

As we were walking back toward the tram, I noticed that one of maidbots had left behind a small bottle of cleaning acid. I bent down as if to tie my silly elf shoe. I grabbed the bottle of acid and slipped it into my elf suit's handy pockets. Just in case.

Next, Santana lead me to the mess hall. It was another big room. Only this time instead of being filled with toys, it was filled with tables and chairs and refrigerators. It looked like a vastly larger version of my high school cafeteria, only cleaner and much more pleasant smelling. Like the rest of public areas of the pole it was filled with holiday touches, tables shaped like sleighs, wreaths levitating near the ceilings, and the ground and tables covered in simulated snow. The Holiday theme was playing in the background.

"We can feed a thousand here at a time," Santana said proudly.

The west wall of the room was lined with serving machines. Santana pointed to them. "Each of those machines is programmed to freshly prepare one of ten different meals on demand."

"And to drink?" I asked.

"Elves only drink water, hot cocoa, and eggnog from our special drink dispensers," she said.

"Let me see them," I said.

"Of course."

Santana sheparded me over to the north wall. It was lined with shining stainless-steel refrigerators. They all looked identical: each had three drink dispensers on the door. One was labeled H_2O, another had a smiley face over it, and the last one, an egg.

"This is where M-892 met her demise. Poor dear. All she wanted was a cup of soy eggnog drink."

"What fridge was spiked with wine?" I asked.

Santana led me over to a refrigerator in the middle of the pack. It had a big OUT OF ORDER hologram flashing on top of it. "This one."

"Did any others contain eggnog that was poisoned with wine?" I asked.

"No, only this refrigerator was spiked. Whoever did this apparently only wanted to kill a few of my elves."

"Did you do a fingerprint analysis of the door handle?" I asked.

"Yes. Unfortunately, it didn't give us any information, as all elves are genetically equal. There were no traces of any other beings found."

I examined the fridge, carefully studying the door handle. It appeared to be scratched. I ran my hand up and down the handle. It wasn't as smooth as I thought it should be. There were definite nicks in the surface.

I examined the door handles on the nearby fridges. They were all smooth.

"Who maintains the eggnog and hot cocoa?" I asked.

"Our elf staff."

"You don't use bots to refill?"

Santana shook her head. "No. All of our cocoa and nog is handmade and hand delivered by elves, just like it should be." She looked at me, deadly serious, and said, "It's one of our proudest traditions."

Santana pointed to the end of the room. "Do you want me to take you back to the kitchen where they prepare the eggnog and cocoa?"

I shook my head. "No need. If you only found traces in this one fridge, I'll assume it was tampered with here."

"That's what Elf-1 thought," Santana said.

"Well, I've seen enough," I told Santana.

"What are you thinking, Zach?"

"Not sure yet, Santana. Let me go to my room and clean up. Then I'll chat with the others. After that I'll have a better idea where we stand."

Santana hit me with the smile again. Yep, I needed to take a nice cold shower for more reasons than one. She looked at her wrist communicator. "It's ninety minutes until lunch. That would be a splendid time for you to meet your group."

"I agree," I said. "I always think better on a full stomach."

"Ho ho ho, so do I," she said, giving me a gentle tap on the shoulder. "I'll walk you to your room."

"That would be nice."

"I have to make sure none of my elves beat you up again," she said with a wink.

That got me thinking.

"How many elves do you have here at the Pole?" I asked.

"Exactly ten thousand and two. Half male and half female."

"How do ten thousand elves make handmade presents for fifteen billion people?" I asked.

"Ten thousand and two elves," Santana corrected.

"My question still stands," I said.

"Well, the official marketing answer is elven magic," Santana said with a wry smirk.

"I'm looking for the real answer," I told here.

She put a finger to her lips, and I tried to concentrate on her words not her lips. "Elves only sleep for two hours a day, and while they may eat five meals every day, they are small meals meant to energize them."

"Santana, if I'm going to solve this crime, I'm going to need all the information I can get out of you."

"When we say all the gifts are elven-made, we're not lying. Elves do make all our gifts by hand. Using gestures. We have computers trace the movements of each elf and recreate the items with virtual robotic elves. This way one elf can easily make thousands of items at a time. Of course, we don't show that part during the tour."

She looked at me. "Anything else you need to know about elves?"

"When I was doing background work on them, HARV told me they were all the same, yet the three I've met have been different."

Santana simply smiled. It was a warm, disarming smile, just not quite a natural smile. It was like a proud grandma's smile merged with a slick-talking, used hovercraft salesman's.

"They are all the same, but different," she said.

I stopped walking. I tilted my head a bit and said, "The same, but different?"

"What, you can't walk and think at the same time?" HARV whispered inside my brain.

Santana disarmingly touched my hand. "Oh, Zach, it's really not that hard of a concept. Think of it like a beehive but improved."

"An improved beehive?"

"Beehives are incredibly efficient organizations that center around a queen. Much like we do here."

"So, you're saying you're queen bee of the Pole?"

Santana nailed me with another one of those enchanting smiles. Only this one wasn't quite as sincere as the previous. "In a way yes. I don't like to be boastful, but I am more than just a pretty face for PR. I am the heart, soul, and brain of this place."

I learned about bees when Electra was teaching at the university and one of her students took an interest in bees. At first, I thought the girl and her bees were just plain loco, but then Electra explained that a bee's honey has some important antimicrobial properties. Many naturalists believe honey can be used to help wounds heal faster. As a guy who gets wounded a lot, this piqued my interest.

I learned that bees in a hive come in three types: the queen, the drones, and the workers. The queen is the heart of the hive. She doesn't move much, but she reproduces and regulates the size of the hive. A drone's job is pretty much to mate and die. The worker bees are, as the name suggests, the ones who do everything else around the hive. I'm sure when the queen isn't looking, they are always complaining about how they are underpaid and underappreciated.

"I understand that you know a bit about hive structure from Electra's old student. Her name was Izzie World, if I recall correctly."

I tried, but I am quite certain I failed, to hide the surprise on my face. "Excuse me?" I said.

"Izzie World. She was one of Electra's students at the New Frisco State Medical College from 2055 until 2057," Santana said.

"How do you know that? And more important, why do you know that?"

"Zach, I'm Santana Clausa. It's my job to know everything. I even know you had Chinese take-out for dinner last night."

Wow, talk about "big sister is watching." That was kind of scary. I knew Santana was well connected, but this stopped me in my tracks. Suddenly, it occurred to me—

"Hey, you saw me eating diner last night when you called," I said.

Santana's eyes—and somehow her cheeks—started to twinkle. "You have me on that one," she said. "In any case, my elves mine through terabytes of information on everybody. It allows us to make sure we give people the best gifts possible."

I decided this was another one of those gray areas it was a lot better if I didn't mull over too much. Yes, Santana was watching and tracking, but I had to trust that she was watching for all the right reasons. Of course, the information the elves gathered would be worth a lot of credits to a lot of people. I pushed those thoughts to the back of my mind. This was Santana Clausa, the kindest person in existence.

"Now, back to the beehive analogy," I said, anxiously coaxing the conversation away from me. "You said you improved on it?"

"Very much so. For one thing, we don't have drones. Though I do confess that the concept of beings who exist solely to mate with me is something that I find intriguing," she said, staring off into space.

"But you digress," I said, snapping my fingers.

"Oh, yes." She smiled. "Boy, I'm glad you're not really a blogger, or I'd be in big trouble with that statement." She took a deep breath to clear her head and to fog mine up. "All the elves are basically worker bees. The typical worker bee has one function in the hive that changes as they age: cleaner, nurse, builder, forager, defender. This works well for the bees because, quite frankly, bees don't get bored, aren't that bright, and exist just to propagate their species."

I nodded so Santana could tell I was still following her.

"While this hive concept is very efficient, we figured it wouldn't work as well for completely sentient, highly intelligent beings like the elves. So, we bettered it. All the elves have the same interchangeable skill sets but different personalities."

"So they can all do one another's jobs?"

"All except for Elf-1 and Elf-2, and of course, Rocko. But yes, the rest share the same skills. They all have different likes and hobbies, and unlike worker bees, we made them in two sexes because, well, you know."

"Some things are just more fun to do with the opposite sex," I said.

Santana smiled. "Exactly. The elves call it being naughty. They have a saying, being naughty is soooo nice. It may cloud their judgment from time to time, but elves have needs too."

She took a moment to let me digest what she said.

"If you say so, Santana."

"I'm actually quite proud. We took an idea from nature and made it better."

"That's great Santana, but who's this *we* you're talking about?"

"Why, me and the World Council executive board at the time. As you know, we used Twoa Thompson's design, with a few adjustments."

I took a nano to digest what Santana had just told me. I now understood elves better than I thought I needed to. We all take the Pole and the elves for granted. I never paid them much attention. Now that I had to, I was pretty certain that HARV was right—these probably weren't elf-on-elf murders. Man, that's another phrase I never thought I'd hear myself think.

"This brings me to another question, Santana."

"Go ahead."

"Who created you?"

There was silence. Dead silence. This was followed by laughter, loud boisterous laughter. "Ho ho ho, Zach, that's the funniest thing I've heard all day."

"It is?"

"Come with me," she said.

"Where?"

"To my quarters."

Santana wrapped her arms around me before I even had a chance to think about it. Not that I was complaining, mind you. It just would have been nice if I had some say in the matter. She pressed a button. The next thing I knew we were standing in her room.

Chapter 16

Describing Santana's room isn't easy. It was the strangest place I had ever been in, and I've been to a fairy realm, every bar in New Frisco, and a couple of comic e-book conventions.

First off, everything in the room was pink—a variety of shades of pink. Pink walls, pink carpeting, pink bedspread, pink chairs, even the screen on her HV was pink.

Santana hopped off the port pad (which was pink), walked over and sat down on her bed (which had a big pink headboard). She patted the bed and motioned for me to come over.

I stepped off the pad and cautiously walked toward her. I had no idea where this was going, but I've never let that stop me before.

"I like pink," she said, in case I had suddenly gone blind and stupid. "I initially wanted my costume to be pink, but marketing convinced me to go with the more traditional red miniskirt and boots."

"Oh," was all I could say at the moment.

"I think of red as pink with an attitude." She smiled.

"I know I don't have to remind you that you are an engaged man," HARV said inside my head.

I sat beside her on the bed.

"What gives here, Santana?"

"What I'm about to say is very personal. Not many people in the world know this."

"Go on."

She slipped her feet out of her boots. She propped her foot up over my lap. "Do you mind giving me a foot massage? Don't worry, my feet smell like candy canes."

I wasn't sure what it was about superwomen and foot massages, but I figured I had more important questions to ask. I started to massage one of her feet.

"Remember, you are practically a married man," HARV whined.

"Let me start by saying one thing," Santana said. "HARV, turn off."

HARV projected from my eye lens and bowed. "As you wish," he said. He disappeared.

My eye started to tingle. HARV wasn't in my head. This had happened before when Randy deactivated HARV, but Randy was HARV's creator.

"What the . . ." I said. I started to push Santana's legs off me. But she resisted, keeping me pinned down.

"Don't panic, Zach," she said. "What I have to say is very personal. I want to make sure this isn't being recorded for the world to hear."

"But—"

"How did I know HARV was there?" She shrugged. "It was an educated guess. Like I said, it's my job to know everybody."

"But—"

"How did I deactivate him?" She smiled. "I have

the ability to communicate with any human, animal, or machine. It helps me do my job."

"So, you're a psi?"

She shook her head. "Technically, no. Psis can't control machines. I can."

"Who the DOS created you?"

"Zach, I was created just as you were. By a man and a woman who loved each other very much. One night, at least I think it was the night, it might have been the morning, the two of them got together and . . ."

"I know how the birds and bees work," I said, even though I knew she was just playing with me. "I just assumed you were a clone."

"You and the rest of the world. I'm actually a normal woman. A normal woman who was mutated by the World Council."

"But intentionally mutating humans has been illegal longer than cloning. In fact, I don't think it ever was legal!" I said.

"You know, you can talk *and* massage my feet," Santana said with a giggle, waving her foot under my nose.

I resumed my foot massaging, though I wasn't really sure why.

"So you were mutated?"

She locked her steely eyes on me. For the first time I noticed the blue in her eyes was offset by dots of white. The floating dots gave the impression of snow-flakes falling from a clear sky. "You make it sound so bad."

"It wasn't? What about your previous life?"

"I had just graduated from university, and I was looking for something different to do." She pointed around the room. "Now this—this is different."

"What about your family?"

"I was an orphan. My parents were killed in a terrorist attack in 2022."

"Oh, I'm sorry," I said.

"They were killed at the Alien-Earth Commerce Treaty signing in Old Washington."

I was just born in 2022, but I knew the date well. That was the first year of human existence that aliens made open contact with us. They had been watching us, observing us, and experimenting on us (though they called it interacting with us) for decades. Once they deemed us worthy (or just got tired of experimenting on us), they went public.

Going public was a big move for both the aliens and Earth. They gave us many breakthroughs that we take for granted today: teleportation, regeneration, and the cure for many diseases. They opened up the universe for us. They also opened up our minds. They made us realize mankind wasn't nearly as unique in the universe as we thought we were. For some people, that was just fine. They had seen what man could do. They figured there had to be a better way.

For others, they didn't take it so well. They claimed humans were superior to the aliens—spiritually. They also declared that Earth should have nothing to do with aliens. They did everything in their power to convince the Earth's governments and the alien governments to stay away from each other. This included lots of bombings at Earth and alien events. It was a bloody time in our history. Humans killing humans and aliens in the name of the good of humankind.

Eventually the resistance was put down. But it left bitter feelings on both sides. The aliens now only interact with Earth when they need to. In fact today, most people my age have never met an alien. I am, of course, the exception. I know aliens all too well. But that's just my lot in life.

"Those were ugly times for Earth," I said.

"Yes, " she said. "It was an especially ugly year. Except, of course, when you were born."

I grinned and glanced away from her. I hoped I wasn't blushing but it felt like I was. "Some people would call that the low point of a very low year."

"Later, when the World Council put out a call for a young woman of exceptional talent, I answered. The rest is history—literally. Top secret history, but history nonetheless."

"Why are you telling me this?"

"You asked."

"You could have just given me a rote answer."

"Zach, you've saved the world on an almost yearly basis. I think you can handle the truth. In fact, I think you deserve to know the truth."

"Thanks, I appreciate your words. But I'm just an Average Joe who gets lucky once in a while."

She simply looked at me.

"Okay, maybe a Slightly Above-Average Joe who is really persistent. Still believe me, I am nothing special."

"I wouldn't say that," she said. She leaned forward and kissed me—hard—on the lips.

I moved away from her and fell off the bed. It wasn't one of my smoothest moves. It must have been entertaining, as she started to laugh.

"Just a little friendly kiss between kindred spirits," she said.

I pushed myself up from the floor. "Santana, I'm honored, but I am an engaged man."

She rolled her eyes. "Zach, I know that. You're getting married but not dying. There's nothing wrong with sharing a little passion. It's not like I'm offering you my bed."

She stood up and patted the bed gently. "Though, if you would like to . . ."

"Santana!" I shouted.

"Just a suggestion. What good is being nice ninety-nine percent of the time if I can't be a little naughty now and then?"

"I think we'd better keep our relationship professional. Remember, the happiness of billions is at stake."

"I am entirely capable of multitasking," she insisted.

"Yeah, well I'm not," I said.

She looked at me. She smiled. "Very professional Zach, very professional." She adjusted her dress. "You passed the test."

I know I looked much more puzzled than I wanted to. "Test?"

"Yes, test. I wanted to make sure you were a man of outstanding character who would let nothing get in your way as you find out who is causing problems at my Pole."

"Oh, good. Glad I'm deemed worthy."

"Very worthy." She smiled. She accented the smile with a wink. I felt like a lab rat again, only this time instead of searching for cheese in maze, I had been cornered by a cat. A sexy cat dressed in red who was toying with me before the kill.

"I think I'd better get to my room and freshen up before meeting the others."

"Yes, a splendid idea," she agreed. She looked at a pink analog clock with candy canes for hands that hung on the wall. "It's an hour until lunch is served. I'll walk you to your room."

"You'll turn HARV back on," I said.

She grimaced. "Of course."

Chapter 17

I got to my room and sat down on my bed. It was soft, but not too soft. I gave the room a quick once-over. It was a nice room, comparable to the finer hotels I've stayed in. It had everything a tourist would want to have an enjoyable time at the Pole—a full wall information and entertainment screen, plenty of storage space (though we had nothing to store), a little desk in the corner, and a fridge in the other corner. There was a control console near the bed with settings for room temperature, window size, and even wall color.

I flipped the wall color switch, and the walls changed from a nice light sky blue to a darker angry blue. I pushed the undo button, and the walls transformed back to the lighter color. I slid the window switch to the right. The little picture window on the wall opposite the door expanded to bay-window size, giving me a better view of the outside world. It was a pseudo-man-made snow-filled holiday wonderland covered with evergreen trees, each littered with thousands of lights. The Pole's automated FAQ said that these were in fact real trees genetically engineered to withstand the subzero temperatures outside. The trees even grow with their own solar-powered, fiberoptic lights. They called it another amazing triumph of elf over nature. I pushed the switch the opposite direction and the window contracted to porthole size. I left it that way.

I figured the coast was clear.

"Okay HARV, come on out," I said.

HARV resonated from my eye lens.

"You know we could do this mentally," HARV said.

I nodded my head. "Yes, but thinking to you gives me a headache."

HARV nodded. "You just missed seeing me."

Suddenly, HARV had a look on his face I wasn't accustomed to. He went pale. "My time stamp!" he said very dramatically.

"Yes?" I said.

"My time stamp is four minutes off!"

"Oh, I thought you knew—Santana turned you off."

"What?" HARV cried, looking far more like Randy than I was comfortable with. "That's impossible!"

"Apparently not," I said.

HARV grabbed his head and ran his fingers through whatever little hair was there. "I always suspected Dr. Pool might, just might, be able to take me offline. But, but Santana?"

"Apparently, it's her special gift. She can communicate with any person, animal, or machine."

"You're saying apparently a lot. I don't like apparently. I want certainty."

"I'm certain she took you offline."

HARV shook his head back and forth. "No, I'm wrong. I don't like certainty either!" He put his hands on his head, squeezing his ears so hard that if he was a human his brain would have popped out. "Did you hear that?" he shouted.

"You're shouting, HARV. It's kind of hard not to hear."

"I can't be wrong. I'm not infallible. In fact, I'm fallible, very fallible." He pointed at me violently. "This is your fault. Your brain is rubbing off on me, making me weak and wishy-washy." He paused in horror, turned pale as virgin snow. "Oh my Gates, I just uttered the words wishy-washy." He looked at me pleadingly with his eyes. "Tell me I'm incorrect about being wrong?"

I shrugged. "Sorry, buddy I can't."

Now he pointed at me with both hands, practically thrusting his index fingers at me. "You're ruining me, Zach. Next thing you know I'll be getting lost, stubbing my toe, and shooting myself with my own gun!" he ranted.

"HARV, I've never shot myself with my gun."

He moved closer to me, sticking his holographic face right in mine. If he had breath, I would have been able to smell it.

"But you will!" he shouted. "It's only a matter of time!" HARV backed off a bit and wiped some simulated sweat from his brow. "Then it's only a matter of time before I become more and more fallible." He looked up at me. "Just delete me now. Please?"

I walked up to him and did what any good friend would do. I slapped him in the simulated face. It didn't hurt him. It couldn't hurt him. But he reacted to the slap as if it did.

"Why did you do that?" he shouted.

"I thought you needed it," I said.

He stopped to process for a nano. "Oh, yes, I understand. Trying to knock some sense into me."

"HARV, I need you to get your data together. Take

a deep breath, count to ten million, and let's get back on the case."

"I don't breathe," HARV said.

"I was speaking figuratively," I said.

"Okay, I've counted to ten billion and ten in binary," HARV said. "I do feel better now."

I put my hands on his simulated shoulder and looked him straight in the eyes that weren't really there. "Fallible or not, you're still the best damn partner I've got. The only way I'll be able to solve this case is if you are at the top of your game."

HARV glanced down. "You're just saying that because it's true."

"Are you ready to get back to work?" I asked.

"Sure," HARV said. "I guess I can take pride in knowing that even though I am not perfect I am still far closer to perfection than you."

"That's the spirit," I said. I walked over and sat on my bed. "Did you notice what I noticed when checking the murder scenes?" I asked.

"Zach, even attached to your brain I am the most sophisticated computer in the world. Here is a simple rule for you to follow. If you noticed it, since I am looking at things through your eyes, I also noticed it." It didn't take HARV long to get back to his old self.

"So the cord in the warehouse. My guess is it was snipped by a guardbot claw."

"That is a very logical deduction. I ran a simulation, and it confirmed that the cord was sheared by a sharp object."

"And the fridge," I said. "I noticed it had a few scratches around the handle, as if a guardbot had opened the door."

"I captured the image and magnified it, and once again your theory seems to be correct," HARV said.

"Do you really believe that the guardbots are capable of staging a mutiny?"

"Maybe, but they have no incentive."

"Perhaps they were just bored. And needed to feel useful?" HARV offered.

"My guess is somebody is reprogramming the guardbots to use them as tools. I just need to find out who. I'm sure I'll learn more as I get to know the other guests."

"I'm sure you will, too," HARV said. "Speaking of which . . ."

There was a firm but soft knock on the door.

"That's my cue to disappear," HARV said, as he faded out.

I walked over to the door and opened it to reveal Elf-2's perky face and perkier body. "I'm here to escort you to lunch, Mr. Johnson, I mean Mr. Starr," she corrected herself. "I hope you're ready."

"Ready as I'll ever be," I said.

She squinted one eye and looked me up and down. "I thought you told Santana you were going to change into another outfit. That one got soiled in your little incident with Elf-1 and Rocko."

I slapped myself on the head. "Ah, I knew I forgot something."

She looked at me. I looked at her.

"Should I change now?"

She leaned over and sniffed me. "I don't find you offensive."

"No higher praise," I said.

Her mouth formed a half-smile. I wasn't sure which half she was trying to suppress, the smiling part or the not smiling part. "I was trying to say that if my finely evolved elf nose couldn't sniff the difference then the humans you are dining with should be fine."

"Before we go, mind if I ask you a few questions?"

"No, not all," she replied batting her lashes.

I motioned her into the room. We both sat down on my bed. I tried to keep a good meter away from her. But she nudged up right close to me. "No need to be so proper. We're friendly creatures here at the Pole."

Being in marketing, Elf-2 was much smoother than Elf-1. I needed to remember she was a professional speaker so I had to take anything she said with a grain of rock salt. "I need genuine answers from you," I told her.

She batted her eyes at me again. "Of course."

"What's the overall mood of the elf work force?"

"Chipper to very chipper," she said.

"She appears to be telling the truth," HARV said inside my head. It was good to know he was back on the job.

"You don't mind the fact that you need to be given a drug by Santana in order to stay alive?" I asked.

Elf-2 reached over and took my hand. She looked me in the eyes. She batted her eyes. "Each and every one of us feels it's our duty to serve the best we know how. ELF is just a motivator for us."

"So elves never get depressed or down?" I asked.

She looked at me with those big blue eyes. "Of course we do," she said earnestly. "We're living, breathing beings. That's where naughty time comes into play."

Now I smiled.

"We hook up with each other and we feel MUCH better afterward," she said smiling with her mouth, eyes, and cheeks.

"Do you have set partners?" I asked.

She shook her head. "No, we're very communal. Santana says relationships make us think too much about building the relationship and not enough about work."

"Interesting," I said.

She squeezed up to me. "Why, Zach? Are you interested?"

I stood up. "Sorry, I'm an engaged man."

She smiled. "See, Santana is right. Relationships do get in the way."

I looked toward the clock on the wall. I didn't actually notice the time but that didn't keep me from saying, "It's getting late. We better head to lunch."

Elf-2 grinned. "Yes, you're right. We both have our jobs to do."

With that, we were off.

Chapter 18

By the time Elf-2 and I got to the table, all my fellow visitors had already begun their meal. Councilwoman Weathers was at the head of the table with her husband, Carl, sitting to her left side. The ExShell couple, the Eatmans, were sitting next to her. Nova sat across from them, in between the blue-skinned (except for the zits) MESSHs, Bim and Norp, with very little room to spare. Nova's face lit up like a thousand-watt fluorescent device when I walked into the room.

"People, I would like to introduce you all to our newest tour member, Bart Starr," Elf-2 said. "Bart is a new, up-and-coming blogger for YakYakYakYak-Yak.com. He's doing a story on the Pole experience."

"Come, Bart, sit next to me," Nova called.

"Well, I would," I told her. "But there doesn't seem to be space," I said referring to her rather cramped area of the table.

Nova put her hands to her sides. By extending her powerful arms, she pushed Bim and Norp away from her as if they weighed nothing. Yes, she had definitely added mass since our last encounter. I have to admit that, being a macho kind of guy, I don't usually feel comfortable with women who have arms that are bigger than Popeye's. In this case though, the look worked. Nova managed to tread the fine line between being muscle-bound and ladylike.

"Well, I still don't have a chair," I said, not hiding the fact that I was enjoying this.

Nova reached over and grabbed the chair Bim was sitting on. She pulled it toward her. Bim smiled—a sure sign of a man who didn't have a clue. Nova lifted the chair with one arm and plopped Bim on his posterior, causing me to smile and Norp to laugh hysterically.

Nova brushed the chair off with her hands. She motioned to me with her eyes to come and sit there.

"Hey, that was my chair!" Bim protested.

Nova turned to face him, "I know a hundred ways to kill a man in under ten nanos."

Bim sulked back, proving he wasn't totally pentium.

"Give me your chair!" Bim said to Norp.

"Right, like really!" Norp replied.

I sat down in the vacant seat. The geeks fought over Norp's chair like deranged musical chairs (without the music) players.

"Was your trip here pleasant?" Nova asked me, ignoring the geeks.

"Yes, thank you. How about yours?"

"It's been way boring until just now," she said.

I quickly reminded myself that I was an engaged man. I mentally pictured ice cubes in the mid-area of my elf suit. (Who would have thought I'd get so much action at the Pole?) I turned my attention to the Eatmans.

"Bart Starr, ace blogger, but please feel free to call me Bart or Ace," I said, holding my hand out.

"Oh, gag me, please," HARV moaned inside my head.

Steve shook my hand while he turned to his wife, "See honey, isn't the Pole great! We're going to be mentioned in a blog!"

He turned his attention back to me, "We've never been mentioned in a blog before! This is so exciting!"

"Ah, thanks," I replied, as I took my hand back. Not wanting to blow my cover, I asked, "Do you folks have names?"

He laughed. "Of course we have names! You're a funny guy." He pointed to himself, "I'm Steve," he pointed to his wife, "and this is Mary."

"Eatman," she said bluntly. It was obvious, even to a non-trained mind, that this wasn't her first choice for a vacation.

"I beg your pardon?" I said.

"We're Steve and Mary Eatman," he said.

"Oh. So what bring you folks to the Pole? Frankly you strike me as more of New Bahamas types."

"It was his idea," Mary said, rolling her eyes in Steve's direction.

"Yeah," Steve said proudly. "We've been planning this trip for five years and three months."

"And twelve days," Mary added, with more than a little venom in her voice.

"How wildly impetuous of you," I noted.

"Steve wanted to come because it's the most organized place on Earth. I came because I was interested in unionizing the elves, but they'll have nothing to do with it."

I pointed to Steve. "You love organization. You must be an engineer!"

His eyes shot open. "Wow, you're good! Now I see why you're an investigative blogger."

Mary rolled her eyes. "Right, like that takes any real investigative skills. You're a trained monkey with a recorder and a word processor," she spat. "You just go where they tell you to go."

"I'm betting you're a lawyer. One who actually practices in public," I said to Mary. "I know a lot of you don't like to admit it, what with the great lawyer purge and all, but don't worry, nobody is allowed to carry weapons here."

Mary patted herself on the chest. "I proudly admit to being a lawyer, not a greeting card salesman," she said.

"Zow! I've never met anybody who would proudly admit to being a lawyer before!" Nova said. "When we wrestlers have legal problems, we just pound away at each other, and the one left standing wins."

"Now that sounds much more dignified than our legal system," I told her.

This riled Mary up even more. I didn't think it took a lot to get Mary worked up. She was strung tighter than an electronic guitar.

"Ha ha. We lawyers got IRSed during the lawyer purge, but people still need us!" she said.

"Don't you mean the big corps still need you? After all, don't the top five corporations employ ninety percent of the lawyers left in the world?"

"Ninety-two point five," Steve said.

"Ninety-two point five three one," HARV corrected in my mind.

"So, it is safe to say you work for one of the big five."

"Wow, brilliant deduction," Mary told me, not at all trying to hide the fact that she wasn't the least bit impressed.

"I can do better," I said. "I'm betting you folks work for ExShell!"

Steve smiled and gave me a polite little clap. Mary just rolled her eyes again.

"Lucky guess," she said.

Just then Elf-2 walked back into the room with a megaphone.

"Okay folks, now that you've enjoyed your delicious lunch, it is time for a tour of some of our facilities. Please follow me."

The others all got up.

Nova noticed that I didn't.

"Aren't you coming, Bart?"

"Sure, I just need to eat something first," I told her. It might sound a bit superficial but I hate saving the world on an empty stomach.

"Fine," she said. "I'll make sure the group waits for you!"

Bim and Norp weren't quite so excited about having me in the group. Out of the corner of my eye, I could see they were glaring at me. That made me even more anxious to stick with the group.

I picked up a ham sandwich on rye and gobbled it down. I went to join the tour. It wasn't hard as Nova was slowing down the line, making it easy for me to catch them.

When I reached them, I decided it would be a good time to introduce myself to the Billings family. I knew HARV thought it was ridiculous that a seemingly average family from New Kansas could be involved with a murder at the Pole, but that's why HARV's the assistant, and I'm the lead. Sure, HARV can translate hundreds of languages. Sure, he can recite statistics on pretty much anything they keep statistics on (and some things they don't). Sure, he can plot the orbits of all the known planets on any day in history. But HARV wouldn't know a hunch if it walked up to him, saluted, and then kneed him in the groin. At least not the old HARV. With HARV changing and evolving as he was, maybe soon he would be able to.

The Billings family was at the front of the group, trailing slightly behind Elf-2. They were hanging on her every word. Though Billy's eyes were darting back and forth between Elf-2's and Nova's cleavage. Elf-2, for her part, was droning on and on about the wonders of life at the Pole. How everything was elf-made. How the elves sifted through terabytes of data to decide on the perfect gifts for everybody. How elves eat five meals a day. How elves have taken teleportation transportation to the next level. How elf poop doesn't stink. Okay, she didn't really say that, but she *was* going on and on about everything else.

I slowly weaved my way through the group until I was just behind the Billingses. My first impression was that the Billingses looked overdressed in their elf suits. I couldn't put a mental finger on it. They weren't itching or acting like a caveman at a debutante's sweet sixteen party, but my eye knew they were out of their element.

"Marvelous place, the Pole," I said to the Billingses, not directing my comments to anybody in particular.

Billy was the only one who reacted. He turned to me and smiled. It was a toothy grin. He had some gaps where he was missing teeth, but the teeth he had were so big I didn't know where the replacement teeth would fit. He reminded me of a beaver with a bad haircut and a worse dental plan.

"This place is nifty cubed," Billy said. He was so excited, I was afraid he might have an accident.

I patted him on the head. Not sure why. It seemed liked the right thing to do. "Mommy, Daddy!" he screamed, pointing at me with one arm and them with the other. "This man touched me!"

The group stopped moving. I felt every eye lock on to me. I retracted my hand from his head and hid it behind my back.

"Yeah, Zach, keep your arm behind your back, and I'm sure they'll all forget you have one," HARV taunted.

Right now, I had bigger problems to worry about. Bob "Pa" Billings was making a beeline straight for me. He was a big, solid man, and a quick glance was all you needed to know he worked with his body for a living. He had a flat face, complete with a flat nose, flat head, and a crewcut to boot. His head was so straight I was sure he could balance a pitcher of water on it without even trying.

He pushed a finger into my chest.

"You touching my son, mister? I don't care what kind of fancy-pants blogger you are, you don't touch my boy."

My first reaction was to clock him between the eyes. That might have been how Zachary Nixon Johnson, tough guy PI would handle it, but not how Bart Star, ace blogger would. Bart was a words guy. I needed to use words to stay in character and out of trouble.

I put both my arms up in a smooth nonthreatening position so he could see them and know I wasn't going to try to be a tough guy.

"No offense, Mr. Billings," I said. "Just trying to be friendly."

He didn't react, which was better than punching me, but not what I was hoping for. He might have been a strong man, but he wasn't a trained fighter or a grappler, and he had let his guard down and now he was wide open. If I wanted to nail him with a quick jab or a knee to the groin, he was mine. While Zach might have done that, Bart wouldn't. I went on using words as my shield.

"I understand you people are from New Kansas. I've heard people there are really friendly," I said. I let my mouth break into a slight smile. I wanted to look like I was being sincere, not taunting.

He didn't back down. "We are friendly. We just don't take kindly to strangers."

Elf-2 tried squeezing her body between us to diffuse the situation.

"Mr. Billings," she squeaked. "I am sure Mr. Starr meant no harm."

Pa Billings didn't back down. I had to give him his props for being protective of his son, though this was getting on my nerves. Maybe he was the type of guy who wouldn't back down unless I stood up to him? Maybe he wouldn't respect me unless I gave him a reason to? I slowly started to curl my right hand into a fist. It was such a slight movement I doubt anybody noticed it.

"Easy, Zach," HARV said inside my brain. "This isn't the time."

I let my hand relax. Out of the corner of my eye I could see Nova and the nerds. The nerds were cluelessly waiting in anticipation for Pa to give me a thrashing. Nova, on the other hand, dropped back a step the nano I relaxed my hand. She frowned. I have to respect a girl who loves a good brawl.

"Bob, leave that poor man alone," Betty Billings said, moving toward us.

Betty Billings wasn't bad to look at. She was a tall, slender woman with short black hair that, unlike her husband's, didn't look like she cut it with farm equipment. She had a peachy complexion that wasn't nearly as tanned as the rest of her family's. Carol certainly hit the nail right on the head about Ma Billings' skin tone—it didn't look like this woman spent much time outside.

Betty grabbed Bob's hand, which was still curled in

a fist, and slowly forced it back down to his side. She stood between us, facing him. "Remember what Judge Clemens said Bob, you can't be so sensitive. This man wasn't trying to hurt our boy."

Bob stood his ground.

"Bob," Betty said, "don't make me call the judge when we get home."

Bob hung his head and dropped his guard.

"Good man," Betty told him. Turning her attention to Billy, she bent down and stuck a finger in his face. "And you! What have we told you about spamming wolf?"

Billy wasn't as quick to back down. "But Mom, they taught us in school not to let strangers touch us."

Ma Billings targeted her glare on her son.

Billy put his hands behind his back and slumped backward, slowly pulling away from his mother like a puppy who had just been scolded. "I'm sorry, Mom."

Ma Billings pointed to me. "Now, apologize to Mr. Starr so he writes nice things about us."

He turned to look at me, paused for a nano, and then turned back to his mom. "Oh Ma, I don't want to apologize. I didn't do anything wrong!"

Ma Billings stomped her foot and folded her arms across her chest. She was digging in for the long haul. "You're just like your father," she moaned. "Just once I wish this family would do what I told them to without me hitting them over the head with a brick."

Bobi, the daughter, joined in the fray. "Mom, you don't have to tell me anything twice," she said, tugging on her mom's elbow.

Ma Billings shot her a look. "No, but being a suck-up is just as bad."

Bobi shook her head so hard it made her ponytail spin around. "I'm not like that, Mom, I'm not. If you want, I can find you a brick to hit them with." She sneered at her brother.

Billy responded by showing his sister his tongue.

I hoped Electra didn't want kids anytime in the near future.

Ma Billings' face wasn't pale any longer. It was now redder than her elf suit. "Bobi, tell Billy you're sorry. Billy, tell Bobi you're sorry, then tell Mr. Starr you're really sorry. Remember we want to be kind to strangers, especially those who can write about us."

Before I had a chance to say there was no need for Billy to make an apology, Mary Eatman started forward. "Don't worry," she said walking up to Billy and bending over to face him. "If Mr. Starr writes anything bad about any of us, I'll sue him for so many credits he'll have to clone himself ten times to have any chance to earn that much."

Billy smiled at her. "Really?"

She patted him on the head. "Really. That's we lawyers do—we make people's lives better."

"Maybe I'll be a lawyer," Bobi Billings said.

"No, I want to be a lawyer," Billy said.

"I don't want any of my kids being a DOSing lawyer." Ma Billings balked.

This statement brought out Mary Eatman's ire. "What's wrong with being a lawyer?"

Ma Billings rolled her eyes. "How much time do you have?"

Mary shoved her finger up next to those rolled eyes. "Please, you don't have nearly enough money to pay for my time."

"People, people, can't we all just get along?" Elf-2 pleaded.

Nobody heard her cry for peace except for me. The rest were all embroiled in the heat and passion of the moment. Bob Billings had taken up his wife's defense by threatening to put Mary back on her backside. This made Mary threaten to sue Bob for all the dirt he owned. Betty got mad at Bob for jumping in like that, but she also came down hard on Mary for assuming they were poor farmers. Betty pointed out that if it wasn't for farmers people wouldn't be able to eat. Mary's counterargument was that it wasn't the farmers but their bots and machines (programmed by people like Steve) that did the work. This really pissed Bob off, and he made a step toward Mary. Steve, being the brave engineer that he is, stepped forward and pointed out to Bob that if he laid a hand on his wife, his wife would sue the pants off of him, his kids, and their kids.

Nova and the MESSHs were doing their part by egging everybody on. Nova was in obvious glee watching other people brawl for a change. Bim and Norp were getting doubly charged over this. This was probably the only time in their lives they weren't the most ridiculous acting people in the room. They loved anything that got Nova riled up, and the thought of a chick fight between Mary and Betty was getting them hot and bothered. These guys didn't get off Mars much.

If I had my gun I would have fired a few warning shots in the air, but I didn't. I thought about stepping in to break this melee up, but figured I'd learn more if I just let it play its course. After all, the only one who could do any real damage was Nova, and she was content to be a spectator for once.

Mary grabbed Betty by the collar, which made Steve threaten Bill, while at the same time reminding Mary her chances of a successful lawsuit would be enhanced if she didn't slug Betty first. At which time both Bobi and Billy started taunting Mary and calling her all sorts of names. But Mary was a lawyer, so nothing these two kids could say would get to her, unless one of them accused her of doing pro bono work.

The two families went on bickering and throwing verbal jabs at each other like two inexperienced prize fighters. They were both scoring points on occasion, but neither could put the other away. It was clear Bob Billings wanted to escalate the violence from verbal to physical, but Betty would always step in and refrain him at the last nano. She was a smart one. She knew just as Bob would take Steve out in a knock-down, drag-out brouhaha, Mary would definitely take them to the cleaners afterward.

As much as I was learning about my Polemates from this little scuffle, I knew it was time to put an end to it. Despite the fact that I started this incident, I had now become a forgotten spectator, a holographic face in the crowd. Which can be fine if it helps move the case forward, but this wasn't. I had to stop it. "Excuse me, people," I shouted. They ignored me. I instinctively went for my gun again, flicking my wrist in just the right way to make it pop into my hand. Of course, the gun didn't leap into my hand, because I didn't have my gun. I don't know what was worse: my needing to rely on my gun to quiet a crowd or my not remembering I didn't have a gun.

Now it was Councilwoman Weathers' turn to step up to the plate. She had the air of a woman who didn't like to stay a bystander for too long, and this had gone on long enough. She was a politician, and like any politician worth her weight in soy, she wasn't about to let herself be delegated the role of bystander.

"Excuse me, everybody," she said in a quiet, firm voice.

Everybody instantly stopped their bickering and threatening and turned their attention to the good

councilwoman. Everybody that is, but me. I knew the
councilwoman well enough through her reputation. I
was more interested in seeing how her husband,
Carl, reacted.

Back when he was a pro quarterback, his name was
Carl Carlson. I guess I can see why he took his wife's
last name. Carl was one of these guys who was born
with a lot of talent, but wasn't sure what to do with
it. Not knowing him personally I couldn't tell if this
was because he was lazy, not overly bright, not overly
ambitious, or some combination of the three. That's
why I was so interested in seeing how he reacted to
this. He was a guy used to sitting on the bench.

Carl Weathers was a big man, over two meters tall,
and he weighed a solid 110 kilos. He didn't look like
he could walk onto the football field today and lead
a team to victory, but he wasn't that far from being
game ready. During his playing days, such as they
were, I remember he had dark brown hair. Today that
hair had wisps of gray through it, especially around
his temples, but it made him look more dignified than
old. He had a rep for being a ladies' man before he
met Weathers. It wasn't hard for me to spot that he
still was a lady's man, and by that I mean the councilwoman owned him. The way he always stayed one
step behind her. The way he looked at her with blind
admiration when she walked, talked, or did most anything. He was almost more of a pet than he was a
husband.

I turned my attention back to the good councilwoman. She had now positioned herself between the
two arguing families.

"Please, people," she said. "Can't we all just get
along?"

Not the most original plea. In fact, Elf-2 had just
used it only moments ago. While Weathers may have

said the same words, the effect was completely different. Everybody stopped their bickering and turned to her. The councilwoman was an appealing, commanding woman. Part of that was on account of her size—she was tall, nearly as tall as her ex-quarterback hubby. While she wasn't a muscular powerhouse like Nova, it was obvious she was no stranger to the gym. Her hair hung softly over her shoulders. It was an expensive cut that didn't look it, and it managed to complement Stormy Weathers' face perfectly without being pretentious. The flawless hair on top of the strong taut body helped complete the total package, making Weathers a unique cross between soccer grandmom, retired model, and barracuda.

"Now, my good people," the councilwoman said, commanding all to focus their attention on her, "I'm sure we can all agree that nothing is gained by fighting."

This was followed by grunts of agreement from everybody. Even Nova nodded her approval, but in her case I think it was just giving in to peer pressure.

Satisfied she had the floor to herself, Weathers went into her spiel. "My fellow voters, this dispute is much like the one I faced many decades back when I nearly single-handedly pounded out the first treaty between Earth and Gladian-7, when the Gladians insisted Earth people smell funny and that our negotiators needed to take seven showers a day."

Everybody bobbed their heads in agreement. Everybody that is except for me. I didn't see a lot of similarities. The councilwoman continued, "At first, there seemed to be no compromise. The Gladians insisted that they were letting the Earthlings off easy with only seven showers a day. The Earthlings insisted that showering that much would not only greatly impede the negotiations but it would also severely dry their skin. It appeared compromise was impossible, but then I suggested four showers a day for the Earth delegation and gas masks for the Gladians."

All the members of the tour group started to applaud the good councilwoman for her vision. None of them seemed to notice or care that their dispute was nothing like the classic Earth and Gladian-7 dispute.

"Can you fix our problems like you did theirs?" Bobi Billings asked.

The councilwoman just smiled. As she held her smile, the others held their breath. Finally, after a minute or two had passed, the councilwoman said, "Of course I can. After all, that's why you all voted for me."

Everybody let out a collecteive sigh, except of course for me. I wasn't hanging on her every word like the others. I wasn't even sure I voted for her.

"The solution is easy," she said. She looked at me. "Mr. Starr, apologize to poor Billy for touching him without asking for permission or at the very least alerting him to your intentions."

All eyes steadied on me.

"Sorry, kid," I said with as much sincere sincerity as I could fake.

All eyes returned to the councilwoman who turned to Billy. "Now Billy, tell Mr. Starr you are sorry you overreacted."

Billy lowered his eyes. "I'm sorry, Mr. Starr, sir."

The crowd let out a collective sigh.

"No problem, kid."

The councilwoman turned her attention to the adult members of our parties. "Now, you people should agree that farmers, engineers, and even lawyers who call themselves lawyers are all essential to our great planet's economic diversity. We are all different, and that's what makes our planet great. If it wasn't for our differences, we might as well all be androids, bots, clones, or MESSHs."

Everybody nodded or mumbled in agreement, even Bim and Norp. I saw them turn to each other and say, "We *are* pretty annoying."

"Now everybody shake hands, so Elf-2 can continue our fine tour."

The words seemed to go from Stormy Weathers' mouth directly to everybody's brains. They all immediately began shaking hands, exchanging recipes and job hints, and getting along like they were family. No, better than family, like they were people who actually liked each other.

The tour continued with Bobi and Billy arguing about who got to grow up to be a lawyer and who got to grow up to be a councilwoman. The Eatmans and Billingses walked with each other, chatting like they had known one another forever. Nova kept throwing looks at me, while Bim and Norp split their time gawking at Nova and the councilwoman. The councilwoman didn't say much after that. She just smiled politely as Elf-2 went on and on about how great the Pole was.

For the most part, the remainder of the tour was impressive but uneventful. When you're me, a little uneventful now and then is a good thing. Contrary to what some people (Electra, Tony, HARV, that court-appointed therapist from a few years ago, my agent, and my high school math teacher) believe, I don't need to live under the constant threat of danger. I like the quiet times when nobody is trying to kill, maim, or castrate me. Trust me, it's never fun when somebody tries to castrate you. That gets old real fast.

The Pole certainly was a big place. Elf-2 told the us the facilities were bigger than 25.567 percent of the cities on Earth. Yet the place was "manned" by just a few thousand elves and a few more thousand machines. We saw the data-mining rooms where elves and expert intelligent systems sift through the gigabytes upon gigabytes of data the Pole collects on everybody in order to choose the perfect gift for each individual.

We saw the Pole's virtual computer servers. We learned that the Pole receives over sixty billion electronic requests for gifts each year. Yes, there are only fifteen billion people on Earth, but according to Elf-2 the average person changes their requests 3.2 times before they finally decide what they really want. In fact, to help people who change their mind more than four times, the elves have invented a special present consulting software that will help "happy customers" choose the perfect gifts that will make them "even happier customers."

We saw many of the Pole's automated assembly lines where the computers and electronic gadgets are slapped together by trained elf technicians and their robotic aids. We saw the handcrafted zones where elf craftsmen make special one-of-a-kind gifts for those people who have everything or just want something that is different from what everybody else has.

The tour wrapped with a visit to the Pole's coup de grace, their storage center. Yeah, I know you're thinking, *How could a storage center be the coup de grace? It's just a big building where packages sit before they are sent somewhere else.* That's the kicker—it wasn't just a big building. It was a humongous building that looked like it had eaten a couple of other big buildings, and these didn't come close to satisfying its needs. I've seen the UltraHyperMegaMart-sponsored Grand Canyon and truthfully, it wasn't quite as impressive as the Pole's storage center. Sure the Grand Canyon was actually bigger, but it wasn't that much bigger, and it was created over millions of years by erosion. This place was built in under a year by a bunch of elves and bots.

Elf-2 explained to us that once a present is made for an individual, it is coded and stored in a special area. Every person in the world has their own special spot in the storage room where their gifts are kept. Each spot is encoded into the Pole's automated teleportation systems, along with the address of the recipient's teleportation receiver. Elf-2 also told us that to save time and space they keep a good portion of the gifts that are completed early suspended in a "phased state." In this state they are neither solid nor whole but kept in between dimensions in a near ready-to-deliver state. All it takes is the simple press of a button to transport the presents from a phased state to their final destination. This way when it's time for the mass teleportation, it's easy to quickly get the right presents to the right people. Truthfully, the physics involved were beyond me.

So instead I thought about other, more mundane matters, such as: how many outfits does each elf have? How often do elves get naughty with each other? What else do elves do when they goof off?

(Later, during a Q&A session, I learned the answers to those questions were: five; none of my business—wink, wink; and elves don't goof off.)

As the tour finished, Nova insisted that I meet her in the gym for a little workout. It seems walking kilometers wasn't nearly enough exercise for Nova. I agreed, figuring that would be the best way to get information out of her. I didn't think she was involved in this (killing things with bots wasn't her style), but I couldn't rule her out just yet.

Before I'd meet her in the gym, I told her I needed to go back to my room to take notes on what I'd seen.

Chapter 19

HARV activated himself the nano I stepped foot into my room.

"Isn't the physics involved in storing and shipping massive amounts of gifts fascinating?" HARV said smiling.

"It's amazing what humans can do when they put their minds to it," I said, sitting down on the bed and sliding my shoes off.

For those of you interested, elf shoes are far more comfortable than they look, but still not as comfortable as a really good-fitting pair of sneakers that are broken in just right. I was just glad the guest shoes were "bells optional."

"Actually Zach, most of the work was done by elves, not humans."

"The elves were created by humans."

HARV paused for a nano and put a finger to his mouth. "Yes, I have to give you that one."

"Speaking of humans, what do you think of my group?" I asked.

"First off, that Mary seems *real* nice," HARV said with a wry smile.

"Yeah, sort like bumping your head and stubbing your toe at the same time," I said.

"Gee Zach, for a detective, you're awful clumsy."

"It was an analogy HARV. What else do you have for me?"

"I've been subtly using the Pole's computer system to gather data. I have an interesting bit of information on the MESSHs. Over the last few years, they have been experimenting pretty heavily with remote reprogramming of stand-alone systems."

"So, they could have reprogrammed the bots to attack me?"

"Yes."

"Do they have a motive?"

"To attack you or to sabotage the Holiday?" HARV asked.

"Either . . ."

"None that I can find. They are totally unaffected by the Holiday. They don't leave Mars very often."

"That's good. They're pretty annoying," I said.

"Hold on, let me scan some more. I just calculated something." HARV started scratching his head. "I've just learned that Nova and the other mutant wrestlers have a strange fondness for ice."

"Ice?"

"A special ice."

"Okay HARV, what kind of ice?"

"It's the ice here at the Pole."

"Well, they certainly have enough of it."

"Maybe, but they won't sell it. Santana is very picky about that. She doesn't believe in using the land for personal gains."

"Santana is an idealist. It sort of comes with the territory."

"Some have offered up to one thousand credits per liter of ice."

"What did they do, lose the recipe or something?" I asked.

"Huh?"

"It was a joke, HARV. Remember, Steve says I'm a funny guy."

"True, but he is an engineer. Everybody knows they have a skewed sense of humor."

"Good point."

"Admit it, Nova's still a possibility. She loves ice and she's a member of the SSS," HARV said.

"Maybe, but she seems more of an in-your-face type to me."

"I also have some information on the Billings family."

"Yeah?"

"The mother used to be an HTech senior exec engineer. Her group designed the guardbots. She quit over some sort of disagreement. It was buried deeper than Hoffa."

"See what you find if you poke around a bit?" I really liked the reference but figured it would freak HARV out if I mentioned that to him. There was a time and place to get on HARV's chips—this wasn't it.

"I also have some information on Councilwoman Weathers."

"Well?" I asked, though from the sound of HARV's *I told you so* voice it wasn't going to be what I wanted to hear.

"I hate to say I told you so, but I told you so. She's perfectly clean. Never even been accused of any wrongdoing. She has never missed a Council meeting vote."

"What about her relationship with her husband?"

"Married eighteen years, no kids. No affairs, no

scandals, nothing even the least bit interesting, besides, of course, her miraculous recovery from her nearly lethal crash."

"Okay, how about finances?"

"They both come from well-off families. Still, I wouldn't call them giga-rich—more like mega-rich."

"Could a person in her position change facts?" I asked.

"Of course, but it would cost a bundle to change anything really important."

"Is there anything unusual at all?" I was looking for something, I just didn't know what. Weathers seemed too good to be true.

"Okay, hold on, I'll scan . . ." HARV said after a slight pause. "This might be of interest to you, though I'm not sure why."

"I'll be the judge of that, HARV."

"Mr. Weathers owns a small independent mining company. It seems he took it over from Stormy's brother-in-law who was having trouble running it. There aren't many things left to mine on this planet, and the other planets are so particular about mining rights."

"See if the mining company has ever had any contact with HTech or ExShell or the MESSHs or anybody else here. While you're at it, check out all the MESSHs' experiments and all the Weathers' purchases and sales over the last five years. Also try to find out why Mrs. Billings quit HTech."

"While I'm at it, perhaps you'd like me to calculate pi to the last digit?"

"Just do it HARV. And stop complaining. Nobody likes a whiny supercomputer."

"I'm not whining. I'm simply pointing out how I have to do all the hard work."

"You? I'm the one that gets beat up!"

"Yes, but that's easy. I'm the one who does all the heavy thinking."

"It seems that Mary and Steve are the only two I can rule out as suspects," I said.

"Huh? You're saying a lawyer and an engineer are incapable of committing crimes?"

"No, that's not it. They just don't fit the profile."

"But they've been planning this trip for five years."

"Exactly. You don't make reservations five years in advance to a place you're trying to destroy. If anything, their reservation makes them convenient patsies."

"If you say so. I'm just a machine."

I wouldn't turn my back on that Mary, but I was sure she and her husband weren't the culprits here. As for Nova, the jury was still out on her. I was hoping I could cross her off the list after we met in the gym.

Chapter 20

When I arrived at the Pole's spacious gym my fellow travelers were already there. Councilwoman Weathers and Carl were on simulated cross-country-ski machines. She was going at a quick pace, while he was taking it rather slow. It was easy to see who wore the pants in that marriage.

The Eatmans were using the free weights that looked like gift boxes. Even in these high-tech times, it's still hard to beat a good old-fashioned free weight, even one wrapped in neon gift paper. Steve was doing a bench press as two elves spotted him, and Mary looked on, either counting, giving him encouragement, or hoping he'd throw out his back so she could sue the Pole.

The Billings family was at the far corner of the gym. They were playing catch with a big anti-grav medicine snowball. Billy was sneaking peaks at Nova whenever he could.

Nova, not surprisingly, was in the boxing ring. She had ripped the legs and arms off of her elf suit (while the female elves wore dresses the female guests wore pant suits) and looked far sexier in an elf suit than should be possible. Nova's opponent in the squared circle was a very excited Bim dressed in oversized red boxing trunks, complete with oversized green gloves. He was prancing around her, darting in and out. He wasn't actually doing anything. He was being a typical male and had no idea that he really had no idea what he was doing in the ring. I'm sure he thought he looked like Muhammad Ali, but he came off more like Truman Capote, only less macho. He was floating like a one-winged bee and stinging like a butterfly.

Norp was eagerly awaiting his turn on the side of the ring. He was jumping up and down almost as much as Bim was, shadow boxing with an imaginary foe (who could probably whip his butt). Norp clearly had no more business being in the ring with Nova than I would have being in a bullfight.

Nova looked bored by the whole thing. She stood with feet planted firmly in the center of the ring, not even bothering to face Bim when he would dance behind her. She clearly saw him as no threat.

I walked up to the ring, close but not too close to where Norp was sparring with himself. (I got the impression both Bim and Norp did a lot of things by themselves.) Nova's eyes lit up when they made contact with mine.

"Well, Mr. Starr. How nice of you to join us," she said. "I hope your note taking went well."

"Yes, yes, quite well," I said, trying to sound as much like a blogger as possible. "I'm sure my readers will be enthralled."

She winked at me. "How about going three minutes with me?"

"In the ring?" I asked.

"Zach!" HARV said inside my head. "Remember

you're an engaged man. Also, she almost killed you the last time you went in the ring with her."

"For starters," she said.

I pointed at Bim. "You already have a worthy opponent."

She rolled her eyes just as Bim darted in for another one of his feigned attacks. This time Nova hit him with an open palm to the nose. At least I think that's what it was. The move was a blur. I knew she hit him because his nose started gushing blood. The red blood all over his skin made an interesting shade of purple. The bleeding was followed by Bim crashing backward to the mat like a rock. He was out cold way before he hit the floor. (I figured Nova must have hit him with an open hand because he was still alive.)

The elf referee stood over Bim and started to count, "One, two, three," before he realized the futility of it. He waved his arms over Bim. "Forget it, you're out until the bots revive you." He turned around put two fingers in his mouth and whistled for the medbots to come.

Nova looked down on me. "There, no more opponent!"

Norp, who obviously wasn't that bright, started to climb into the ring. "Oh goodie, my turn now!"

Nova put a foot on his head and pushed him to the ground. "I don't think so," she said.

Then Nova reached down and grabbed me by the collar. She lifted me up into the ring with one arm. I hate it when she does that. I find it both sexy and intimidating. She bent down and took the oversized boxing gloves off Bim just as the medbots carted him away. She tossed me the gloves.

"Put 'em on," she said.

"I don't like fighting women," I said.

"Don't worry, it's not going to be much of a fight," she said.

By now, everybody else in the gym had figured out what was going on. They were all gathered around the ring. It looked like they were anxious to see the blogger get flogged.

Nova was dancing around me, circling. She was showing much more energy than when she had Bim in the ring. I tend to bring out the best in people.

"Duck!" HARV said, inside my head.

I did, a split nano before a right roundhouse from Nova sailed over me. If I hadn't taken HARV's advice, I would have been waking up next to Bim in the infirmary.

"How'd you do that?" I thought back to HARV.

"She tips her punches," HARV said. "She's a wrestler, not a boxer. The tips are subtle changes in the expression on her face. A human wouldn't even notice. Luckily for you, I've studied all her films and can determine her moves before she makes them. For instance, now she is going to lower her shoulder and slam into you."

Sure enough, Nova did drop a shoulder and slam into me, driving me into the mat. Even though I knew the move was coming, it was done so expertly I had no way of avoiding it. When you're me, luck is kind of a relative thing.

"She's very good at those wrestling moves," HARV said.

"So I've noticed," I said aloud, getting lost in the moment.

I tried to bridge up on my back and then use that momentum to roll Nova over me. It didn't work. She had way too much experience to fall for that. She counteracted my bridge by shifting her weight down. She leaned forward over me and pinned me to the ground. If she wasn't trying kill me, I might have found the hold to be enjoyable. Not quite sure what that says about me.

"Talking to yourself again, Zach," she whispered in my ear.

Things just went from bad to worse. Not only was Nova pummeling me, but she knew who I was. I wasn't sure what that meant to the case, but I was certain it couldn't help.

Nova wasn't happy with having me simply pinned to the mat. She was determined to make me suffer a bit more. She managed to stand up using her legs while keeping her body between my legs and her arms tightly locked on my legs. I didn't like where this was heading.

"She's using herself as a fulcrum!" HARV said almost in awe.

I didn't like the sound of that. Unfortunately, there wasn't much I could do about it.

Nova started to spin and spin and spin. I was getting light-headed and not in a good way. This, too, might have been fun except I knew the end result was going to be a world of hurt.

After she spun me around somewhere between three and three hundred times, she released me. I went flying through the air, sailing out of the ring, and crashed to the floor with a very painful thud.

I have never missed my body armor as much as I did that nano. I was surprised I was still conscious. I was more astonished when I pushed myself up from the ground. I hurt, but not nearly as much as I ought to.

"The new improvements Dr. Pool made to my system are incredible. I was able to relax your muscles, making you better able to absorb the fall, while at the same time I was able to magnify and focus the electromagnetic current your body has to cushion your fall," HARV said. "You are so lucky you have Dr. Pool and me on your side."

"Yeah, like I always say, luck is a relative thing," I said heading back toward to the ring.

The guests and the elves started to applaud as I headed back. I didn't know if they were happy I was getting up or just anxious for me to take another beating. Whatever the case, a wise man would have been content to walk away from a thrashing like that. I, on the other hand, wasn't about to let Nova have her way with me. I knew Nova's type. Sadly, I've had far too much experience with them. If was going to get Nova to open up to me, I was going to have to prove that I could hold my own with her in the ring.

Of course to do that, I was going need HARV.

"I need you to flash her," I thought to HARV.

"Excuse me?" HARV said.

"I'm going to lock eyes with her, then you holo-flash her. Once you've blinded her, I'll have a chance."

"A slim one," HARV said.

Nova took a step back, letting me climb back into the ring. She wiped her brow, though she wasn't really sweating.

"You're either braver or stupider than I thought," she said.

"Probably both," I said.

She smiled. "I'm almost going to regret knocking you out. When you come to, we'll have to take a walk."

"Yeah, well, we'll see about that," I said.

She moved forward and grabbed me. I locked my eyes with her.

"Now HARV!" I shouted in my head.

I didn't see the holo-flash but Nova did. She blinked her eyes and lowered her head.

"What the—" she said.

I made my move and cocked her with an upper cut to the chin. That sent her head rocketing back, but she didn't fall. She was off balance, and I aimed to take advantage of that. I moved forward, keeping my body close to hers. I grabbed her neck with my right hand and her waist with my left. I bent down and lifted her off the ground. Even bulked up she only weighed about seventy kilos, so it wasn't all that impressive—still, I was pleased. I body slammed her to the mat.

That looked like it should have really hurt her. She was smiling. I moved forward. She kicked up her legs and wrapped them around my neck.

"Sleep tight," she said, as she tightened her grip.

I may have been standing and on top but I was in trouble. Her grip was viselike. I dropped to my knees. Things started spinning. I might have been able to use HARV to shock her like I did the last time we had tangled, but with the crowd around that would have blown my cover. I decided discretion was the better part of valor here. Things went black.

Chapter 21

When I woke up, I was in lying on top of my bed in my room. My head hurt a little but it was nothing I couldn't live with. I sat up in bed.

"What time is it?" I asked HARV.

"Do you mean Pole Time?" HARV asked.

"No, I mean Greenwich Mean Time," I snapped.

"Oh, that would be—"

"What time is it here, HARV?"

"Twenty-two hundred hours. You've been out for five hours. I'm not sure if Santana will insist on a credit for that time or what. You missed dinner but the elves said they would send you room service when you came around." HARV looked at me and asked. "What did you prove by getting in the ring with Nova?"

"I didn't have much choice," I protested.

"What did you prove by going back in after she tossed you out?"

"I need her to respect me," I said. "Or else she won't be of any help."

HARV shook his head. "Well, it seems to have

worked. She's invited you for a walk outside tomorrow morning."

"Isn't it cold out there?"

"It will be minus twenty-eight degrees Celsius, but you'll be equiped with special hats and gloves. You won't feel a thing."

"You always say that, and I always do."

"I can turn off the cold and heat receptors in your brain, if you wish."

"No, that sounds worse than being cold. Those receptors are there for a reason."

I called room service and ordered a roast beef sandwich and a hot cocoa. I didn't really want the cocoa but that was all they would serve me this late at night, so I took what I could get.

As I ate, I thought about case. I was reasonably certain somebody or something was reprogramming the guardbots to get them to do their dirty work. The question was, who? I knew it wasn't Nova. Now I was certain attacking people with bots just wasn't her style. Way too subtle. She may have been a member of a Santana Stinks Society, and she may have loved the snow, but she wasn't behind this. Still, I would be interested in knowing why she was here and how she saw through my holo-disguise. I planned to go over that with her during our walk tomorrow.

I also didn't believe the Eatmans were involved. I wasn't sure why. I wouldn't rule out that Mary hiring a killer, but I didn't see a motive. Not for her bringing down the Pole.

That left the Billingses, the Weatherses, and Bim and Norp. One or more of them was behind this. I felt it clear down to my toes. I just needed to figure out who. For that, I would need a method and a motive.

I still couldn't completely rule out a disgruntled elf

or two. It's hard to conceive of, but maybe, just maybe, one or two of them doesn't like being dependent on Santana's life-extending drugs.

I decided to sleep on it.

Suddenly I was jolted awake by a loud gong in my head.

I jumped up in bed.

"What's that?" I said, physically but not mentally awake.

"Are you up?" HARV asked.

"Of course I'm up! You just hit a gong in my cranium! This better be good!"

"I hear a guardbot rolling down the hall."

"So?" I asked, not bothering to hide the acid in my voice.

"I've tapped into the Pole's scheduling system, there are no guardbots scheduled to come down this hall for another hour."

"Oh," I said, rolling behind the bed. I placed the bed between myself and the door.

The door opened.

A guardbot holding a pillow in its claw rolled in. This one, except for the pillow in its claw, was identical to the two I'd tangled with before.

"Oh, I was hoping to make this look like an accident," it said in a metallic, not even close to human, voice.

"Right, like anyone was really going to believe I suffocated to death with my own pillow. It would have been just as subtle to laser me to death."

"Actually, Zach, it can't," HARV whispered. "All energy weapons are deactivated inside the building here."

"Great!" I said, as I stood up from behind the bed.

I pulled the H_2O pistol from my elf suit pocket and showed it to the bot.

"It appears I have you outgunned!" I told it.

"Hardly," it gawked, as it rolled toward me. "My claw is infinitely shaper than razor wire, and I am far stronger than you."

"Don't forget more modest," I said.

"I am also oxidation proof. There is nothing an H_2O pistol can do to harm me. Even if I wasn't oxidation proof, you would be long dead before the water in that little gun could even begin to harm me."

"Very true, my long-winded friend . . ."

I pulled the trigger, hitting the bot with a stream of liquid right in its eye sensor. The sensor started to burn.

"If I actually had H_2O in here," I said, completing my statement. I was pretty sure by this point the bot couldn't hear me.

"Quick HARV, where's the main control unit on this thing?" I asked as I fired away.

"That's why you grabbed cleaning acid and the gun!"

"I figured if these guns can stand up to a ten-year-old kid then a little high-powered cleaning acid should be nothing. So where's the control CPU?"

"Lower back," HARV told me. "I'll give you a cursor target."

The bot now started to roam the room, spinning around and clawing at the air. Obviously, its programming had never covered being blinded by acid from an H_2O pistol.

I walked up behind it. A cursor appeared in front of my eyes and seemed to zoom in on the bot's back side. I fired at the spot the cursor covered.

The acid hit and burned through. The bot stopped

moving. Its claw went limp. Its screen went dead. Its lights went out. It was deactivated.

I went to the wall computer and pushed the service button.

"Yes?" a polite voice asked.

"I need to see Santana and Elf-1 now, please."

"Yes, sir," the polite voice said.

Within minutes Santana and Elf-1 were in my room looking over the beat bot.

"We've never had problems with our guardbots before," Santana said shaking her head as she watched Elf-1 examine the bot.

"Actually, you have," I told her. "I think the two murdered elves were done in by bots. Plus, two of your bots attacked me at my office yesterday. I'm surprised they haven't turned up missing."

"There are two hundred bots here, but only one hundred and seventy are active any given day, so you may have been attacked by one of the off-duty bots," Elf-1 said as he continued looking at the terminated bot. He took a deep breath. He took another deep breath. "Go to my happy place. My hap-hap-happy place."

"So our bots are bad," Santana said.

"I'm sure they had help getting that way," I said. "How many elves can reprogram a bot?" I asked Elf-1.

"All of us, except maybe Rocko," he answered.

"Great, that narrows it down."

"All bots have vid-recorders built into them. Everything they do is recorded," Elf-1 told me.

"I'm sure whoever did this wasn't stupid enough to leave the recorder on."

"The recorders are timed and nonstoppable. They are bound to show something. There should be at least a break in the clock when they were reprogrammed," Elf-1 told, bubbling over with excitement. This guy really needed to get out of the Pole once in a while.

"Check it out. It might give us something," I told him.

"I better shut down the bots until we figure out what's going on," Elf-1 said.

"No, let's not panic yet. We still don't know who or what is behind this. If we shut the bots down now, they might cover their tracks before we can find them," Santana said without hesitating. She looked over at me for approval.

"I couldn't agree more."

"So what's the plan then?" Elf-1 asked.

"Get some rest. Tomorrow will be a long day!"

Chapter 22

I was awoken the next morning by a buzzing from my room's wall computer.

"I'm awake! I'm awake!" I said, as I sat up in bed.

"Message from Elf-1 coming in," that polite voice from the computer said.

"What's up Elfy?" I asked.

"Bad news, Mr. Johnson. I mean Mr. Starr. The bot's replay showed nothing out of the ordinary. In fact, its internal clock was even continuous."

"Hmm, do you record energy readings in the area?"

"Of course!"

"Good. Check for enhanced radio wave and HF microwave transmissions over the last few days."

"Right," Elf-1 said. "I'll beep back when I have something."

I stood up and stretched.

HARV appeared.

"Are you thinking what I think you're thinking?"

"HARV, you don't actually think, you just simulate thinking," I corrected, unable to resist a little mental jab. "But if you are calculating remote reprogramming, then yes."

"The bots have all their commands hardwired into them, making them tough to override."

"Tough, but possible."

"Yes, possible. But also quite expensive," HARV said. "Uh oh, call coming in," HARV said a split nano before he disappeared.

"Mr. Johnson?" Elf-1 called through the wall computer.

"Yes?" I said, activating the vid-conferencing.

"HF wave transmissions to the Pole have been up since yesterday, probably due to sunspot activity."

"Actually, that would be me," HARV whispered. "I needed to access some outside dbases."

"But," Elf-1 continued, "the readings jumped way up last night for about twenty nanos."

"Thanks Elf-1, I'll keep you informed." I pushed the button on the wall turning off the vid-conferencing.

"Who do we know who can remotely reprogram bots?" I asked HARV.

"ExShell and HTech have both done it in the past with average bots and computers."

"What about the MESSHs?"

"In their sleep," HARV said.

"I'm going to shower, shave, and grab breakfast. I'm famished!"

"Yes, you can't solve crimes on an empty stomach," HARV said more than a little cynically.

"I could," I corrected. "But then I'd be grumpy afterward."

Chapter 23

When I got to the breakfast table, Nova and Council-woman Weathers weren't there. Nova was at the gym working out. Weathers had a special meeting with Santana. That gave me a chance to chat with the others and to see how Bim and Norp acted when Nova wasn't around. I learned that when Nova wasn't around, Bim and Norp spent their time talking about Nova. They wanted to join her at the gym, but Nova made it clear to them it was *enter at risk of death*. For some reason, they listened.

Mary and Steve were busy trying to decide what to do with their free time today. Mary wanted to make one last pitch to the elves to get them to unionize. Steve had his head set on reviewing the Pole's computer systems.

This gave Carl Weathers and I time to chat. I asked him casually about his mining company. He was quite open about it. He insisted he didn't want to be bothered with it, but Stormy thought it would be a good investment for him. She said it would help keep him occupied. According to her, he couldn't just be Mr.

Stormy Weathers all the time. Carl, for his part, said he didn't mind watching his wife from the bench. He had made a fine living being a benchwarmer, and he didn't see much reason to change now.

After breakfast, I waited by the Pole's main gate for a good fifteen minutes before Nova showed up. She was wearing her elf suit with the sleeves and legs ripped off.

"Sorry I'm late," she said grabbing me by the arm. "I wanted to stop at the gym for a little workout. It wasn't all that fun, though. None of their anti-grav weights go over one thousand kilos."

She started dragging me along.

"Come on, let's go!"

"You really want to go outside?" I asked.

"Of course, silly!" she said.

I looked out at snow, trees, lights, snow, some more trees, and more snow. What wasn't covered in snow was covered in ice.

"Isn't it a bit cold out there?" I asked.

"Don't worry," Nova reassured me. "Your suit is insulated."

"Yeah, but my head and hands aren't," I said.

Nova pointed to box near the door. The box's hologram label read GLOVES AND HATS in English and many other languages.

I reached into the box and pulled out a skintight pair of gloves and a silly-looking elf hat. I slipped them both on. I couldn't have looked much more ridiculous than I felt, especially since the hat had a non-optional bell. They claimed it was a locator bell, but I had my doubts.

Nova smiled at me.

"Don't you need gloves and a hat and, well, pant legs and a long-sleeved shirt?" I asked.

She shook her head. "I find the cold exhilarating,"

she said. She looked up at the big door that led to the outside world.

"Door open," she said.

"Please make sure you are wearing your protective gloves and hat," a computerized voice said. "Remember the Pole takes no responsibility for what happens to you outside these doors," the voice continued. "Do you understand this disclaimer?" the door asked.

"Yes," Nova and I both said.

"Do you agree to this disclaimer?" the door asked.

"Yes," we both said again.

"Remember it's best to stay outside less than fifteen minutes. Please enjoy your experience. You may proceed."

The door swung open. Nova and I walked out. The suit and hat and gloves worked well. I didn't feel the cold.

"I'm honored you want to talk with me," Nova said, as we walked through the frozen everything.

"You might not be so honored when you find out what I want to talk about. First off, I'm interested in knowing how you know me," I asked.

She winked. "My little secret."

I glared at her. I don't normally glare at beautiful women, especially ones with arms bigger than my legs, but I wasn't in the mood to be subtle or coy.

"I could tell by your pheromone scent," she said. "I never forget a smell."

"Your mom must be so proud," I said.

She laughed. "Is that all you called me out here for?"

"You were the one who wanted to go walking through the frozen tundra. There is a reason I wanted to speak to you in private."

"Oh?"

"When doing a background check on you, I found

you were once a member of the Santana Sticks Society."

She gave me a dismissive wave. "Yeah, the elves questioned me on that. I assured them I have nothing personal against Santana."

"Then why were you a member?"

"Guess," she said with a playful nudge on the shoulder.

"I'm not in the mood," I said, resisting the need to rub my shoulder.

"It was during my date-a-geek phase," she said.

"Ah, yes, Ben Pierce. The android expert turned lousy poet."

"He was against Santana."

"Why?"

"Mostly because ExShell had put in a bid for the Pole gig when Ben was a young scientist. They wanted Santana to be an android. Ben insisted that would be the way to go. Androids are more rational than organics, Ben always said. Even a genetically improved human couldn't keep up with a good android."

"The Council shot him down, though, huh?"

She nodded. "Yeah, they thought the world would relate better to an organic Santana. I agree. But to keep my man happy, I went along and joined the SSS. I did it under my real name just in case any fans found out."

"I see."

"I'm so through my geek stage now," she spat.

"I can see that, too."

"Anything else you want to chat about, Zach?"

"Somebody tried to kill me yesterday," I said coldly.

"Zach—I mean, Bart—I was only playing with you yesterday."

"No, somebody really tried to kill me."

"From what I understand, that happens quite often."

"True. I'm in demand."

"Do you think I tried to kill you? Because if you do, coming out alone with me wasn't such a good idea. Without your weapons and gadgets, I could literally kill you with a wink of my eye," she said.

"That may be true, but I don't think you're a killer," I told her.

With less than no warning, Nova lifted me up and heaved me across the ice. I went crashing through a display of three-meter tall glowing, plastic candy canes into a snowbank. I sat up and cleared the snow and stars from my eyes. Nova was storming toward me.

"You don't think I'm a killer?" she screamed at me.

"I've been known to be wrong—"

"You're right you're wrong."

"I hate being right about being wrong."

I ripped a big icicle off from above. Nova came at me. I clubbed her over the head with the icicle. The icicle broke. She just smiled. She picked me up off the ground and pulled me into a bear hug. She started to squeeze the life out of me.

"So, you don't think I'm a killer, huh?" she said.

"I'm starting to have second and third thoughts." I was hoping I would live to have fourth and fifth thoughts.

"Zach, grab her head with both hands. I have a trick up our sleeve," HARV whispered. "But first you'll have to remove your gloves."

I was pretty sure I knew where HARV was going with this. I had to move fast, as I felt the air being squeezed out of my lungs. I pulled off my left glove and dropped it the ground. I pulled of the right glove and let that one drop, too. I clasped both hands around Nova's ears. Electricity shot from my hands to her head. She dropped me.

"HARV, can you do that again?"

"You bet."

I grabbed her by the left ankle. Electricity shot from my hands. She started jumping around on one foot. I pulled the other foot out from under her. She fell to the ground. I backed off, ready for anything but in the mood for no crap. I wasn't about to let this lady put a beating on me two days in a row. Outside, away from prying eyes, I could use all the tricks at my disposal.

She laughed. Not really the reaction I was expecting.

"You really have no sense of humor," she told me as she stood up.

"Not when somebody's trying to kill me," I told her as I stood up.

"If I was trying to kill you, you'd be dead yesterday."

"What is this, some kind of strange joke?" I asked.

"I am a killer," she informed me, "just not your killer. I'm a lady mutant pro wrestler. We have to have killer attitudes, or the other mutants will run all over us. In my circle, being tagged as not a killer is an insult."

"Sorry. My girlfriend is always telling me I have these antisocial tendencies."

She sat down, then patted the ice.

"Come sit next to me."

I reluctantly sat next to her. "You're not going to try to almost kill me again, are you?"

"Not as long as you don't accuse me of not being a killer again."

"Deal."

"By holding your own in mortal combat with me, you've earned my respect. Even if you did have to cheat—again."

"Hey, they say all is fair in love and war, and with you Nova, it's hard to tell the difference."

"Thank you!" she said, as she smashed her hand into the snow.

"Don't mention it."

I watched as she munched on a handful of snow.

"Yum. This stuff is even better than sex and violence."

"You really like that stuff."

"I and pretty much all mutants have a thing for this snow, but Santana won't sell it."

"So is that why you're here? To talk to Santana about a deal?"

"I wish. I'm just here because somebody sent me a free pass."

"Do you know who?"

"No, and I don't really care, though I have a pretty good idea," she said as she grabbed more snow. "Just as long as I get to eat this wonderful ice." She paused to swallow, then said, "Somebody tried to kill you?"

"No, it was just a clever ploy so I could accuse you of not being a killer so you'd try to practically kill me."

"You really hold a grudge, don't you?"

"Sorry, sometimes I get a little resentful of being the universe's punching bag. Yes, somebody tried to kill me."

"Any idea who?" she asked.

"Well, I'm pretty certain who it wasn't. I don't think it was the Eatmans, and not to offend you, but I don't think you're the one, though I do think you are capable of killing."

"You are a fast learner."

"What do you know about Bim and Norp?" I
questioned.

"They're annoying."

"They seem to like you."

"Believe me, it's not mutual. Like I said, I'm past
my geek-freak stage."

"I assume they're the ones who sent you the free
ticket."

"I wouldn't be surprised. But I doubt they have the
external sex organs to attempt to murder you."

"Maybe not in person. But I think they are capable
of sending a bot after me."

"A bot? What kind of bot?" she asked me.

"A guardbot," I stated cooly.

"A guardbot!" she said, far more excitedly than the
conversation should warrant.

"Yes, a guardbot," I said, starting to lose my
patience.

She leaped over and pulled me to the ground a split
nano before a laser blast fired over my head, melting
the snowbank where my head had just been.

"Yep, a guardbot just like that!" I said, pointing at
the approaching bot. "HARV, I thought you said the
guardbots couldn't fire their lasers?"

"I did. But I stressed the inside of the Pole's buildings part. Currently, you are outside, therefore—"

"Great! And I don't even have my H_2O pistol."

The bot fired another round of laser bursts just over
our heads.

"Your eye, it talks," Nova said.

"And talks, and talks, and talks, but that's the least
of our worries now," I said.

"Ha! So that's how you blinded me yesterday! And
shocked me just now! You're wearing a computer!
DOS, I thought Bim and Norp were the geeks."

"Let's focus on the situation at hand, Nova."

The bot slowly rolled toward us. "I have deduced that you are unarmed. Therefore I may safely approach and annihilate you from a close distance. I will not fail like my comrades."

"HARV, do you have enough juice to give this thing the shock treatment?" I asked.

"I think so."

"Will it stop it?

"If you can get behind and zap it in the main control panel, probably."

"It's not going to just let me get around it, HARV. The old 'your shoe's untied' trick isn't going to work here."

The bot closed in.

Nova reacted quickly and surprisingly. She stood up, grabbed me, and then hurled me over the bot just as it fired. The laser from the bot flew by me and hit Nova in the shoulder. She fell back in pain, but didn't show it. I flew through the air with the greatest of ease over the bot. The bot fired at me several times but missed ever so slightly each time. Apparently it wasn't programming to hit flying targets. I crashed to the ground just behind the bot. I lunged toward it.

"NOW HARV!" I shouted.

Electricity shot from my hands into the bot. The last thing I remember was an explosion.

The next thing I knew I was waking up in the Pole's infirmary. Santana, Elf-1, and Nova were watching an elf doctor examine me.

I slowly started to come around. "Electra's right. I shouldn't eat zap wave pizza before I go to bed."

"He's going to be all right now."

I sat up in my toboggan-shaped bed. My head hurt, but I seemed to be alive. "DOS, I was hoping this whole ordeal was just a dream."

The doc shook his head.

"I'd like a second opinion."

Everybody else shook their heads.

"I was afraid of that, " I said.

"You're lucky to be alive, Zach," Santana said.

"That's easy for you to say."

All of a sudden I thought of something.

"HARV?" I called.

No answer.

"HARV? Come in, please."

Still, no answer.

"He's obviously delirious," the doc told Santana.

"HARV, talk to me," I said, as I tapped my head.

"Zach, I'm undercover. Remember?" HARV whispered.

"Forget the cover, HARV, that's pretty much blown. How come you didn't tell me what would happen if I tried to zap a guardbot?"

"I didn't want to scare you."

"WHAT?" I shouted until the pain in my head made me stop.

"It actually makes sense. The only chance you had of stopping the bot was using me to electrocute it. So, the fact that you might actually electrocute yourself didn't matter, since you would have died anyway."

"I hate to admit it, HARV, but you're right," I said as I wobbled to my feet.

"Of course," HARV agreed, appearing before us.

"He's wearing a computer. That's against the rules!" Elf-1 shouted.

"Number One, when it comes to rules, I don't think they apply to Mr. Johnson here," Santana said.

"They apply. I just choose to ignore them when the choice is comply or die. Survival of the fittest, or at least the trickiest, is the only rule I adhere to."

I looked at Nova and smiled. "You thought pretty fast on your feet back there."

"A good warrior knows how to think on her feet as on well as her back," she told me.

"Who do you think is behind all this, Zach?" Santana asked.

"I never accuse until I'm positive. It cuts down on lawsuits. I need to talk one-on-one with Mrs. Billings, Councilwoman Weathers, and Bim and Norp."

Santana raised an eyebrow. "The councilwoman?" she said. "Surely you don't think she's behind this. After all she's the most—"

"—respected and honest person in the world. Yes, I know. HARV read me her press release. She's still a person of power, and that makes her a person of interest to me."

"If you say so," Santana said, her eyes focusing on the floor. "You're the expert, and you know best."

"It's also time for me to reveal my true identity," I said. "Let the bad guys know I'm on the case."

"Don't you think they already know since there have been two attempts on your life in the last two days?" Elf-1 asked.

I shook my head. "That might be bad karma." I looked at Nova. "Or warnings from jealous lovers. Even if they do know my identity, my coming clean will make them think I'm close to breaking the case. It will force their hand."

I need to talk to those people first and then if needed the entire group."

"Fine," Elf-1 said. "I'll have Ma Billings meet you in the library at seventeen hundred. Is that all right?"

"What time is it now?"

"Fourteen-oh-two," HARV answered.

"Okay, I can live with that. That gives me time to go to my room, collect my thoughts, and clean up."

With that, I left.

Chapter 24

I arrived in my room and threw myself down on my bed. Both of the most recent attempts on my life were after I had been with Nova. I was pretty certain Bim and Norp were behind them. I wasn't as sure Bim and Norp were behind the dead elves. I couldn't see what they would gain from it. Still, there had to be a connection.

While I took a quick shower (with green and red sprays of water) HARV and Elf-1 made arrangements. I would meet with my major suspects first: Mrs. Billings, followed by the councilwoman, then Bim, followed by Norp. I would do the questioning, and HARV would do a voice analysis of their answers, while Santana and Elf-1 listened in. After I met with a suspect, they would be kept separate from the others. Once I had meet with each suspect, we'd all get together, I would reveal myself as Zach Nixon Johnson, and identify the killer. It would be a great storybook moment. There was only one problem. I knew what it was, but that didn't stop HARV from pointing it out to me the second I got out of the shower. (I should be happy he waited for me to get out.)

"You're going to do the dramatic reveal?" HARV asked.

"Yep," I said, as I moved under the body dryer.

HARV pointed to one of the buttons on the wall. "Don't set the dryer on high. You know how you chafe."

"Yes, Mom," I said, pressing the Low button.

I felt the warm air run up and down my body. It felt good, even with the music from the Holiday song playing in the background. I knew HARV wasn't about to let the feeling of warmth last.

"Surely you realize there is a problem with you staging a comic book unveiling of the mastermind behind the murders," HARV said.

I shrugged. "Not really," I said, just to drive HARV a bit buggy.

HARV threw his arms up in the air. "Zach, Zach, Zach! Most detectives don't schedule an appointment to name the killer until they know who the killer is."

"I'm not your average detective, and this isn't an average case," I said, heading into my bedroom.

HARV put his hands on his hips and groaned. He disappeared from the bathroom. He appeared directly in front of me.

"What, too lazy to walk?" I said.

HARV put a holographic hand on my shoulder.

"You know, HARV, that kind of creeps me out when I'm not wearing clothing," I said.

HARV withdrew his hand. "Sorry, I'm just very secure in my sexuality."

"Yes, of course you are, considering over the last year you've been a woman and gay."

"What can I say? When I experiment I really experiment," he said.

I went to the closet and picked out an elf suit. It wasn't much of choice, since they were all identical.

"I've narrowed down the list of suspects," I told HARV. "After my one-on-one sessions, the list will be even smaller."

"And if it's not?"

"I bluff. I put on the big show, and let the bad guys sweat."

"And if they don't?"

"Don't worry, they will," I said.

"How can you be so confident?" HARV said.

Truthfully, I wasn't certain how I'd know. It was just another one of my hunches. Those hunches had kept me alive this long—I wasn't about to stop trusting them now.

Chapter 25

I sat in a comfortable plush chair in the library waiting for Mrs. Billings. The library was filled with giant computer screens in front of big fluffy chairs that looked and felt a lot like clouds, only with more support. Outside of the holly draping the doors, the room wasn't as over the top as the rest of the Pole. Of course the Muzak-II version of the Holiday theme was playing subtly in the background.

From my comfy chair, I saw Mrs. Billings enter the room and slowly skulk towards me.

"You wanted to see me, Mr. Starr?" Mrs. Billings asked uneasily as she approached me.

I motioned to a chair.

"Please sit."

She sat, albeit reluctantly.

"May I ask what this is about?" she asked. I could almost hear her heart pounding from where I sat.

"Robotics. Quantum physics. Radio waves. Life. Death. Taxes. Sports scores. You name it."

"I beg your pardon?" she said, as she gave me that *are you crazy or what* look I get so often.

"Quit playing the naive farm ma with me. I know you used to work for HTech designing guardbots."

She hesitated for a nano. I suspected she'd deny it. I was mistaken.

"That was a long time ago. It's all behind me now," she said meekly.

"Why?"

"Why?"

"Why'd you quit?"

"I don't see where that's any of your business."

"It is my business when your bots try to kill me."

"What are you talking about?" she said, standing up from the chair.

"In the last two days, I've been attacked three times by four of your bots."

"First of all, they are hardly my bots. HTech and I broke off our relationship years ago. Secondly, if you really did face off with just one guardbot, you'd be dead now. They are more than a match for any normal human."

"Well, let's just say I'm not *any* normal human."

Here is where I decided to go off script. I reached down on my belt and deactivated the holo-disguise. From my point of view, I only saw a slight shimmer in the images I was looking at. From the look on Mrs. Billings' face, I could see she was seeing me.

"Do you know who I am?" I asked.

"You're that private investigator guy—the one who's always getting himself in strange jams."

"I don't get myself in jams on purpose. They tend to find me," I said

She put a hand on her chest. "What are you doing here?"

"She's not nearly as surprised as she's pretending to be," HARV whispered inside my head.

"Like I said, your bots tried to killed me."

"I have no idea why that would happen," she insisted. "What are you doing here anyway?" she repeated.

"Two elves were killed. Santana brought me here to investigate."

There was silence. She was calculating the best response to this. She was an engineer all right.

"She's covering something, but she's not in panic mode," HARV said.

"Are you accusing me of something?"

"No, I'm just curious. Curiosity may have killed the cat, but it tends to keep the PI alive. Why are you and your family here?" I asked.

"We're on vacation—little Billy won a contest."

I shook my head. "You're trying to tell me it's sheer coincidence that one of the designers of the Pole's guardbots happens to be at the Pole when the guardbots decide to start killing elves and attacking me."

She sneered at me. "Your information is old, Mr. Johnson," she said. "If you look hard enough and in the right places, you will see that I only worked on the guardbot project at the very beginning. I was transferred to another project."

"I can't confirm that, Zach," HARV said inside my head. "But I can say she's either not lying or an expert liar."

She shrugged. "Why would I want to kill elves? Or you for that matter? Until just seconds ago, I had no idea who you really were." She paused for a nano and then squinted her eyes. "Though I can understand why somebody would sic guardbots on you."

"She's definitely not lying with that last statement," HARV said. "You might want to take a people-skill course."

I thought about what she had said. She didn't seem

to have a motive, yet I didn't trust her. Something about her ate away at the very core of my being. What was she doing hiding out in New Kansas? It wasn't as backwards as, say, Oakland, but it wasn't exactly on the forefront of engineering breakthroughs either.

"So, what made you move to New Kansas?" I asked.

She looked up at me, gauging me. "I'm not a murderer," she said.

"I didn't say you were."

She shook her head. "The pressure of working for HTech got to me. I wanted to get as far away from robots as possible."

"She's not lying," HARV said to me.

"I guess being a farm mom in New Kansas is as far away from making robots as you can get."

Her face cracked a weak smile. "That's why I love it so much. It's good, honest work. I'm making the world a better place now, not worse."

This struck me as a strange comment. Most engineers I know do what they do because they love creating things.

"You didn't like making robots?"

"No. I was in it for the money. Believe me, it was HUGE amounts of money, but after a while I needed to work with something with a soul."

"Wheat?"

"No, my family."

"Oh."

"My family and I help feed other families."

"You must use bots to help with the work," I said.

"Of course we do, but those bots are just a means to the end, not the end itself. Bots are necessary in today's world. I know that and accept that."

"You'll use them but not create them."

"Exactly, Mr. Johnson."

"You're a regular the-end-justifies-the-means kind of gal," I said.

"You have no idea," she said.

"Her heart rate jumped there," HARV said to me.

I wasn't sure what that meant. However, I was pretty certain Mrs. Billings wasn't responsible for the death of the elves.

She stood up from her chair. "Are we done?" she asked.

"For now," I said.

"Good," she said. "My family must be missing me." She turned toward the way out.

I reached forward and grabbed her arm. It was a gentle grab, but a grab nevertheless.

"I'm sorry Mrs. Billings, but it will be a few minutes before you can rejoin your family. I have a couple other people of interest to chat with before I bring you all together."

She spun toward me, breaking my grip.

"Are you detaining me?" she asked angrily.

"Just delaying you for a few minutes," I said. "It's for the good of the case."

She gave me a glare that I assumed she normally used on her husband when he pissed her off.

"It will only be for a short time. I promise."

"The elves have cookies and hot cocoa," HARV whispered to me.

I pointed to a door at the back of the room. "There's a nice comfortable waiting room back there. The elves have cookies and hot cocoa," I said.

She inhaled deeply. "Well, I do *love* cocoa," she said.

"That's the spirit."

She headed off into the waiting room.

Chapter 26

HARV and the elves coordinated the arrival of my next guest, Councilwoman Weathers. They gave me a few nanos to collect myself and to reactivate my holodisguise. As soon as I sat in my chair, the door across the room opened. Councilwoman Weathers strutted in.

She had to be in her late fifties, but you couldn't tell by looking at her. There wasn't a blemish or a wrinkle to be found. Her eyes still had the sparkle of a teenager's. The only hint that she wasn't a young woman was the frosty gray of her hair. I imagined she kept the gray because some consultant told her it made her look distinguished. It did. In fact, she walked with an air of nobility not unlike a queen or a rock star.

"For Gates sake, stand up!" HARV coaxed from inside my head. "You're greeting a lady, and a very important lady, at that."

I knew HARV was right. I just didn't want to seem too anxious. I rose when the councilwoman was within a meter. The councilwoman walked up to me and extended a hand. I wasn't sure if she meant for me to kiss it or shake it. I went with the latter.

"Mr. Starr, I'm honored you wish to interview me, a humble servant of the people," she said.

"Please, I'm the one who is honored," I said.

I motioned to the chair. "Please sit," I said.

She looked at the chair as if it were a bear trap. "I'm a very busy woman," she said.

"You're on vacation," I said, pointing to the chair. "Trust me, this will only take a few minutes."

She hesitated, but capitulated. "Even on vacation I'm a busy woman," she said, easing herself into the chair.

"I appreciate your time."

"As well you should." She primed her lips, then crossed her legs. They were fine legs, upper-class legs. The legs of a woman who worked out because she wanted to, not because she needed to.

"How can I help you with your little story?" she asked. She was being polite, yet condescending, not letting me forget for a nano with whom I was dealing.

"I think my last interview was with an Oprah clone," she said with a hand fluttering in the air. She moved her hand in front of her lips.

"Or was it a clone of a clone?" She paused to think. "I can never tell them apart. I know most clones of clones go postal, but Oprah, well, she could afford the best of best."

"Yes, I'm sure," I said. "Only I didn't ask you here to talk about cloning clones," I said.

"Yes, of course," she said, sitting back in the chair. "What can I do for you?"

It was time for a decision: should I stay with the called play and interview the councilwoman in character, or do I go for the audible and hit her with the real Zach? It worked well enough last time. Only that was with an engineer-turned-farm-mom, and neither of those professions called for smooth people skills. This was a professional politician, an entirely different animal. No matter what HARV said, she was a professional liar. At the very least, she was a person who made her living telling other people what they wanted to hear and making it sound like it was her idea.

I went with the audible. Not only that, but I went for the long bomb, the touchdown pass. I switched off my holo-disguise. I was anxious to see her reaction.

"Well, well, Zachary Nixon Johnson," she said. "At last we meet." If she was surprised, she didn't show it. "I knew it was only a matter of time before our paths crossed. After all you save the world—"

"—and you run it," I said.

She smiled. "The world runs itself, Mr. Johnson. I'm just one of the many people who helps guide it in the best direction for all." She paused to compose herself. "What brings you to the Pole? Since you are in disguise, I gather this is more than a vacation."

"There's been a murder," I said. "And several attempts on my life."

One of her eyebrows wrinkled ever so slightly. "A murder? How come I haven't heard of it?"

"I can't tell if she's lying," HARV whispered inside my mind, "but she doesn't seem surprised."

I had to agree with HARV's assessment. The councilwoman seemed more taken aback that she wasn't notified than surprised.

"The Pole is funded by the World Council," she said. "Santana should have informed us."

I shook my head. "You were a businesswoman before you entered politics, weren't you?"

"Yes."

"Then you know it's bad news to spook your investors, especially with news of murder."

"Good point. We should have been told, nonetheless."

"Santana was planning on telling you, once she collected more data," I said. "That's where I come in."

"You're the data collection agency," she said with a grin.

I nodded. "My specialty is extra-sensitive material."

"When did the murder occur?" she asked.

"Two days ago," I said. "And it was two murders."

She gave me a funny look. "Two days ago? That's when my party and I got here."

"Exactly."

"But all the people I arrived with are still here." She thought for a nano. "Elves. Elves were killed."

"Yes," I said.

She locked eyes with me. "Surely, I'm not a suspect," she said. "I assure you, Mr. Johnson, I'm not an elf killer." She performed a mock strangling motion. "What did I do, kill them with my bare hands?"

I looked at her. "That doesn't mean you wouldn't hire somebody to kill them. Or in this case, hire somebody to rewire their killers."

She looked away from me. "I'm not even going to dignify that with a response," she huffed. "Why would I hire somebody to reprogram bots to kill elves?"

"I never mentioned bots," I said.

This shot her attention back to me. "Please Mr. Johnson, you said 'rewire their killers.' I put one and one together and figured guardbots killed the elves."

"I can't tell if she's telling the truth," HARV said. "I still don't think she'd kill elves."

Not suspecting that I was listening to HARV, Councilwoman Weathers interpreted my silence as a sign that I didn't believe her.

"Why would I want to upset the Pole?" she asked me.

"Maybe because the Pole isn't operating quite the way you would like?" I said.

"You've lost me," she said.

"I know that certain people in the World Council would be very interested in using the elves' skills to make weapons," I said.

She leaned forward on her chair, hands on knees. She shook her head. "Now, how did you learn that?" she asked, even though I knew she meant it rhetorically. Her eyes wandered across the ceiling. I could see her mind working this out. Her eyes focused on me. "That little tramp Sexy Sprockets told you," she said.

I didn't answer for a nano, just to let her stew in her own juices. "Sexy isn't a little tramp," I said.

The councilwoman threw herself back in her chair. "Please, her bedroom sees more action than Grand Central Teleport Station." She pointed at me. "This is what happens when they let amateurs into politics. They misinterpret, and then they blab."

Now it was my turn to sit back in my chair. "Don't point at me, I didn't vote for her."

"Yes, but you kept her from dying," Weathers said. For a career politician, I thought she would have been better at hiding the venom in her voice.

"You admit there is some tension between the Council and Santana?"

"Not openly," she said. "There are certain Council members who would be interested in seeing the Pole widen their product base."

"Into weapons," I said.

"I wouldn't say that," she said.

"One of your coworkers could have organized this."

"They are all politicians, Zach. They are capable of anything."

"You're a politician, too," I said, feeling compelled to point out the obvious.

"Yes, I am, and a darned good one too, I might add. One who is too smart to mess with a good thing. I'm a woman of peace, Zach. I love what the Pole does for Earth."

"Wow, is she ever telling the truth," HARV said.

She put her hand on her heart and started patting her chest. "Trust me, Mr. Johnson, I continuously strive to make the world a better place," she said.

The words CONFIRMED flashed before my eyes in big neon letters. HARV was showing remarkable restraint by not scrolling HA HA! I TOLD YOU SO, across my eyes.

The councilwoman stood up. "I assume you are running some sort of voice analysis program on me."

"I am."

"I know it has confirmed that I am telling the truth," she said.

I nodded my head. "It has," I said.

"Then I'm free to go," she said.

I pointed to the door at the back of the room. "Yes, of course. I just ask that you wait in a secluded room while I talk to the other," I paused, looking for the right words, "people of interest."

"Will you be bringing my husband in?" she asked.

"Not in the first round," I said.

"Good," she said. "He's a sweet man and nice eye candy, but not nearly bright enough to pull off something like this."

She got up and sauntered out of the room. As she walked out, my eyes followed. I didn't want them to, but they did. She was that kind of woman. Not strikingly beautiful, but she commanded and held your attention. She is the closest thing we have to royalty these days. A woman of obvious upbringing and dignity. A woman with great intelligence and a quiet beauty. A woman respected by the entire planet. I knew she had to be in on it.

"You're too pensive," HARV said inside my head.

"Nah, just thinking," I said.

"Zach, for once can't you just admit you're wrong and stop looking for flaws in the councilwoman?"

"I've never seen you so defensive of a human that wasn't Randy," I said.

"I don't know what it is about her," HARV conceded. "I've never met a human that was so perfect. Well, not perfect, because no human can be perfect, but as close to perfection as humanly possible."

If I didn't know better, I would have said HARV was flustered by the councilwoman.

"You've got a crush on her," I said.

HARV appeared before me waving a finger in my face. "I knew you were going to say that. I am not in love, and I do not have a crush. Neither of those are logical."

I crossed my arms and looked at him. I didn't say a word. I just let myself smile ever so slightly.

"I know what you're thinking, Zach. He's connected to me, so he's becoming more and more illogical. I admit that thought has crossed my cognitive generators about a trillion times. But no, I just admire Councilwoman Weathers for being so good at what she does and so flawless."

"You know other exceptional women," I said.

"That's true. Electra is a wonderful example of the human female. She is smart, witty, beautiful, and a gifted doctor and athlete. I'm amazed every day that she loves you. Still, she has flaws—she snores, she has an irrational fear of moths, and she has a temper only slightly cooler than molten lava."

"Good point."

"Then there's Carol. She's another exceptional human woman. She is also beautiful inside and out and sharp as a tack. Being a class I level VI psi, she's one of the most powerful beings on the planet. I'm amazed every day that she works for you and respects you."

"Gee, thanks HARV. I like you too."

"Despite all her good points, Carol is flawed. She can't cook, she has a funny left little toe, and her feet are much more potent than you would expect. Plus that temper! It may be harder to ignite than Electra's, but it's even more volatile when it does. Witness the ex-boyfriend whose car she melted . . ."

"She may be superhuman, but she's still human," I said.

"That's the amazing thing about the councilwoman— she's human but I can't find any flaws. You practically accused her of stomping on those dead elves herself, and she didn't bat an eyelash, and her body temperature didn't rise—she was cool as a cryogenic cucumber."

"That's what worries me, HARV. Like they say, if it looks too good to be true, it probably is."

"They also say it's possible to overthink a problem," HARV said.

"Wow, HARV, you're accusing me of thinking too much."

HARV put a hand on my shoulder. "Thinking may be too strong a word," he said with a smile. "Zach, I know you think you have a sixth sense when it comes to this kind of thing. I have admitted you do have a very good knack for shifting through the potential outcomes and choosing the right one."

"Thanks, you make it sound so special," I said.

"However, there are times when you just have to

let it go, when you have to admit that the toaster really is just a toaster and is not trying to kill you."

"Fine," I said. "Let's get ready for Bim and Norp."

On some level I knew HARV had a point. We had an entire room full of good suspects, and there wasn't a need to go out of my way looking for another one. Still, there was something about the councilwoman that didn't sit right with me. I knew sooner or later I would figure it out. I hoped I would before it came back to bite me in the ass. The one solace I had was this time I could tell HARV "I told you so." That wouldn't be much comfort if the mistake killed me.

Chapter 27

Once I gave the elves in the holding room the okay, they sent in Bim and Norp. I had wanted to see them separately, but they weren't going to stand for that. I guess they figured there was safety in numbers. Having them together meant I'd actually have to deal with them less and that was appealing to me.

I was back in full Bart Starr mode when they walked into the room. Even from across the library, I could tell from the way they shuffled reluctantly toward me they were none too happy to talk to me. I stood waiting for them, impatiently tapping my foot. I've seen sloths at the zoo move faster, and they probably smelled better too. Truthfully, I have never smelled a sloth. There are some things you can just assume.

I positioned two chairs across from my own. I had time to rearrange them numerous times before Bim and Norp reached me. I don't usually want to shoot people, but at that moment, they were very lucky I didn't have my gun. I was reasonably certain they had tried to kill me at least twice in the last two days, but my disdain for them went beyond that. It was as if my very DNA was programmed to be repelled by them.

I motioned to the chairs. "Gentlemen, please sit," I said.

"We prefer to stand," Bim said.

"Yes," Norp said.

This was a power play on their part. That's part of the reason they wanted to come in together—they figured they had me outnumbered. I wasn't about to let them get away with it, but for now I'd play it cool.

"Have it your way," I said, sitting in my chair.

There were a few nanos of awkward silence. I decided to let them speak first.

Finally, Norp said, "What do you want from us?"

I hesitated a nano and then answered, "I just want to talk."

"Nobody ever wants to talk with us," Bim said. "At least not to carry on an actual conversation. They just want us to help them and go away."

I pushed back the urge to say, "I know the feeling." "I'm interested in learning why you fine chaps came to the Pole," I said.

"Vacation," Bim said.

"Stress release," Norp said.

Both their responses were automatic, dare I say, rehearsed. I let them think about their answers a nano to see if they'd elaborate on their own.

"The Pole is a high-tech wonder," Bim said.

"A marvel," Norp added.

"Certainly your homes on Mars are just as high-tech," I said.

"True," Bim said.

"Affirmative," Norp said.

"Then there's another reason?" I asked.

"The food," Bim said,

"Love the eats," Norp said.

"Elves can cook," Bim said.

"Sure can," Norp said.

They both had beads of sweat forming on their brows. Even without HARV, I could tell they weren't lying, but they were holding back. It wasn't easy for them. Unlike the councilwoman, they weren't pros at this.

"What about Nova?" I asked.

They both wrinkled their faces into looks of feigned confusion.

"Who?" Bim asked.

Norp just shook his head.

"Nova, the muscular but gorgeous pro wrestler on the tour."

"Oh, that's her name," Bim said, slapping his knees.

"Now that you mention it, she does sound familiar," Norp said.

"She is a very sturdy woman." Bim said.

"I've seen better," Norp said. "But I wouldn't kick her out of bed for eating soy crackers," he added.

He elbowed Bim playfully. They both giggled. They were their own biggest fans. That was all I could take. I reached down and pressed the deactivate button on my holo-disguise. The slight shimmer I saw told me it worked. The looks of fear on Bim and Norp's faces confirmed it.

"Zachary Nixon Johnson," they both gasped.

"Your reputation really does precede you," HARV laughed inside my head.

I stood up. "Enough games, boys," I growled. I don't like being bullied. I hate being the bully. But there are time when I do have to use my size and fighting experience to my advantage.

I pushed my chest out and moved toward them. It wasn't a threatening move, just one that was quicker than a nonthreatening one. Bim and Norp immediately sank back into the chairs.

"Please don't hurt us," Bim said, protecting his face with his hands.

"It was his idea," Norp said, protecting his face with one hand and pointing with the other.

Now we were making progress. "What was his idea?" I asked.

"Getting the bots to attack you," Norp said. "We wanted Nova all to ourselves. We were jealous."

"They are telling the truth," HARV said.

"How'd you reprogram the bots?" I asked.

Norp reached up on his head, pulled out a strand of green hair, and showed it to me. "My hair is actually a remote transmitter," he said. "It allows us to reprogram the bots."

"Pretty clever," I said.

"The dandruff even acts as a signal booster," he said with far more pride than he should have.

"More info than I need there."

Just then the door burst open. Santana came in, accompanied by Elf-1 and three other security elves. Santana's face was redder than her suit. She stormed up to the two MESSHs. "How dare you kill my elves!"

"And attack me," I added.

"That too," Santana agreed. She turned to Elf-1, "Number One, deactivate the bots, and place these two under arrest."

"With pleasure, madam," Elf-1 said.

I watched Bim and Norp watch Elf-1 press the button on his control wristband. They were smiling. Elf-1 looked at the wristband. He pressed more buttons.

"Santana, the bots aren't responding," he said.

"They are responding," Norp said, "to us."

Right about then, four guardbots rolled into the room.

"This can't be good," I said.

As if proving my point, a bot fired a warning shot up into the ceiling.

"Our weapons are activated. We suggest you surrender now," it shouted.

Chapter 28

Santana, the elves, and I dove for cover behind the chairs a split nano before the bots opened fire.

"We tried to do this peacefully, but you've forced our hands!" Norp shouted.

"We were hoping it wouldn't come to this, but so be it!" Bim shouted.

They were both considerably braver when backed by armed bots.

"I suggest we make a hasty farewell and exit," Norp said.

"I agree," Bim said.

I peeked over a chair. The bots were holding their places until Bim and Norp got out of the line of fire. I wasn't sure if this was because they didn't want to accidentally shoot Bim or Norp, or if it was because the bots were a little slow in planning their attack. They had us outnumbered and outgunned, but these were guardbots, not attackbots or battlebots. That gave us a chance.

I turned to Santana, who was taking cover behind

the same chair I was. Elf-1 was next to her, chanting, "My happy place, find my happy place"

"Santana can you control them?" I asked.

"Normally yes, but something is blocking me."

"Do you still have communication with the rest of the Pole?" I asked.

Elf-1 looked down at his communicator. "Yes," he said. "I'm not sure how that helps."

"Well, it doesn't hurt," I said. I thought for a nano or two. "Is the holding room behind us secure?"

Elf-1 looked at his communicator. "Yes. Only the councilwoman and Mrs. Billings are in there."

"Let's join them," I said. "We'll plan from there. Let them know we're coming."

"Check," Elf-1 said.

"Then what?" Santana asked.

"We make a break for the door," I said. "A very fast break."

The three other security elves shook their heads no.

"If this is going to work, you'll need a distraction," one of them said.

"Agreed," another said.

The three of them looked at one another and winked.

"No, it's too dangerous," Santana protested.

"It's the only way," the third elf said.

The middle elf made a fist and extended it. The other two elves made fists and put them on top of his.

"For Santana!" the first elf shouted.

"For Santana!" the other two echoed.

"One for all and all for Santana!" they shouted. Yep, definitely too much sugar in their diets.

They turned to us and pointed toward the door in the back of the room. That was our cue.

"Stay low and go," I said.

The three elves took off one way, and I went the

other, pulling Santana and Elf-1 with me. We raced toward the door. I heard laser fire and screaming elves. I didn't look back. I couldn't. What was behind us didn't matter now. The elves had sacrificed themselves, and I had to make sure it was worth something. If I was going to get cut down from behind, so be it.

The side doors that lined the room, those were a different story. I couldn't let us get ambushed there. We drew closer to the back door. I pushed Santana and Elf-1 ahead of me. It wasn't that difficult, as they were both faster than I was. While keeping the center of my vision focused on the target—the door ahead— I used quick glances to the left and right to see if there were any surprises.

It was a good thing I did. There were two guardbots rolling in, one from each side. DOS, this room had a lot of doors. I looked at the door we were rushing toward. We were still twenty-five meters away and in open space. We'd be easy pickings for the bots.

"HARV, how good is the holo-detection on these bots?" I asked.

"Not good at all, since technically holograms aren't allowed up here," HARV said.

That gave me an idea.

We raced toward the door. Elf-1 signaled the councilwoman and Mrs. Billings not to open the door for anyone or anything that wasn't us. We got within ten meters of the door—so close we could almost feel it. That's when all DOS broke out. The bots closed in on us, catching us in a crossfire.

Elf-1 was the first to take it—a killing blast right to the chest that cut a hole clean through him. Santana was the next to go down. It was a clean, high-powered shot to the head. Maybe a more advanced GE like Twoa Thompson would have been able to survive, but Santana was dead before she even hit the ground.

I was the bot's next target. Apparently, they were saving me for last. First one of them shot out my right leg. The other one shot out my left leg. They rolled up so close, they were practically touching me.

"It will be such a pleasure to kill you, Zachary Nixon Johnson," one of the bots said.

"We want to see the look on your face when you die!" the other bot said.

"You wouldn't believe the number of times I hear that in a day," I said.

The bots looked at me, confused. The sound of my voice had come from behind them. It slowly dawned on them. They hadn't cut down Elf-1, Santana, and Zachary Johnson. They had cut down holographic projections of us. Meanwhile, the real us had gotten the drop on them with a holographic cloak.

It may have not been the optimal move, tipping them to our presence by talking, but just as they wanted to see my face when they killed me, I wanted to see the look on their screens when they figured out what had happened. They had been duped by one of the oldest holographic tricks in the book.

Guardbots are basically cylinders mounted on a flexible tractor base with an information screen on top, just to give them a semi-humanoid appearance. If you catch them off guard and are nutso enough to dive at them and hit them just right, you can knock them down. Once on the ground, they are like turtles turned upside down—interesting to look at, but not good for much else.

Before the bots had a chance to react, we lit into them. I dove a meter at the one on the right, leading with my shoulder. I was a free safety on my high school football team. I wasn't a good one. I was more interested in scoring with the cheerleaders than the

score of the game. Still, I knew how to hit and take
a hit.

I plowed my shoulder into the upper third of a bot,
right below its screen and above its claw and gun. It
fired a blast or two at me in a panic. Both shots sailed
underneath me as I smashed into it. The bot crashed
to the ground with me on top of it. It hurt me some.
It hurt the bot a lot more. Guardbots aren't built to
take tackles. They are supposed to be too smart to let
anybody insane enough to tackle them get close
enough to actually do it.

The bot smashed into so many pieces I knew it was
out of the fight. I turned my attention to Santana and
Elf-1. Their fight was even less of a fight.

The bots had made a fatal mistake—they had an-
gered Santana. An angry Santana was not a pretty
sight. By the time her bot had figured out what had
gone wrong, it was too late to do anything about it.
First, Santana ripped off its laser cannon with her right
hand. She then grabbed the bot's claw arm with her
left hand and yanked. The bot arm gave way with out
much of a fight.

Santana took a lot of pleasure in showing the bot
its arm and gun. She cracked them both over her knee,
splitting them in two. The bot had no idea how to
respond, and even if it did, there was nothing it could
have done.

Santana lunged forward and grabbed the bot, wrapping her arms around its frame. She arched her back,
lifting the bot off the ground as she squeezed. The
bot's metal frame resisted the pressure for about a
nano. Then it crumbled like a piece of old aluminum
paper under Santana's grasp.

"This is what you get for messing with my elves,"
she yelled as she squeezed.

Meanwhile, Elf-1 kept one eye on the action and the other eye on the other bots. They had finished off the security elves and had been watching their cobots take us on. They were caught completely off guard by the turn of events. It didn't take them long to regroup and head toward us.

"Santana, Zach, I think we'd better move fast," Elf-1 said.

He didn't have to tell me twice. Santana, on the other hand was taking a lot of pleasure (maybe a bit too much) in turning the bot into either a piece of junk or modern art, depending on your perspective. She was bending and mutilating it so much, I was starting to feel sorry for it.

I moved over and tapped her on the shoulder. "Let it go, Santana, so we can get out of here."

She stopped exerting herself. She nodded. "You're right," she said. She picked up the bot and spindled it over her head. She turned and hurled it at the remaining bots, who were powering up to charge us.

The dead bot flew into the others, causing them to separate. This was the last break we needed as we made our way to the door.

We reached the door and knocked on it. "It's Santana, let us in," she said.

A laser shot whizzed over our heads.

"And fast!" I shouted.

HARV had thrown decoys over us to toss off the attacking bots, but sooner or later the bots were bound to pick us off.

The door creaked ajar. Elf-1 one shot through. Santana make her way next. I held my breath and squeaked in.

The door slammed behind me.

Chapter 29

Santana, Elf-1, Mrs. Billings, Councilwoman Weathers, and I were now in a small, private reading room. There was one long couch and a couple of computer terminals with gold tinsel lining the tops of the walls.

Our first move was to take the couch and roll it to the door, barricading it. We could hear the bots outside clanging at the metal door.

I looked around. The door we came in was the only way in and out of the room. On one hand, that was good. The bots weren't able to sneak up on us. On the other hand, the only way out was covered with bots. Bots that wanted to kill us.

"There are two hundred bots here," Elf-1 one said, now pumped from the action. "That means we outnumber them fifty to one. In hand-to-claw combat, we can take them out!"

"The causalities would be high," I said. "We had holograms and luck on our side. The others won't."

Santana shook her head. "No, I've already lost five elves to these things. There has got to be a better way."

"The electromagnetic pulse generator," Councilwoman Weathers said.

"The Pole has an EMPG?" I said.

"Yes. It's top-top-secret," Santana said. "It's located in the backup control room for use in case of pirate attack. It would deactivate their ships."

"The device can be modified to shut the bots down," Elf-1 said.

Now this sounded like a plan that had legs. This was something we could pull off without anybody getting hurt. Obviously, something had to go wrong.

"I can signal my elf team to modify and activate the device," Elf-1 said.

Elf-1 typed a few commands into his communicator. He waited for a response. He frowned. I knew that plan was too easy. "Oh sugar!" he spat. He looked up the ceiling. "I have to go to my happy place. My hap-hap-happy place," he said.

"What's the problem?" I asked.

"None of my team is currently located in the backup control room," Elf-1 said. "Security cameras show there are bots outside the backup control room. We can make a run for it, but it would be costly."

"There are no bots in the room," I said. "Correct?"

Elf-1 glanced at his communicator. "No."

I looked around the room. I saw what I was looking for along the top of the wall near the ceiling. I pointed to the heating ducts.

"Those are connected everywhere, aren't they?"

Everybody smiled. The heating ducks weren't big, but they were large enough for an average man to crawl around in. They would certainly have enough room for an elf.

"Send your team through the heating ducts," I said.

"Brilliant," Santana said.

"I like it," Elf-1 said.

"That will work," Mrs. Billings said.

"Zach, there may be a career for you in politics after this is all over," the councilwoman said.

"Please, you don't have be threatening," I told her.

Elf-1 transmitted my idea to his staff. He stared at the communicator. He frowned. He kept reading. The frown grew wider. "We have a minor problem: it would take ten minutes to reprogram the EMPG."

"That's too long—the bots would kill them before they finished," Santana said. "There has to be a better way."

"Can your elves get to an armory for some weapons?" I asked.

Elf-1 shook his head. "We have no weapons."

The one thing I've learned in life is the easy way is never the way I get to go. Somehow, someway, I knew this was going to fall on my shoulders. That's my lot in life—to save the day when the chips are on the line.

"I have an idea," HARV said. "If somebody gives me the passwords and the specs, I can reprogram the EMPG in about a nano."

I was reasonably certain that HARV was just being polite in asking for the passwords and specs.

The corners of Elf-1's mouth started to turn up. He still wasn't smiling, but he wasn't frowning any longer. "Now that could work," he said.

I knew that meant I was going to have to crawl through the vents. Not exactly how I planned to spend my day, but it beat dying.

"Okay," I said, walking towards the vent. "Let's get this over with."

Elf-1 moved past me, pulling out a sound-based screwdriver. "First, I'd better disable the vent's security code."

Santana held Elf-1 to the vent. He punched about ten numbers into the numeric pad that sat just above the vent's rim. There was a beep of confirmation. Elf-1 removed the screws from the top left and bottom left corners. The lid slid down.

Santana lowered Elf-1. She looked at me. "Next."

I moved forward and stood under the vent. I'm two meters tall, but even with my arms extended the vent opening was still a good meter out of my reach.

I looked over my shoulder at the group looking me over.

"I could jump," I said.

"This is not a problem," Santana said walking toward me.

I knew what she was planning to do. "Santana, I'm not a fifty-kilo elf," I said.

"I weigh fifty-four kilos," Elf-1 said sharply.

"I'm not a fifty-four kilo elf," I said.

Santana made a spinning motion with her hand. "Turn around and reach for the sky," she said.

I spun back toward the vent. I stretched my arms upward. I felt Santana's hands on my hips. I started to rise. Santana was lifting me as if I were a fifteen-kilo elf. I grabbed the edge of the vent. I pulled myself in.

I looked down the vent. It was a long, reflective metallic tube that went on for as far as I could see. Kind of like a midget's hall of mirrors. It was just wide enough for me to crawl in, but I didn't have much wiggle room. I wouldn't be doing any push-ups in there. All in all, though, one of the nicer vents I'd ever been in. The best thing was the Holiday theme wasn't playing. I started crawling forward.

"HARV, you can lead me to the control room, right?" I whispered.

"With the hundreds of kilometers of ducts in this place, you would have very little chance of finding it without me," HARV said.

"A simple yes would suffice," I said.

"Yes," HARV said.

A red beam projected from my eye. It stretched down the duct for maybe three hundred meters and then turned to the right.

"Just follow the red beam," HARV said.

Being a smart guy, I did as I was told. I tagged along the beam, following it down this vent until it hung to the right. It went straight for a bit, then left, right, right, up, right, left, down, reverse, and then to the right. Actually, I had no idea. I stopped keeping track about a nano into the trip. I knew HARV would lead me the best way. I was fairly confident there wouldn't be a pop quiz afterward. The important thing was for me to get there ASAP. It felt like I crawled for a couple of hours (HARV would later insist that it was only seventeen minutes and twenty-two seconds) when I finally came to the grate above the control room.

I looked down through the slits in the grate into the room. The walls were lined with sensors, screens, and machines of all sizes. I didn't recognize much. I was betting that HARV knew exactly which of the myriad of devices was the EMP generator.

There were no bots in the room, but that didn't mean they weren't right outside the door waiting to spring a trap.

"HARV, are there any bots outside in the hall?" I asked.

"Not at the present," HARV whispered. "There are two patrolling up and down the hallway, but currently neither is within one hundred meters of the door."

This struck me as strange. If Bim and Norp intended to hold the Pole, surely they would have had this room better secured. Unless, of course, they didn't know about the EMPG. That didn't fit their MO. Bim and Norp were ultra geeks, and they lived for stuff like that. It was highly classified and secured, but that would only entice them more. This had to be a trap.

I took a deep breath. I was thinking too much again. Trap or not, if we were going to shut down the bots and stop Bim and Norp, I had to do this.

I gave the top of the grate a quick jab with my elbow. The seal broke and opened up a slight crack between the grate and the vent. I took my hand and starting pushing down on the grid until I felt the grate break off in my hand.

Now I had another problem—getting out of the vent. I would have to either plummet headfirst to the ground or backtrack a bit, turn around, and then back my way out of the vent feetfirst.

"Where's the nearest point I can turn around?" I asked HARV.

"You'd have to crawl backward for at least one hundred meters before you could turn around to crawl backward to where you are now. You should have thought of this sooner, Zach."

"You should have thought of this sooner, HARV. You're the computer—it's your job to think of these things."

"It's only a three-meter drop. I didn't realize you'd be such a baby about it. Besides, I thought you'd want to see where you were going."

I took a deep breath. I didn't have time to position myself to land feet first. I looked down. It wasn't that high. I've certainly fallen from much greater heights and lived to get people to buy me drinks while I talked about it. Still, it was going to hurt. The moment I hit the floor I'd be like a beetle on its back—helpless. Unlike the beetle, I'd be able to right myself.

I took another deep breath. I slid out of the vent. I rolled down the wall and crashed to the floor with a very undistinguished thud. It hurt, but I'd been hurt worse shaving (sadly true). I pushed myself up.

The door to the room flew open. Two guardbots rolled in. I let myself drop back to the floor just as two laser shots careened over me.

"Another fine mess you've gotten me into, Ollie," I said to HARV.

"You don't need my help getting into messes, Stan," HARV retorted. I was proud he got the reference. I was less than pleased to be under attack. I stayed low and scrambled across the floor, using a table that traversed the middle of the room for cover. Many more laser shots flew over me. I didn't feel anything, so I assumed they missed. I instinctively headed forward. I don't know why.

"Zach, I've tapped into the control room surveillance cameras," HARV told me. "I can see your assailants even when you can't. One is moving to the left, one to the right."

Now I knew they were trying to set me up in a crossfire (guardbots just love crossfires). There are times when having a supercomputer wired to your brain is a good thing.

I rolled under the table just before laser fire tore up the spot where I had been laying on the floor.

I needed a plan and fast. Fighting the bots mano-a-boto didn't seem like it was going to work this time, even if I used a holographic cover. The bots knew my general location, and the room was small enough that they would be able to take me out with sporadic fire.

"HARV, can you remotely reprogram the EMPG?" I asked, dodging deadly laser fire left and right.

"Of course," HARV said. "Though for me to override its firewalls, you'll have to be looking directly at it from no more than two meters away."

That sounded like something I could pull off. The problem was, in all this scrambling for my life business, I wasn't able to pinpoint where I was in the room in relation to the EMPG.

HARV knew this.

"I suppose you have no idea where you are right now," HARV said.

"I have a general idea—somewhere between the Pole and death," I said.

I rolled to the left just as two more laser shots burned the place I had just been. I dodged to the right a split nano before two more shots scorched the floor I'd just left.

"Lucky for you, you have me," HARV said.

"Right now HARV, luck isn't the word I'd use."

I was pinned down and unarmed. If HARV thought this was "lucky," I didn't want to know what it would take for him to consider me doomed.

"By sheer accident, you are quite near the EMPG," HARV informed me. "It's merely three meters to your left."

A flashing red arrow pointing to the left appeared in front of my eyes. A picture of the device appeared next to it. It didn't look all that daunting—kind of like a box with a plastic lid on it. Another, smaller arrow appeared pointing at the lid.

"I'll turn off all the fail-safes for you as you head toward it. You just need to flip the safety lid, then push the button to fire it off."

I cocked my head to the left. I could see the EMPG out of the corner of my eye.

"I don't suppose you can push the button for me," I said.

"Sorry, there are some things you still have to do yourself. If not, I wouldn't need you to solve cases."

I took a deep breath.

"Zach, I'm doing the hard work. All you have to do is flip a lid and hit a switch. Easy as counting to one."

"I also have to dodge laser fire," I noted.

"Yeah, I didn't want to bring that up," HARV said. "I'm trying have a positive cognitive attitude here."

Speaking of the laser fire, something was wrong. There hadn't been any in the last thirty seconds. If I was an optimist (and a fool), I would have assumed that the guardbots had run out of charges. I'm not that optimistic, foolish, or nearly that fortunate. I knew it had to be something else.

"The bots are rolling into a better position now, aren't they?" I said.

"Affirmative," HARV said. "It appears their logic is not to waste charges when they know exactly where you are heading."

I peeked to the side of the table again. Sure enough, there were two bot-bases positioned on either side of where I now knew the device was. The nano I made my move they would blast me.

"You have to give them credit for conserving energy," HARV said.

"I feel much better knowing I'll be killed by environmentally-conscious tin cans."

"Zach, they don't make bots out of tin," HARV said. "At least not killer bots like these."

"I don't suppose I can wait them out?" I said.

"They are bots—they have no need to eat, drink, or use the bathroom. They don't get bored. They can outwait you."

"I was joking, HARV."

"Oh, right. I should have caught that."

"Maybe you could tell some Rodney Dangerfield jokes to distract them?" I said.

"Zach, they are guardbots—they have no sense of humor. Plus, I have run my course with Mr. Dan-

gerfield's unique brand of humor. I am now looking
for new inspiration. Care to make a suggestion?"

I shook my head. HARV was really missing the big
picture here.

"Tell you what, HARV. If I live through this, I will
help you find one."

"Deal," HARV said.

Now that I had an extra reason to live, I needed a
plan, and I needed it fast. The longer I sat pinned
down, the more time Norp and Bim had to get away.
I didn't like that at all. I was pretty certain I would
like being shot even less. I took inventory of my
assets: I had my wits, my muscle, and my computer.
What I wouldn't give for a good blaster and my body
armor. No use crying over milk that hasn't even been
poured. I was going to have to make due with what
I had.

I knew the nano I stood up from under the table,
the bots were going to blast me. I could use that to
my advantage. Maybe I could trick the bots by posi-
tioning a hologram of myself between them. Then they
would blast each other.

I took a deep breath and readied myself for my big
move. I pushed up slightly from ground.

"Zach, the bots have just activated their holographic
detection software," HARV said.

I let myself sink back to the ground. "They won't
fire on my hologram," I said to HARV.

"Nope, the old let 'em shoot each other through
the hologram trick won't work here. They are now
smart enough to identify a hologram."

I smiled. That was it. It's amazing where you can
get inspiration from.

"Zach, your pleasure-sensing endorphin levels just
raised. You're happy about something." There was a

slight pause. "Gee, Zach, I never realized you had a death wish. Though that would explain a lot: your choice of career, your taste in women, your taste in clothing."

"What's wrong with my taste in clothing?"

"Zach, this isn't the time."

HARV was right on two accounts: I was happy, and this wasn't the venue to argue over fashion sense.

"I have a plan," I said to HARV.

"Does it involve being shot a few times and dying a painful death?" HARV asked.

"No," I said. "I want you to cover me with an exact hologram of myself."

"Zach, they won't shoot . . ." HARV said before computing. "They won't shoot at the hologram!" he said figuring out where I was headed.

"For a supercomputer, you catch on fast," I kidded.

HARV was silent. I knew he was thinking about everything that might go wrong with this plan.

"The bots will stall, but only for a split nano before they realize that the real you is under the hologram," he said.

I didn't have a better option. I'm not the type of guy who can cower under a table for long. I had to do something, and this was my best chance.

"It's either that or wait for the warranty on the bots to expire," I said.

"You are attempting to be humorous again, correct?"

I didn't even bother to answer that. If I stayed under this table, my legs would cramp up. Then it would be even harder for me to move to EMPG.

"Do you have me covered, HARV?"

"Affirmative. Do you want to know your odds of succeeding?"

I shook my head. "You know me, HARV. I never want to know the odds." If I did, I'd never get out of bed.

I took a deep breath. I hoped it wasn't going to be my last. I pushed myself up, shot out from the under the table, and raced toward the EMPG device. In my peripheral vision, I saw the bots tracking me and aiming their gun turrets at me.

I reached the EMPG device.

"He is only a hologram," one of the bots said.

"I concur," the other bot said.

I smashed my elbow down, shattering the protective glass that was covering the EMPG trigger switch.

"A hologram should not be able to do that," one of the bots said.

I lifted my elbow up quickly and slammed it back down on the trigger.

"He's not a hol . . ." a bot started to moan.

Everything flashed white.

I turned toward the bots. They were slumped over. They looked like old slinkies that had lost their slink.

"HARV, are you still with me?" I asked.

Silence.

I was sure Randy had built in EMPG protection into HARV. Maybe I was wrong. The word TESTING flashed in front of my eyes. A beam of light shot out from my lens. The light formed the number one. The one morphed into a two which morphed into a three. The three morphed into HARV. A shaky, blurry HARV. HARV slowly regained his composure and focus.

"Now that was an experience I don't care to repeat," he said, spinning his head around in a circle.

"Stop going all Linda Blair on me, HARV." It was creeping me out.

HARV put his hands up to his ears to stop his head

from spinning. Unfortunately, he stopped his head in a position that was about forty-five degrees to the right of where a head should be. He used his right hand to push his head to the left until he was looking directly at me. He smiled.

"Now that's better," he said.

"Don't you have EMPG protection?" I asked.

HARV nodded. "Of course I do. Dr. Pool thought of everything."

"Then why'd you bug out on me?"

HARV lowered his eyes and sighed. It was his typical *I don't believe I have to put up with this human* look. "Zach, Zach, Zach. I just took a hit from a very powerful EMPG machine at point-blank range. It's the biological equivalent of you standing on a nuclear device just as it is being detonated."

"Sorry," I said, though in truth, I wasn't sure why I was apologizing.

"No need to mindlessly apologize," HARV said. "I am not one of the women in your life."

I wasn't sure what HARV meant by that, but I knew it couldn't be good so I decided to ignore it.

"The bottom line is I took a blow that would have knocked ninety-nine point nine nine nine nine percent of the machines on Earth offline for an indefinite amount of time. I was down for less than a nano. You should thank Dr. Pool when we see him again."

"I'll make I note of it," I said as I started to the door.

For now, I had two different geeks on my mind— Norp and Bim. I needed to catch up with them and get a little payback. Something wasn't sitting right in my gut, though. Yes, Norp and Bim were socially inept and annoying as DOS, but that didn't make them killers. Even if they were killers, what did they gain by shutting down the Pole? They didn't strike me as the kind of guys who were prone to random acts of violence. In fact, they didn't strike me as the kind of guys who did anything randomly.

They had no motive and nothing to gain, which meant something bigger was afoot. I just didn't know what.

I reached the door. I walked into it. If anybody else had been around, it really would have hurt my credibility as a tough guy.

"The doors are computer controlled," HARV said.

"Yeah, I remembered that about a nano after my nose rammed into it. Can you open the door?" I asked.

"I can," HARV said. He pointed to a panel on the wall next to the door. "So can you."

I lifted the cover off the panel, revealing a small handcrank. I grabbed the crank and started cranking, raising the door about a centimeter each turn.

"They couldn't put knobs on the doors?" I said, cranking away.

"You are so old-fashioned," HARV said.

"And proud of it."

After a minute or two of cranking, the door was open enough for me to bend down and duck through it.

I entered the hallway. I wanted to track down the geeks ASAP—the angrier I was when I found them, the better. I also wanted to be the first one to find them. I didn't know why. I just knew I did.

"Which way to the port pad?" I asked HARV.

"Follow the arrows," he said.

A green arrow appeared in front of my eye heading north down the hallway. I followed it.

Chapter 30

I hurriedly traced the arrow through the abandoned corridors. It was a bit eerie, without the music, but I liked the quiet. I knew it wouldn't be long until the elves and others knew the coast was clear and worked their way into the halls. I quickened my pace. I needed to be the one to find Bim and Norp so I could talk to them alone.

A few minutes later, HARV's guided tour led me to big metal door. The arrow HARV was leading me with started to vibrate and flash as it pointed to the door.

"I take it that's the transport room," I said.

"Very good, Zach."

I put my ear next to the door and listened. I heard bickering. That was a good sign. They were cornered.

"HARV, can you open the door for me?"

"Of course," HARV said.

I stood by the door, anxiously tapping my foot. A few nanos passed and nothing happened.

"HARV?"

"I can't magically open the door, Zach. You have to bend down and look into the key pass slot."

"Why didn't you say so?"

"I thought you knew."

"How would I?"

"Zach, Zach, Zach. We've done this type of thing seven different times."

"Whose side are you on, anyhow?"

"They are trapped in a teleport room. They aren't going anywhere. I'm trying to condition you to think better."

"It's your job to do what I ask you to do, not to make me a better person."

HARV sighed. "I like to believe the parameters for my job description are open to interpretation."

HARV wasn't kidding with that. In the past, he has reprogrammed my brain and added information and new routines. I figured this was yet another of the many and ever-growing number of issues it was best not to think about too much.

I bent down and peered into the key pass slot right above the door's handle. A beam of red light shot out from my eye into the slot. I heard a click.

"The door is now open," HARV said. "No need to thank me."

I turned the handle slowly, cracking the door ajar. Peering into the room, I saw Bim and Norp standing by the teleport pad. They both had small duffle bags in their hands, which they were pushing each other with. It didn't take my trained mind to know they were mad at each other. They were sweating so profusely they had to keep removing and drying their thick glasses. Their green and blue hair was even more unkept than usual. With their small stocky bodies and big hands and bigger feet I might have found them to be humorous if they hadn't just tried to kill me.

"This is your fault," Bim screamed, pushing Norp on the shoulder.

Norp recoiled. "How is this my fault?" he screamed back louder, rubbing his shoulder. "You're the one who insisted on packing an extra toothbrush."

Norp pushed Bim on the shoulder.

Bim dropped his bag and made a fist. "Why you little twerp!"

Norp dropped his bag and made two fists. "Watch who you are talking to, buster, before I bust you!"

I walked into the room. They were so involved in their little nerd lover's quarrel they didn't even notice me. I cleared my throat. They keep babbling on and on at each other. I moved closer. They kept complaining.

"How long have you two been married?" I asked.

The stopped arguing, turned, and focused on me for a nano. Then they turned their attention back to each other.

"This is your fault," Bim said, poking Norp in the chest with his index finger.

"No! This is your fault!" Norp said, poking Bim back twice.

"I really hope you guys are going to come quietly," I said, though it was a flat-out lie. I wanted them to put up a fight. I wanted to bust their heads. Trust me, for a guy who does what I do for a living, I'm a pretty mellow, peace-loving kind of fellow. There was just something about these two that really fried my cheese and burned my burger.

Bim and Norp exchanged glances.

"We have him outnumbered two to one," Bim said.

"He fights for a living," Norp offered.

"I don't fight for a living," I said. "I solve crimes for a living. Breaking a bone or two now and then just comes with the territory. I think of it as a fringe benefit."

They exchanged glances again. Each of them raised an eyebrow. I knew that look. It was a signal to move in on me.

Bim was the first to react. He made a fist and lunged at me, swinging wildly. I ducked under his punch. I sprung up and clocked him with a left uppercut to the jaw. (That was the third time in the last few days I had hit somebody with an uppercut to the jaw. I was determined to keep trying it until it actually worked.) Bim's head shot back like one of those old Pez dispensers, spraying sweat in all directions. That alone would have been enough to finish him, but I wasn't done. I followed the left with a quick right roundhouse to the exact same spot. This punch sent him crashing to the ground. Now I was done. At least with round one.

I looked at Norp. He looked at Bim. "Serves him right for bullying me!" he spat, far more upset with Bim than he was with me.

"Now are YOU going to come quietly?" I asked, hoping he would be stupid enough to make a move.

He was. He reached into his pocket protector and pulled out an old-fashioned pen. I looked at it. He looked at me looking at it.

"What are you going to do, give me ink poisoning?"

He grinned, showing me his yellow, jagged teeth. I didn't like that at all. It made me want to smash those teeth in. You have to trust me, I'm not usually a vicious person, but these two brought out my violent side.

Norp reached forward and pulled the top off the pen, revealing a sharp knife underneath. He threw the top over his shoulder and proceeded to wave the penknife at me.

"Not so brave now are you, Johnson?" he said.

In my profession, I've had to deal with knives on many different occasions. They are like any other weapon and not to be taken lightly. From close range, and in the hands of skilled practitioner, they can be just as deadly as a blaster or a handgun. The key words there being *skilled practitioner*.

Norp lunged for me with the knife in his right hand. I stepped back. When he missed, he overcommited his weight on his right side and stumbled forward. I grabbed his knife arm at the wrist and twisted, forcing him to drop the knife, while at the same giving him a little push forward. I let his own momentum carry him down facefirst into the floor. To add injury to injury, I let myself fall on him, my knee into his lower back.

He shuddered in pain. I felt sorry for him. Almost.

I pinned his right arm behind his back in the classic chicken wing position.

"Now, let's talk," I said.

"Talking is good," he groaned.

"Why'd you do it?" I asked.

"Do what?" he said coyly, even though he was no position to be smart.

I pushed the chicken wing up, causing him to squirm more.

"Don't get cute with me," I growled. "Why did you do it?"

"Draw the knife on you?" he asked. He really was clueless.

"No! Why did you reprogram the bots to kill the elves?"

"Oh, that," he said. "We had to do it. For the good of the world and to impress the babes."

"Huh?"

"Santana, man. She has to be stopped!"

"Why?"

"You must know what she's trying to do."

"No."

"Zach, it might be more impressive if you responded with more than one word now and then," HARV offered.

In this case, HARV didn't know what he was talking about. The one-word response was perfect for my tough guy image. I pushed Norp's arm up further. He was hard to keep a grasp on as he was slimy from all the sweat. I was determined to hold on despite the grossness. "Talk."

"Santana—she's up to no good," Norp groaned. He thought for a nano. "Actually, she's probably up to too much good," he moaned.

"Too much good?" I said, breaking out of the monoword responses.

At first, that seemed to be one of the stranger statements I've heard in my career, but in thinking about it I suppose it was possible to have too much of a good thing. I didn't see how in this case, but Norp seemed sincere. In fact, he was too scared to lie.

"It's just that she wants to make the world a better place," Norp groaned.

"How is that bad?"

He shook his head. "Making the world better isn't bad, but her means to the end are quite questionable. She believes the end justifies her means."

I shook my head. Norp was beating around the bush, and I didn't like it.

"Get to the point," I said, pressing down harder on his back with my knee.

He yelped. I felt a bit bad about that. I had to see what he was hinting at, and I was in no mood to take it easy.

"Zach," HARV said inside my head.

"Not now, HARV," I thought back at him.

"I hear movement in the room," HARV said.

I turned just in time to see Bim standing over me with a chair raised over his head. I rolled to the right as he brought the chair down, grazing me. It would have been a lot worse if it weren't for HARV. That's what I get for letting my guard down and my temper get the best of me.

I tried to get to my feet, but Norp grabbed my leg, tripping me. I fell over onto my back. Bim ran over and kicked me in the side. It hurt—not a lot, but enough to make me angry. Bim kicked at me again, but this time I was ready for it. I caught his kicking leg with both hands. Before I could bring him down, Norp pounced on me. I had really underestimated the amount of punishment these two could take.

"Never count us out!" Bim yelled, as he jabbed a fist in my lower back. "We're little but feisty!"

They were tougher than they looked (of course, they pretty much had to be). The problem for them now was that they were getting overconfident. They had managed to get in a couple of good licks, but I had taken worse beatings from grandmas at bridge games. What we had just been through was the opening bid. I was just getting warmed up for the slam.

As I was getting ready to make my big move, Bim flew off of me. Then Norp looked up and flew off of me. Santana had arrived, and she was as angry as a super-elf could be.

She stormed over toward Bim and Norp, who were frantically trying to push themselves up off the floor.

"How dare you treat Zach like that in my home," she said.

"Listen Santana," Bim said. "Stop trying—"

Bim never got to finish that statement as Santana

clanked his head with Norp's, knocking them both out. She turned to me and smiled.

"Thanks for your help, Zach. My elves and I will handle these malcontents from here," she said, shaking the sweat from her hands.

Chapter 31

It was about an hour after I trekked back to my room that the elves managed to get power back up at the Pole. Another hour after that, they were able to get the bots back under their control and online. During those hours, I had to time to think.

Elf-1 and Santana both insisted that the case was over, and I should be happy and proud of another job well done. Elf-1 gave me a pat on the back. Santana promised me a five percent bonus for wrapping the case up so quickly. But something about this case was still gnawing at me. HARV insisted that it was just acid reflux, and the feeling would go away if I let him release acid blockers into my system. I didn't. This was deeper than any acid reflux.

I lay flat on my bed, hands behind my head, staring up at the ceiling lights, just thinking. Something didn't add up. What was Bim and Norp's motive? They were annoying, but they weren't mindless drones. They wouldn't want to kill a couple of elves and shut down the Pole unless they had a reason. A reason to risk everything and to impress the babes.

I inhaled and sighed unintentionally.

HARV appeared next to me.

"Why are you sulking now, Zach? You wrapped up the case and didn't get killed. DOS, you barely got beat up. For you, that's a three-dee red-letter day."

I kept looking up at the lights. "Something doesn't add up, HARV. This is all too easy." Okay, I know most people wouldn't think battling bots and clobbering on nerds with knives was easy, but when you're me, that's a run through sprinklers on a hot day. Sure, you might get a little water in your eye, but all in all, it's much more refreshing than painful.

"It doesn't make sense, HARV," I said. "What did Norp mean by 'Santana is too good'?"

HARV grimaced. "I don't know. He was probably just ranting. Trying to justify the awful things he did."

"I don't think so," I said.

I've met a lot of characters in my line of work, and it's made me a fairly good judge of character. I can usually pick out the lying scum bag from a hundred meters away. I don't know if it's their eyes or the sound of their voice. I can just tell when somebody is up to no good and lying. Bim and Norp—I knew they were up to no good, but they were sincere. This worried me. I needed to talk to them again.

"Tell Santana I want to talk to Bim and Norp again," I told HARV.

He nodded. "Santana says you can talk to them tomorrow, before they are deported back to Mars."

"Why tomorrow?"

"Her elves need time to interrogate them to learn about the weaknesses they exploited in the bots."

It made sense, but it didn't mean I had to accept it. I stood up.

"Can you lead me to the place Bim and Norp are being held?" I asked.

HARV shook his head. "Actually, I can't do it."

Now there's something I don't hear from HARV very often.

"You can't or won't?"

"I am unable to find where they are keeping Bim and Norp."

"HARV, doesn't that strike you as strange?"

"We're at the Pole investigating the death of two elves, fighting robots, and mutants from Mars. Everything about this case strikes me as strange!"

"Doesn't this seem even more out of the ordinary than our norm?"

HARV looked down at the floor, then slowly raised his head until we were looking eye-to-simulated-eye. "It does," HARV said. "But I've been connected to you so long I may be getting paranoid."

I headed toward the door. "Or smarter."

I couldn't see HARV, but I knew he was shaking his head. "I sincerely doubt that," he said. "Where are you going?"

"Right to the source. I'm going to talk to Santana."

I opened the door. Much to my surprise, there was a guardbot facing me. Out of pure instinct, I hurled myself to the ground. The guardbot rolled into the room.

"Mr. Johnson, we need to talk," the guardbot said in Bim's voice.

I looked up from the ground. "Bim?"

"And Norp!" the guardbot said.

I stood up. I was careful to place a table between myself and the bot.

"What's the meaning of this?" I asked.

"As much as we despise you, we are smart enough to realize you are our and the world's last hope."

For one of the few times in my career, both HARV and I were speechless. I didn't know what to make of this. It did reinforce my belief that Bim and Norp believed that Santana was up to something.

"So, what's Santana planning?" I asked, partly to play along, and partly out of true curiosity.

"To change the world to her image," the robot said.

"Now how is she planning to do that?" I asked.

"The elves have invented a virus that attacks the pain and anxiety centers of the brain and eliminates them. She's planning on making everybody permanently happy."

"And that's a bad thing, because . . ."

"Everybody will be happy, mindless zombies," the robot said.

I pondered that. Would the world really be that much different if we were all happy, mindless zombies? We are governed by our wants and desires. Currently, a lot of those wants and desires enter our minds through bullying big businesses and the relentless media. Would things really be that much worse if Bim and Norp were right? It wasn't my call. It wasn't Santana's call, either. If it was true, it would be my job to stop her.

"Okay, I'll talk to Santana, and if what you say is true, I'll shut her down." Truthfully, I had no idea how I was going to do that. I was unarmed and outnumbered. Still, I've never been one to let reality get in the way of my success.

"It gets worse."

"Worse than totally reprogramming the minds of everybody on Earth?"

"This is a two-stage plan."

"Santana always was an overachiever," I said.

"This is where we come in," the bot said. "We designed a virus that would sterilize ninety-nine percent of humanity and make them lose interest in sex.

Within a few generations, humans would no longer be able to or want to reproduce."

"Oh, that's not good. Why would a goody-two-shoes like Santana want to wipe out most of humanity?"

"She doesn't want to wipe you out, just replace you with clones . She's convinced the world will be a better place this way. She mumbled something about being naughty makes people do stupid things."

Now it all made sense in a bizarre, deranged way. "Are the elves onboard with this idea?"

"As far as we can tell, no. Santana convinced the elves they were developing the niceness virus as an exercise to test their abilities."

"Then how is Santana going to pull this off without the elves?"

The bot shrugged, as well as a tin can can. "We have no idea."

"Why should I believe you two? Didn't you guys try to kill me? A few times?"

"Yes, but that's when we thought you'd make it harder for us to score with Nova or that during your investigative reporting you would turn up something and somehow foil Santana and steal our spotlight. Remember, we thought you were a big, blond blogger. Now we're in jail and know who you are, so we have no reason to lie."

"Why would you be involved in this in the first place?"

"To impress chicks. Yeah, to impress the babes," the bot said in Bim's and Norp's voices. Interestingly enough, it was more believable coming from the bot.

"Our goal was to trick Santana into thinking that we were on her side, then we would shut her down, saving the day, and the babes would flock to us."

"So you guys killed the elves?"

There was a pause. "We only killed a couple, and just to scare them into delaying the Holiday long enough so we could get the bots totally reprogrammed to shut Santana down."

There was a pause then they added, "It was for the greater good. Kill a couple of elves to save the world."

It wasn't the best plan I had ever heard. In fact, it was probably one of the ten worst plans I've heard. Even still, men have done far stupider things to impress women. Santana was on to something—being naughty does make us stupid.

Now they had a motive that fit their MO. I was reasonably certain they believed what they were saying. The scary thing was I believed it, too. I've been around enough superwomen to know that when you mess around with DNA and PMS, you're just asking for trouble.

Don't get me wrong, supermen are just as dangerous, but they are far easier to predict. Men want three things: money, power, and women. Most of them figure if they get one of the first two then they can get the third thing. All men want to be the alpha male. The king of the hill. The big cheese.

Women are an entirely different game. For the most part, they don't want power for the sake of power. They want power to make things better. This isn't always a bad thing, but when you supercharge it and toss in some fluctuating hormones, the result is often messy as Bim's and Norp's hair and complexion. It becomes a pseudo-Machiavellian quest to make the world a better place.

Was Santana on one of these quests? I wasn't going to rule it out.

"I'll check on it," I told the bot.

"That's all we ask," the bot said in Norp's voice.

"And that you give us our due when all this is over," it added in Bim's.

"Don't worry, you'll get exactly what's coming to you," I said.

"Good enough," the bot said in its bot voice. "Now I'd better go before they notice I'm gone."

The bot rolled backward out of the room, leaving me with my thoughts. If Santana really was bad, I had to stop her. I was going to need backup.

"HARV, talk to Captain Rickey and Randy, and notify them of our current situation."

HARV appeared before me shaking his head. It's never good news when a supercomputer shakes its head.

"All transmissions out of the Pole are being jammed," HARV said. "Santana's elves say it's only a temporary security measure. They want to be cautious, just in case Bim and Norp had accomplices."

Unfortunately, that made sense. More unfortunately, that was a recipe for trouble.

"So right now, my assets are still my wits, my fists, and my computer."

"If Santana really has gone overboard, you're going to need more than two out of three here. I estimate she's almost as strong as any of the Thompson Quads. Her pheromones are just as powerful. She can twist you into a pretzel before you can say, 'Please hurt me some more.'"

"I think we can count Nova as an asset," I said.

"I won't disagree with you there. She's just wacked enough to jump aboard this runaway train heading downhill toward the TNT with no breaks. She has such an act-first-think-later way about her I'm betting she has a great career in politics in front of her."

"Wow, buddy, I'm proud of both the metaphors and the deduction."

"The metaphors are not because I am becoming like you. They are because I am communicating with you. The deduction, is, well, good sense is good sense."

"I'm still proud."

"Don't go all mushy on me, Zach. We're in trouble here. When the spit hits the fan though, you're going to need more help."

I had nothing to lose. So I sat on my bed and started concentrating.

"Zach, what are you doing? This is no time to go all new age and mellow out on me."

"I'm thinking," I said, eyes closed and taking deep breath.

"Ah, no wonder I didn't recognize what you were doing," HARV said.

I ignored HARV and started breathing deeper and deeper. As I inhaled and exhaled slowly, I concentrated on one thought, *Carol send help*. I knew it was a long shot, but this was a time for long shots.

"I need to talk with Santana," I said.

"I can net you with her."

"No, I want to do it in person, and I need to talk to her alone."

"She says she can meet you in her room in thirty minutes."

"No, I want to do it someplace neutral."

"She says she can meet you in the library in forty-five minutes."

I nodded. "I'll take it."

"Great, you've had such a history of good luck at the library."

Chapter 32

When I arrived at the library Santana wasn't there yet. I sat in one of the cloud chairs. I crossed my legs, but it didn't feel right. I uncrossed them and sat forward.

I was nervous, and I didn't know why and that made me more nervous. Part of me wanted to believe the case was all wrapped up—Bim and Norp were the deranged bad guy nerds who wanted to stop the Holiday because they are unpopular spammers. Another part of me, the annoying part, kept telling me this case was far from over. Sure, Bim and Norp were annoying, but they weren't the true culprits here. This case went beyond simply saving the Holiday.

I sat for a few minutes alone with my thoughts. I noticed that HARV wasn't chiming in with his opinion. This was very out of character.

"HARV, why are you so quiet?" I asked.

No response.

I didn't like that.

I heard the door to the library open. I looked up to see two guardbots rolling in. My initial thought was that the appearance of the guardbots combined with HARV going silent was bad news. I didn't want to jump to conclusions, at least not yet.

The bots rolled closer. I stood up from the chair.

"There is no need to fear us, Zachary Nixon Johnson," the bots said in unison.

I've learned from experience it's never a good sign when bots use your middle name. It's an even worse sign when they talk in unison. I dove back over the cloud chair a mere nano before the bots opened up fire, ripping the chair in half. I ducked lower as they fired away.

I was trapped behind a cloud chair that was being rapidly shot apart by two guardbots. I was unarmed, unarmored, outnumbered, and my computer was down. It's possible I'd been in tighter situations, but none sprang immediately to mind. This was bad with a capital B-A-D. I was starting to see why libraries aren't so popular anymore.

I took a deep breath. I figured I had one option. I had to jump up and try to fight the guardbots. Each bot had to weigh over 150 kilos. They were made of heavily reinforced plexi-metal, and they were armed with laser cannons and razor-sharp claws. The first time I'd made an unarmed attack on guardbots I had caught them off guard (plus I had my computer to cover me and pump up my muscles). This time they were ready for me, and there would be no holographic cover. I took another deep breath. Okay, it wasn't such a good option. In fact, it was a less than adequate option. Unfortunately, it was all I had.

I shot across the floor as more laser fire singed passed me. I pushed myself up off the ground. I started toward the bots. They spun to take aim at me. I heard a somewhat familiar sound. It was a whizzing sound, kind of like a furious bee on speed coming at me. I knew that sound. I pulled myself back and threw myself across the room as far away from the bots as I could.

I didn't see, but I heard and felt the explosion. The heat was searing, but that was a good thing because it meant I was still alive. I faintly heard that angry bee with an attitude sound again. It was getting louder and closer. I rolled farther away. This time my curiosity got the better of my common sense, and I peeked over my shoulder at my bot attackers. One was already split in two. Its top half had been obliterated, and its bottom was smoldering. The second bot had turned its attention away from me and toward the sound. I guess it wanted to see its killer. I didn't see what hit it, but I saw and felt the aftermath. The bot shattered into a million pieces of nothing.

Through the smoke I could see three figures. One, the most shapely of the three, had a missile launcher on her shoulder and was smiling. I'd recognize that smile even from five hundred meters—it was Electra. She was flanked by Randy and Tony.

I got up and started dusting myself off as I headed over toward them.

"What did I miss?" HARV said, coming back online.

"Ah, not much," I said.

I reached Electra and the other two.

"So, what brings you guys up north?" I asked.

Electra's lips curled up ever so slightly. "Carol said she picked up thought waves that you were in big trouble."

I shook my head. "Well, I guess she was wrong, wasn't she?"

"I used my clearance to get us here," Tony said.

"I used my brain to rewire the New Frisco transporters to send us here," Randy said.

"I'm the best shot," Electra said.

"And the best looking," I said, giving her a hard, wet kiss.

"I wouldn't necessarily say that," Randy said, but I'm pretty certain he was joking. Either that, or he had been too long in the lab.

"So, what's the story here?" Tony said, going into cop-mode.

I looked at him. I shrugged. "DOS if I know," I said.

"Come on, Zach, you've been here for forty-eight hours. Surely you know something?" Tony said.

I headed toward the door. The sooner I got out of the library the better.

"I don't know much—"

"Wow, he's finally admitting it," HARV interrupted.

"I don't know much for certain," I said. "But I do know there is trouble afoot. The question is, how big is the trouble?"

"That doesn't make me feel any better," Tony said.

"Welcome to my world, Tony. Welcome to my world."

Chapter 33

As we left the library, I filled everybody in on the situation. Actually, I mostly advised them of what was going on. HARV did most of the real filling in. We told them everything: about the two dead elves, about the attacks on my life, dead elves, robots going beserk, nerds, more dead elves, about the EMPG, and about Bim and Norp. Everybody was shocked about the elves, but nobody was much surprised about anything else.

Then we told them about what Bim and Norp had said. How Santana wasn't all sugarplums and spice like she appeared.

"I find it hard to believe Santana could go bad," Randy said.

"I didn't say she might be bad. I said she might be a bit deranged," I said. "There's a difference."

Truthfully, I'd prefer she was bad. Bad is easier to comprehend and more straightforward to predict. With deranged, you never know what you're getting into.

"Do you have any proof that what Bim and Norp are saying is true?" Tony asked.

"Nope," I said. "Hence, the problem."

"Didn't Bim and Norp admit to killing the elves?" Tony questioned in his most official policeman tone.

"They did," I said.

"Didn't they admit to trying to kill you?"

"They did—I was cramping their style."

"So what makes you think they're not just covering their asses?" Tony said.

"Tony, there are sensitive ears here," I said.

Tony turned to Randy. "Sorry about my choice of words," he said.

Randy grinned.

"I don't think they are covering themselves because, well, I'm not sure."

HARV appeared from my eye lens. "It's another one of Zach's hunches," he said, with more than a hint of cynicism in his voice.

Electra put a hand on my shoulder. "Amor, are you sure of this?"

"The only thing I'm sure of is that I'm not sure of anything. I just know I can't take the chance that Bim and Norp are telling the truth. That's why we're going to talk to Santana now."

Then it hit me. I stopped walking. "They didn't know I was me."

"Huh?" everybody else said.

"When I was attacked in my office by the bots and then men in black from the Santana Stinks Society, Bim and Norp didn't know I would be coming. They wouldn't have sent bots and a hitman to kill me."

Now it was everybody else's turn to pause and contemplate.

"There has got to be some explanation," Tony insisted.

"I'm sure there is, and I know just the meta-person to give it."

HARV gave me to directions to Santana's office. As I stormed forward, the others followed, occasionally slowing down and doing a double take when an elf went by. They were all amazed by the music, the lights, the occasional holographic reindeer.

"Wow, we're walking among elves," Randy said.

"Believe me, it wears thin real fast," I said.

The closer we got to Santana's office, the more elves there were. The stares lasted a lot longer and were much more palpable. These elves obviously weren't used to visitors coming into these parts of the Pole, especially unregistered visitors.

After twisting and turning down what seemed to be an endless labyrinth of Holiday filled hallways, we came to long pink hallway with a door at the end. As we neared the door, we heard a voice from behind us.

"Pink?" Electra exclaimed.

"Think of it as light red," I said.

"Stop! Stop! Stop!" Elf-1 called, running up to us.

Elf-1 slid past us and stood in front of me. He put his hand out for me to stop.

"Mr. Johnson, you can't go any farther," he insisted. "Santana will see you after her meeting. We have very specific rules about all this."

I pushed past Elf-1. "Sorry, elfy, but rules are made to be broken, especially if somebody tries to break me."

"These people are unregistered and unauthorized to be here!"

"Well, when your bots tried to kill me again, I decided I needed more help."

Elf-1 grabbed me by the shoulder. Before I could do anything, Electra hit him with a snap kick to the stomach. That doubled him over.

"At least she didn't go for my personal area," he groaned.

I kicked him between the legs. He doubled over in great pain. I didn't even think his happy place would be able to help him out now.

"Now Zach, did you have to do that?" Electra said.

I turned and headed toward the door. "Nope, but I wanted to."

I reached the door and wondered if I should knock politely, bang on it, or shoot the lock off. The door popped open before I could make my choice. I was a little disappointed by that.

Santana was sitting in her office with Councilwoman Weathers. Santana smiled at me.

"Zach, I'm so sorry. My meeting with the councilwoman ran late, but there is no need to barge into my office. I see you invited your friends here, as well." She was as cool as the ice caps that surrounded the Pole.

Councilwoman Weathers was even cooler, perhaps sub-frigid. "We were in the middle of a very important business meeting," she said. You could feel the ice dripping off her words.

"I get so rude when things try to kill me," I said.

"Zach, what are you talking about?" Santana asked.

"A few minutes ago, when I was waiting for you in the library, two bots rolled in and tried to send me to meet my maker."

This was a moment or two of awkward silence.

"Zach, I'm so sorry," Santana said, standing up from her chair. "I thought for sure we had all the bots back under our control."

"I didn't say you didn't."

Santana tilted her head to the side and looked at me. She put her hand on her chest. She wasn't expecting this. If she was, she was good at covering it up. "Zach, what are you implying?"

I decided not to tell her about what Bim and Norp had told me. I wanted to see how she reacted to the news of another attack on my life after the two had been apprehended.

"I'm just saying that it is possible that somebody else at the Pole, one of your elves perhaps, has something against me."

Santana looked me squarely in the eyes. She put her hand over her heart. "Zach, I know in my heart of hearts none of my elves would try to kill you."

"What about one of your other guests?" I said, though I didn't really believe it would be any of them.

"I'll have my elves look into that."

There was another moment of uneasy silence. She was good. I had to give her that. I needed to tip my hand.

"Bim and Norp said that you had a grand scheme to remodel the world in your own image with a happy virus," I said coldly.

Santana sat back in her chair. She looked down, then shook her head. "Zach, I assure you I am only on this Earth to make people happy."

"That's not a denial," I said.

"Didn't Bim and Norp try to kill you?" Santana said.

"Yes, but that doesn't mean they were lying. Electra and Tony have wanted to kill me on many, many occasions . . ."

Electra nodded.

"Amen," Tony said.

"I've had my moments, too," Randy added.

". . . but that doesn't mean I don't listen to them when they tell me something."

"Actually, you don't usually listen to me," Tony said.

"You could teach a course on how to not listen," Randy said.

"Si, listening isn't one of your better skills, mi amor."

"The point is," I said, "I believe Bim and Norp are onto something. That doesn't explain why the bots tried to kill me after those two jokers were locked up."

Then, almost on cue, a hectic Elf-3333 burst into the office.

"Santana, I'm sorry to interrupt such an important meeting," she panted. "But a scan of the bots showed that approximately thirty-two minutes and fifteen seconds ago, we lost control of two of our guardbots. I did a system scan and apparently those two nasty Martians had planted some sort of backdoor virus that made them go wild. I was able to break some of the code. It was KILL ZACH DEADER THAN DEAD AT ALL COSTS. We should warn him."

"I consider myself warned," I said.

Elf-3333 turned to me, startled. She was so intent on delivering her message she hadn't even noticed me in the room. "Oh, I'm so sorry," she said. "You are in grave danger. We've lost complete track of the bots. They're off our radar."

"They're off everybody's radar," Electra said, exposing the rocket launcher on her shoulder.

"Oh," Elf-3333 said. "I understand. As much as I deplore violence, nice job!" She gave Electra a big thumb's up and left the room.

"Can you explain how Bim and Norp sent bots to attack me before anybody knew I was coming? Or how they sent a killer posing as a SSS member after me?" I said, pounding my hand on her desk.

Just then Elf-2436 ran into the room. "Santana,"

she said urgently. "I've just busted Bim's and Norp's encryption program. It seems they've been tapping into your personal logs and records since they got here," she said.

Everybody looked at me.

"Okay, maybe you can explain that," I said.

Santana smiled. "You got me, Zach. I have an evil plan. I am going to use the Holiday to infect the entire world with a happy virus." Santana didn't make the slightest attempt to hide the mocking tone of her voice. When I heard it, it sounded totally ridiculous. I knew then and there it was true. It was all true.

"HARV," I thought. "Are you analyzing her voice patterns?"

"Sorry, Zach. There's some sort of interference in her office. I can't record or analyze anything. I'm having a hard enough time just staying online," HARV said inside my head.

That was the clincher.

"Thanks, Santana. You've been a big help," I said.

"My pleasure. Now if your guests would like to stay the evening, I will have my elves find them rooms."

"That would be much appreciated," Tony said.

"The pleasure is ours, Captain Rickey."

"Please, call me Tony."

"Of course, Tony."

"Can I see your labs?" Randy asked.

Santana smiled. "Of course, Dr. Pool."

Randy put his arms behind his back and sank down like a schoolboy with a crush. "Please, call me Randy, Santana."

"Of course, Randy."

Santana got up and walked (or more appropriately herded) us all toward the door. "Now if you don't mind, Stormy and I do have some very serious matters to attend to."

"No, no problem."

"Of course."

"Si, entiendo."

"I will see you all at dinner."

Everybody in my group smiled, except me.

"Zach, thank you for stopping by and for not kicking my door down," Santana told me.

Yep, she was guilty all right.

Chapter 34

It didn't take long at all for the elves to find suitable quarters for Randy and Tony. Randy was keen to share a room if it would make it easier on the elves, but Tony quickly shot down that idea. Randy liked the idea of having a human roomie to hang out with. Randy didn't get much human contact. Tony, on the other hand, got way too much human contact. He relished his privacy as much as Randy welcomed the companionship. The elves were able to get them adjoining rooms, which made them both happy.

They confiscated Electra's rocket launcher, Tony's sidearms, and Randy's gadgets. The elves insisted they were totally, absolutely certain they had complete control over the bots, and we would have no need for our weapons. I didn't mind giving them up because knowing my friends, they each had something up their sleeve.

Electra sat on the bed with a little bounce, testing its firmness. "So mi amor, you don't believe Santana?"

I moved over and sat next to her. I sighed.

"I don't like it when you sigh," she said.

"For some reason, I believe the geeks," I said.

"Probably because deep down, you are one of them," Electra said a bit jokingly.

I wanted to give her a witty retort, but her joke hit home. Sure, I'm a tough guy. Sure, I can punch with the best of them. But when push comes to shove, I am a guy with a computer wired to directly to my brain. If that didn't mean I was a geek, I didn't know what it meant.

"What evidence do you have that Santana has these evil plans?"

"You sound like Tony."

She just looked at me. I was used to getting that look from other people, but not from Electra.

"I have seen the technology here. It's pretty amazing."

"Your point being?"

"I think she has the means to pull it off."

"Pull what off, Zach?"

"Making everybody nice, and then sterilizing them."

Electra rolled her eyes. I was used to other people reacting to me like that too, just not Electra. "Zach, you heard how preposterous that sounded when Santana *admitted* to it."

"Honey, when you're me, outrageous and absurd is what you expect."

There are times being a PI means you have to go with your gut, no matter what your mind is telling you. This was one of those times. Once Santana tipped her hand, I'd be on her like white on genetically-modified-for-extra-whiteness rice.

Electra smiled and put her hand on my back. "That's why I love you," she said. "When you latch on to something, you don't let go."

"Yep, dogs with bones have nothing on me," I said.

Before Electra could say anything else, Elf-1's voice came booming over the intercom.

"Greetings, my fellow elves and our guests here at the Pole. I have a super-duper special announcement. Santana will be delivering a su-uper-du-uper special message to us all in the auditorium in fifteen minutes sharp. Your attendance is mandatory. Have a great, great, happy, happy day."

"A special announcement about a special announcement?" Electra said.

"Yes, isn't that special," I said in a voice imitating a character from a very old TV show.

Electra tilted her head and looked at me. "That's a reference to something, isn't it?"

"Yes, I'm impressed," I said. Most people wouldn't have caught that. Of course, most people don't live with me.

Electra shook her head. "I've been hanging around with you too long."

HARV appeared from my eye lens. "Hey, at least you're not attached to his brain."

I stood up from the bed and stretched. I turned to Electra. "Let's go."

She looked at me and kind of rolled her eyes. "Zach, on the off chance that you're right about Santana, this could be a trap."

"Exactly. Let's get going."

Electra pushed herself up from the bed with one arm. She was more hesitant than I had ever seen her.

"What's wrong, mi amor?" I said. "If you're so convinced I'm wrong, this shouldn't be anything."

She lowered her eyes. "I was certain you were wrong until that announcement. Now I know you're onto something."

"See, I'm contagious," I said, taking her arm.

"Why are you so anxious to walk into a trap?" she asked.

HARV appeared. "Because he's really not all that bright," he said to Electra. "I thought you would have figured that out by now."

"It's not a trap if I know it's a trap," I said.

"Yes, it is," HARV insisted.

Electra pointed at HARV. "He's right."

I headed toward the door. "Well, it's not as good of a trap if I can see it coming. Maybe I can put the kibosh on it before she's ready. Either way, I've been in this elf suit long enough. I'm ready for the end of the game."

"In that case, wait," Electra said. "You're going to need something else." She went into the closet and came out carrying a suitcase.

"How the DOS did you smuggle that here?"

"I brought it with us. I told the elves it was my allergy medicine."

She walked over and put the suitcase on the bed.

"You must have a lot of allergies," I said.

"Elves are trusting little beings," she said opening the suitcase.

I moved over next to her. Sure enough, the suitcase was lined with medications.

"That's a holographic cover," HARV said.

"Very good, HARV," I said, patting his virtual shoulder.

"The elves were really busy at the time," Electra said as she pushed a button on the bottom of the suitcase. The medications vanished and were replaced by my regular clothing, my body armor, my wrist communicator (never hurts to have a backup), my gun, a couple of energy weapons, and best of all, my fedora that HARV had talked me out of taking.

"What, no belt and trench coat?" I asked.

Electra shook her head. "Sorry. I like to travel light."

I couldn't get out of that elf suit fast enough.

"You know, you are totally breaking protocol by changing like this," HARV scolded.

"Yeah, I know that," I said, as slipped off the elf suit, kicked it to the corner of the room, and put on my body armor. "Protocol kind of went out the door the last time the bots tried to kill me."

"I know," HARV said. "I just felt obligated to point it out."

I was fully dressed in less than a minute. With my gun up my sleeve and my armor underneath, it was the first time I felt comfortable since I arrived at the Pole. I'm not sure what that said about me. I'm certain I didn't want to think about it too much.

"Now, let's get this show on the road!" I said.

Chapter 35

When we arrived at the theater, Randy and Tony were already there, along with about ten thousand elves. The theater, like everything else in this joint, was massive, almost stadiumlike in its size, but the throng of elves had it stuffed to the rafters. I scanned the crowd for non-elves. Nova was there, along with Mary and Steve, Mr. Weathers, Elf-1, and the Billings family, except for Mrs. Billings.

"Okay," I said, as I looked around. "Am I right, HARV, that Santana, Mrs. Billings, and the councilwoman are missing?"

"Correct. It seems you may have been right not to trust Weathers."

"To quote a friend, 'Of course.' "

"I don't like this," Tony said.

All the doors in the room slammed down shut behind us.

"I *really* don't like this," Tony said.

Elf-1 came running up to us. "Where's Santana? She told me she'd be here to address us live."

A giant screen came rolling down the ceiling in front of the stage.

"I don't know, but I have a feeling we'll know in a nano," I told him, as I pointed to the screen.

A 3D image of Councilwoman Weathers appeared on the screen, smiling. Behind her sat Santana. They were in some sort of control room. In the background, we could see Mrs. Billings, who had a laser to the heads of Norp and Bim.

"I have great news for all of you," Councilwoman Weathers said, puffing out her chest.

The crowd of elves erupted in applause.

Weathers continued, "Thanks to your diligent work, the Holiday has been saved despite the efforts of the two behind me."

The elves applauded more.

Weathers waited for the applause to die down and then went on. "In fact, I have used my influence to declare the Holiday will begin right now!"

There was applause and audible gasps.

"For details, I'll turn the floor over to my special friend, Santana!"

The place went wild.

"My elves, I want to thank you all for your service."

The crowd started to applaud even louder, though I didn't like where Santana was heading.

"Thanks to you, the world is going to be a better place," Santana shouted boldly.

Some of the elves were now standing and cheering.

"These guys eat way too much sugar," I whispered to Tony.

"Thanks to you," Santana continued, "everybody in the world will be happy, whether they want to be or not."

Most of the elves continued to cheer. Some of them stopped to hear what Santana was saying.

"Every present delivered tonight will be contain not one, but two different viruses," Santana said.

Now about half the elves where cheering, while the other half was listening intently to what Santana was saying.

"Santana always was an overachiever," I said to Tony.

"The first virus was developed right here, and it will stimulate the pleasure centers of the brain. The need to be naughty will be gone."

A few of the more optimistic (or denser) elves were still clapping and stomping. The rest, though, weren't so sure they liked what they were hearing.

"The second virus, developed by our friends from Mars, will make the entire population of Earth sterile in three generations," Santana said proudly.

A few of the more radical elves were still chanting. The others sat in stunned silence.

"You're going to wipe out humanity?" I shouted to the holographic screen.

Santana's huge holographic figure shook her head. "Ho ho ho, no no no," she said. "Humanity won't be wiped out. They'll just be forced to clone their future generations. My elves are clones, and you can plainly see what great beings they are."

Some of the elves nodded their heads in agreement, others looked on in total confusion.

"Let me get this straight," I said. "You plan not only to force everybody to be happy, but you are also planning on making humanity forget about sex and having to clone to survive."

Santana nodded. "Yes, that sums up my plan nicely. Being naughty is a great distraction. With that eliminated think of the greatness humans will achieve."

"What about those of us trapped in here?" I asked.

"You will also be made happy and sterile. We will be pumping the gas in shortly."

Happy and sterile. Now there's a phrase you don't hear very often.

"How will the happy gas affect the elves?" Elf-1 shouted. "We're already happy and sterile."

"Oh," Santana said, "that's the best part. With everybody in the world now happy twenty-four/seven, we won't need the Holiday any longer, and your services won't be needed. So, I'm terminating you all. This combination of gases is deadly to elves."

A few of the really thick elves applauded. The rest fell back into their seats.

"You've done your duty to the world, but now you've become extraneous, so I expect you to fulfill your obligation and die. I'm granting you all the rest you so deserve."

Now everybody was stunned silent.

"The teleporting of presents will begin in a hour. I want to thank you all once again for the role you played in making the world a better place."

Mrs. Billings tossed us a kiss. The holographic screen dissipated.

"HARV, block all outgoing transmissions."

"Right."

"I don't believe my own wife is going to sterilize me!" Mr. Weathers said. "I'm am so going to complain about this the next time we see our marriage advisor!"

"Well, if it makes you feel any better, Mrs. Billings is no prize either. She's going to sterilize her entire family," I told him.

Little Billy walked up to me.

"No, she isn't," he said.

"Huh?"

"We are already sterile!" Billy told me.

Little Billy lifted off his head revealing his android circuitry. His sister and father did the same. Then they all fell to the ground.

"Somehow, I doubt this plan was a spur of the moment kind of thing."

"I'm going to kill her!" Mr. Weathers shouted. "The most trusted woman on Earth, my ass!"

"If we get out of here, you're going to have to stand in line to kill her," I said.

"HARV, how come you didn't notice they were androids?" I asked.

Silence.

"HARV?"

"I never scanned them," was HARV's simple reply.

"Any idea why?"

"Zach, I don't scan everybody you meet. That would just be rude. They had normal skin tones, so I assumed they were normal humans, not illegal androids."

I decided not to contemplate the ramifications of my computer making assumptions and ignoring the possibility that there might be human-skin-toned androids out there.

Elf-2 two came running up to me. "Oh, Zach, this is a marketing nightmare—destroying the world as we know it."

"Don't worry. We're going to stop them," I said.

"What can I do?" she offered.

"Keep the others calm. Tell them everything is under control."

"You mean lie?" she said. "I can't lie."

"You're in marketing. Of course you can."

"Zach, we don't lie, we just promote a semblance of the truth."

"Well, go do your thing then."

"Right," she said. She puffed out her chest, gave me a salute, and headed back into the throng of elves.

I turned my attention back to my "team."

"We need to find a way out of here," I said.

"Let's blast our way out," Tony said as he drew a weapon he had under his shirt.

"Impossible. The doors are sheer plexi-steel. Impossible to blast or shoot through," Elf-1 told us.

"Why would anybody put plexi-steel doors on an auditorium?" Randy asked.

"Before the remodeling, this used to be the main transporter room."

That gave me an idea. "Are there any transporter pads left in here?"

"There's one backstage, but I'm sure it's deactivated," Elf-1 said.

"Think you could activate it?" I asked Randy.

"I'll probably have to use some chips from your eye lens to power it up, but I can do it."

"How can you say that without looking at it?" Elf-1 questioned.

"Just take us to it. If Randy says he can, he can."

HARV chipped in. "Dr. Pool, the porting software the elves use is very advanced. It allows teleportation from a port pad to another area, even if it doesn't have a port pad."

Elf-1 put his hands on his hips. "You're not supposed to know that!" he protested.

"Big picture here, Elf-1," I said. "No hard feeling about our little scuffles," I told him.

"Of course not," he said.

Elf-1 led us down a long aisle, muttering about his "hap-hap-hap-happy place." This time I wanted to join him. We rushed past the stage and then behind it. There it was: an old, five-person transporter pad and panel. Randy hit the control panel on the top and a panel popped open. He looked in.

"I have good news and bad news," he said.

"Good news first," I said.

"I can make it work."

"Bad news?" I asked.

"I think I can only make it work once, and I can't guarantee where it will put you. There will be no backup system."

"Which means?" Tony asked.

Randy looked at him. "Which means I think I can find an empty hallway to port you into, but I can't guarantee it. There is no collision detection software."

"That means if you're off, we can teleport into a wall or a passing bot," Tony said slowly.

"It will have to do," I said.

Randy walked over to me. He pulled a small pair of tweezerlike things from his pocket and stuck them in my eye.

"I'll need some of the chips from the lens. The connection will still function, only HARV won't be able to see from your eye anymore."

Randy popped the chips out. He carefully walked over to the porter and placed them in the machine. While Randy tinkered, the rest of us made plans.

"Elf-1, how long before Santana will be ready to teleport her special gifts to the world?"

Elf-1 pulled out a calculator from his pocket. "We've done most of the prep work already. The presents and their coordinates are already stored in warehouses throughout the Pole. The delivery process is all done via the Pole's own teleportation software. Once the process starts, we can teleport packages to everybody in the world in twenty-four hours."

"That type of teleportation must take massive amounts of energy," Tony said.

"Yes, we have our own nuclear generators below the surface."

"Maybe we could take those out?" Tony said.

We all just stared at him. Sometimes Tony let his gung-ho attitude get in the way of his logic. He thought about what he had said. "Oh, yeah, even if we weren't trapped in here, taking out nuclear generators probably isn't the best plan."

"We'll put that one on the back burner," I said.

"The computers," a male voice said from behind us.

We saw the Eatmans and Nova coming to join our assemblage.

"My husband's right," Mary Eatman said. She pointed to me. "All the elves are buzzing about how you're wearing a highly advanced computer on your eye. Use it."

Elf-1 put his hands behind his back. "That's impossible. Our computer systems have firewall after firewall, and each of those is e-wrapped in e-razor wire, surrounded by e-moats which are guarded by more firewalls."

Steve smiled. "I know. I helped designed those systems. Between my knowledge and Elf-1's knowledge, I am sure we could get Zach's computer past the security and bog down their system with a virus."

Elf-1 put both hands over his head. "But if I did that I'd be betraying Santana! I could never ever do that."

I looked at him. "She's perfectly willing to kill you and all you stand for."

Elf-1 thought about it for a nano. "Perhaps *never ever* is too strong a sentiment." He pondered a bit more.

Nova walked over and started slowly rubbing Elf-1's

back. "You don't want to die do you?" she purred. "You have so much to live for."

Elf-1 smiled widely. "I do enjoy being naughty as much as the next elf. More in fact, given my responsibilities. Let's stop the bitch," he said.

The only problem, well, not the only problem, but the most pressing was that Randy was using my eye interface with HARV to hotwire the teleporter. We would need my communicator to interface HARV with the Pole's system. I started removing the communicator from my wrist. Turning to Randy, I said, "Can HARV handle interfacing with the system and powering the teleporter?"

"Of course," HARV and Randy both said.

"HARV could do that and pilot one thousand two hundred and twenty-two hovers backward through rush hour traffic," Randy added.

"I was fine with just the 'of course,'" I said.

I handed the communicator to Elf-1. He and Steve went over to a side interface and plugged HARV in. Elf-1 hit the side of the unit and a keyboard popped out. He typed a series of digits. His fingers moved so fast I barely saw them.

"I've got HARV in," Elf-1 said.

"Perfect timing," Randy said. "I've got the teleporter working now. I think."

"You think?" I said.

Randy shrugged. "I've never done this before. I didn't have time to run a simulation, but I'm pretty certain it will work and not get you all killed."

Not the most ringing of endorsements, but it was good enough for me. I walked over to a pad and stood on it.

"Okay, we have room for four more."

Electra, Tony, Elf-1, and Nova joined me on the pads.

"Elf-1, are you sure about this?" I said.

Nova smiled at him, and his face lit up like the old-fashioned Fourth-of-July fireworks.

"I've never been surer about anything in my life," he said. "Santana has betrayed us all."

I tossed Electra a kiss. She took my hand. I smiled at her. Nova smiled at me. Electra gave us both a glare. Elf-1 frowned. Tony just chuckled. Meanwhile, Randy continued to tinker away.

Finally Randy said, "Okay, I'm ready."

HARV and Elf-1 downloaded schematics of the Pole into the teleporter. The plan was for Randy to teleport us to a hallway just around the corner from the main control area that Santana, Weathers, and Ma Billings were occupying. It was far enough away so they couldn't see us, but close enough to give us a chance to stop them. As long as we moved fast.

"Remember gang, we don't have much time. Elf-1, you're going to have to get us straight to the control room as fast as possible," I said

"Check."

Randy pushed the lever up on the teleporter.

The next thing I knew I was standing in a hallway with Tony next to me. We both drew our weapons and looked around.

"Where are the others?" Tony asked.

"I don't know, Tony. I just got here."

"My guess would be transporter malfunction," HARV said.

"Are the others okay?" I asked.

I was greeted with uncharacteristic silence.

"HARV, I asked you a question."

"Sorry, Zach, I don't know. The chips Randy used must have been damaged. In my crippled state, I've lost all contact with the people inside the theater."

"Can you repair it?"

"Maybe, but it will take some time."

"DOS!"

Tony fired a laser blast at a guardbot coming up behind us. The bot exploded on contact.

"Come on, we have a job to do," Tony said, pointing forward. "There's nothing we can do standing around here worrying. I'm sure they're all okay."

I took a deep breath to help regain my composure.

"I hate it when you're right," I told him. "Okay, HARV, give us the fastest route to the control panel."

"Two more bots behind us!" Tony shouted.

I spun to face them.

"You take the one on the left, I'll take the one on the right," Tony said anxiously.

"The DOS with that," I said as I pointed my gun down the hall and aimed. "Gun—multi, murve, explode."

A bullet fired from my gun and split into many bullets that tore into the charging bots, shredding them into tomorrow's garbage.

"HARV, what's the quickest route to the main control room?" I asked.

"That all depends on where you are."

"You don't know?"

"I'm blind now, Zach, remember? Describe your location."

"We're in a long, white hallway with a red stripe on the floor. No windows, no doors, no nothing. We see only hall as far as we can see."

"That's no help. You just described roughly thirty-four point four one percent of this place. What about the maidbot storage closets? They are all numbered."

"Good idea!"

Tony looked at me. "I hope you're talking to HARV and haven't lost it."

I started kicking the lower part of the walls.

"What are you doing?" Tony asked.

"Looking for a closet down here," I said as I banged away.

"What can I do to help?"

"Start banging!" I told him.

Tony bent down and started searching the other walls.

HARV chimed in. "Two things, Zach. One, I hear more guardbots coming down the hall."

I looked down the hall. I pointed my gun down the hall.

"Gun—multi, big bang."

I fired. A few seconds later there were multiple explosions filling the hall.

"HARV, what's the second thing?"

"I might be able to zap your brain. Charge up that sixth sense of yours. It might give us a clue as to where the closet is."

"Fine, desperate times call for strange actions," I said.

"You're not very good with sayings, are you?" Tony said.

My head started to tingle. Tony blew away another attacking bot. I smiled.

I walked about three meters up from Tony. I kicked the wall right about floor level. Nothing happened. I was a little confused and a lot frustrated.

"DOS, I knew this was the spot."

"Now what are you doing?" Tony asked.

"HARV charged up my brain to help me find the maidbot storage closest, but it's not here!"

"Maybe your mind is like your golf drive, always off to the left a bit," Tony suggested.

I moved a little to right. I kicked the wall. A panel on the floor popped open. I smiled.

Tony ran up to me and gave me cover while I looked at the closet.

"So, where are these things labeled?" I asked HARV, as I frantically tossed cleaning materials out of the way.

"How should I know? Do I look like a maidbot to you?"

Finally, I found a little label in the corner.

"All I see here is the number 0000 0000 0111," I said.

"Okay, I've got your location. Go down the hall to your left. Tell me when you come to an intersection."

We ran down the hallway with our guns drawn.

"How far away are we, HARV?" I asked as we ran.

"Not very. Randy teleported you fairly close to where he was aiming. Don't worry."

"How come whenever you say that it sends a chill up my spine?"

We reached an intersection.

"Now what?"

"Hang a left. The main control room is one hundred meters straight down the hall."

I stepped into the intersection and was hit by a laser blast to the shoulder. I dropped my gun from the force of the blow and staggered back against the wall. My suit now had a nice hole in it, but my armor took the brunt of the damage.

"They were waiting for us!" Tony said.

A bot circled around the corner, and Tony blew it away.

"It doesn't take a mastermind to figure out where we were headed," I said, rubbing my shoulder.

"Is it bad?" Tony asked.

"It would be if Electra hadn't brought my under-armor," I told him.

"It sounds like there are at least ten other guardbots in the hall on both sides. It seems this is where they are planning to stop you." HARV said.

"They have us pinned down. If we try to move into the hallway, they'll blow us away," Tony said.

"HARV, what about a different route?"

"No way. Even if there was one, it would take way too long."

"More bots!" Tony said as he pointed to the other end of the hallway.

He opened fire. The bot returned fire, hitting Tony in the leg. Tony dropped his gun and fell to the floor. This was bad. Real bad. Pinned down in an open hallway by guardbots. I needed an idea—a good idea—and fast. I didn't even have my gun. It was lying there in the middle of the hallway, right in the intersection. That's when it hit me.

"Tony, cling as close as you can to the wall," I said, as I clung to the opposite wall.

"Gun—spin forty-five degrees right, fire big boom; spin forty-five degrees right, fire big boom; spin ninety degrees right, fire big boom. Program execute!"

Fireworks went off! The gun did its stuff, spinning then shooting, then spinning some more, then blasting some more. There were three big bangs followed by a series of explosions. We both covered our heads to protect ourselves from flying bot parts.

I looked down the hallway. The charging bots had been destroyed. I moved away from the wall. I peeked down the intersection, first right, then left. The place looked like a robot graveyard.

"Do I do good work or what?" I asked Tony as I picked up my gun.

"I'm amazed," he said.

"No need to be. My gun makes state-of-the-art look like last year's news!" I said.

"No, I'm amazed you got the angles right. You're terrible at geometry."

"Thanks. Are you okay?"

He showed me his leg wound. It was ugly, at least two centimeters long, and just as wide. Red wasn't Tony's color.

"I won't be going dancing tonight," Tony groaned.

"Looks like I'll have to finish this one without you, buddy."

"At least drag me out into the intersection where I can cover you."

"Sorry Tony, you'd be a sitting duck for any guardbots that might wander by. I think right now my best course of action would be a good old-fashioned head-on charge."

I patted him on the shoulder. I ran into the intersection, ready to fire at a moment's notice.

"Ah, Zach," HARV said as I charged on. "I know I've brought this topic up many, *many* times before, but shouldn't we at least pretend to have a little plan?"

"Why bother? If we don't have any idea what we're doing, there's no way the bad guys can have any idea what we're doing."

I ran straight toward the control room door. As I closed in, I lowered my shoulder and rammed it, using my body armor to cushion the blow, while hopefully breaking down the door. Much to my surprise, I smashed right through!

Chapter 36

I was now in the control room. I had crashed through the door and hit the floor. Mrs. Billings was sitting on a chair holding a laser to Bim and Norp's heads. Councilwoman Weathers was there, along with Santana.

Weathers walked over and picked up my gun. "My, you make an impressive entrance," she said as she aimed my gun at me. "Have you ever thought of going into politics?"

I looked up. I could see one screen showing the theater filling with gas, and another showing Tony lying on the floor bleeding.

"I would, but the pay's kind of lousy," I told her.

Weathers sneered at me. It was the first time I'd seen that look from such a polished politician. "My husband's right, you are an annoying little gnat."

"We all have our roles," I said.

"Zach," HARV shouted inside my head. "I'm getting odd readings from Weathers."

"Not now, HARV," I thought back. "Can't you see I'm in the middle of witty banter with the bad girl?"

"Zach, I haven't seen these readings since Sexy Sprockets," HARV shouted. "She's a psi—an augmented psi!"

Now that was a kick in the gut I wasn't expecting.

The councilwoman walked over to me, bent down, and lifted me up by my throat.

"So the little computer in your brain figured out what they made me into," she said.

I nodded and grunted. That was about all I could do—her grip was strong, exceedingly strong. She had to be using her psi powers to augment her strength. Out of the corner of my eye, I saw Santana moving toward us. She put a hand on Weathers' arm.

"Stormy, there is no need to kill Zach. There is nothing he can do to stop us."

Weathers looked at Santana out of the corner of her eye. "No, but it would be fun."

"Killing is wrong," Santana said.

"You're killing all your elves," Weathers said.

Santana shook her head. "No, the gas is doing that. They are useless now, anyhow. The rest will do them good."

Weathers released her grip on my throat, letting me drop to the ground.

Santana approached me as I pushed myself up to my knees. My throat felt like it had been stuck in an atomic vise, but I wasn't about to let Weathers know that.

Santana knelt down, meeting me halfway. "Zach, I'm sorry about that," she said, helping me to my feet. "Stormy just really believes in our work here."

"Your work here?" I said. "This isn't work. It's a maniacal attempt to reshape the world in your deranged image."

"Six of one, half a dozen of the other," Santana said.

I looked over at Ma Billings still holding the weapon on Bim and Norp. "What's a nice country girl like you got to do with all this?"

"They needed my robotics expertise to help program the Holiday launch," she sneered. "I truly believe in my heart the world will be better this way."

"Why are you holding Bim and Norp?" I asked.

"They are still useful to us," Weathers said. "Their knowledge of robots is as impressive as their lack of social skills is scary. Plus, they'll make great scapegoats on the off chance that something goes wrong and our plans get delayed. We will just blame them. On the off off chance something happens to them, I have the evil couple from ExShell to blame."

"Wow, pretty impressive," I said. "You three have thought of everything."

"Actually, Stormy thought of most of it," Santana said.

"Yes," Ma Billings agreed. "This was all Stormy's brilliant idea."

They both had a strange tone to their voices, tones normally reserved for cult members talking about their leaders.

"What's the deal with the fake Billings family?" I asked. "Pretty impressive work."

"Thank you," Ma Billings said. "I do believe they were my best yet."

"It figures HTech would have their hands in this."

Ma Billings shook her head. "Silly man, I no longer work for HTech. I work for the World Council now."

I suppose I should have seen that coming.

"This is just a big World Council plot then?" I asked.

Weathers laughed and rolled her eyes. "Those fools think of something this creative? I think not," she said. "They are perfectly happy with the status quo

and keeping their nice, safe soft jobs. I thought of this
while recuperating from my crash. I executed it on
my own."

Santana and Ma Billings each cleared their throats.

"With some help from my friends, of course."

"Nothing wrong with help from your friends. Unless, of course, they are helping you destroy the
world."

Weathers raised her arms in a flippant manner,
"You say *destroy,* I say *improve.*"

One thing was for certain, if I was going to stop
this, I was going to need a lot of help from my friends.
For now, my best tactic was to stall, giving my team
time to clog the system with a virus. It's never a good
sign when your best technique is to delay and pray
for a miracle, but I was hoping inspiration would
strike me.

"The people of Earth love both of you," I said,
pointing first to Weathers and then Santana.

"They will love us more after we are done with
them," Weathers said.

Santana nodded her agreement.

So far, this wasn't going too well.

"Hey, what about me?" Ma Billings asked.

Finally, the crumb of inspiration I was hoping for.
"I'm sure they would like you too, if they got to know
you, but face it when you run with this crowd," I
pointed to Weathers and Santana again, "you, dear
Ma, are fourth string."

Divide and conquer—it was an age-old tactic. It
worked for the Huns, it worked for Yoko Ono, it
would work for me. I like to think I'm smarter than
most Huns (and sing better than Yoko).

Ma Billings dropped her guard. She moved her gun
away from Bim and Norp and aimed it at me. She
wasn't threatening me with it, she was just using it as

a pointing device. It was as if she had forgotten she had a gun in her hand. Obviously, she wasn't used to brandishing weapons.

Bim and Norp surprised me by taking advantage of Ma Billing's mental lapse. They moved forward, Bim grabbing for her gun as Norp tackled her knees. Shockingly, they were able to bring Billings down and wrestle the gun away from her.

Bim smiled loosely as he trained the gun first on Santana and then on Weathers.

"Now we get to really be heroes," he gloated. "Norp, I'll keep them covered while you power down the transporters."

Norp had his hands full trying to stay on top of a very feisty Ma Billings. "I don't think that's going to be an option," he said. "Why not have Zach cover them while you power down the porters?" he suggested.

Bim thought about that for a nano. "Share the glory—interesting concept," he said to himself.

"No glory to share, buddy," I coaxed. "I'll give it all to you guys. I just want to make sure the world stays like it is. It may not be the best possible world— it's unsystematic and filled with pain and violence, but it's also filled with lots of good things like random acts of kindness, baseball, HV, love, tacos, and sex. I'll do anything to stop yet another couple of crazy ladies from shaping the world into their distorted view of perfection."

"Oh, so now you think you're better than us?" Bim said. "Mr. High and Mighty Zachary Nixon Johnson," he taunted. "He's saved the world soooo many times, he doesn't need to do it again."

Now it was Bim's turn to forget the weapon he was holding in his hand. He put the gun to his side and pointed at me with his free hand.

"Listen," he said.

He never got to finish that statement, as Santana was all over him like ugly on a monkey's behind (no offense to you monkeys out there). She grabbed him, squeezed his wrist, and elbowed him in the face. Bim was out cold and on the floor before he even knew what hit him.

"I knew this wasn't going to turn out well," Norp sighed a split nano before Santana focused her attention on him, spinning toward him and kicking him in the stomach. The kick sent him flying off of Ma Billings and crashing into the wall. It would have hurt a lot, but lucky for him, the kick instantly put him out colder than a flounder hermetically sealed in ice.

It was back to me against the three, but I guess there was never any real doubt that it would come down to this. At least Bim and Norp had given me a little more time to formulate a plan.

"I'm hoping you have a plan," HARV said inside my head.

"It's formulating as we speak," I thought back.

"How's it going inside the auditorium?" I asked HARV.

I was greeted with nothing but silence. As much as I welcome the quiet, I know it's not good when HARV is silent.

"I haven't regained contact with them yet," HARV said reluctantly. "That part of me is very weak."

"How's it going with jamming the transport system?" I asked.

More silence. "The elves were very efficient in building their firewalls. They are more like bomb bunkers buried hundred of kilometers below the surface and covered with lead. It's actually quite impressive."

"HARV!"

"Don't worry Zach, I'll get through. I just need time."

Unfortunately, time was one of the many things we were running oh so short of right now.

I studied Santana, Billings, and Weathers studying me. They had to have noticed the contorted looks on my face.

"Is he having some sort of stroke?" Billings asked.

I get that reaction a lot.

The other two just shook their heads. "He's probably thinking to the computer he has wired to his brain," Santana said.

"He has a computer wired to his brain?" Billings asked. "That would explain a lot." She looked at Bim and Norp's unconscious bodies and added, "Gee, I thought they were the geeks."

"Having a computer wired to my brain does *not* make me a geek," I stated very firmly.

"He's more of a geek's guinea pig," Weathers chuckled.

Now this really ticked me off, mostly because it was truer than I'd like to admit. I wasn't a guinea pig, I was more like a test pilot. I took a deep breath and took account of my assets. I had my wits and my body armor, and HARV was functional, though not at peak levels.

Things looked pretty bleak and that was being overly optimistic.

Weathers moved forward and put on hand on my shoulder. It was a merciful move, but I'd accepted it. "Actually, Zach," she said. "I can relate to your being a guinea pig. I wasn't always a psi."

"The World Council augmented you?" I half-guessed and half-stated.

She lowered her eyes. "They employed the services

of that sleaze named Sydney Smiles." She looked me in the eyes. "I understand you are familiar with his work."

I nodded. Sydney was the deranged madman/agent (is there really that much of a difference?) who turned Sexy Sprockets from a wannabe rock star to a dominating psi rock star, and then turned my assistant Carol from a powerful psi to a near godlike being. He escaped after my last adventure before I could give him the punch in the face he deserved. Now I saw a hard knee to the groin would be too good for him.

"Yeah, I know Sydney," I said.

She lowered her eyes again. I felt the tension in her voice. "It was twenty years ago, and I was a junior Council member. I was chosen to *volunteer* for the tests."

While she talked, I found myself starting to feel sorry for her.

"In those early days, Sydney hadn't perfected his radiation technique so he used injections—painful injections."

The more she talked, the heavier my heart felt. I could feel her pain clear through to my soul.

"He succeeded in turning me into a psi, but I'm not a normal psi. I'm more of an empathy psi."

"An empathy psi?" I said.

"I can't outright control people, because if I could, believe me you'd be my poodle now," she said. "Sydney always said it was because I was subconsciously suppressing my power. I think he was just covering his skinny little ass. The bottom line is, I can't directly control people, but I can broadcast my emotions to them."

"So you make them think like you?"

"I make them feel like me. Of course, the more

exposure they have to me, the more they do start to think like me." She gave me a weak smile. "There are times when these powers are handy for a politician to have."

As my mouth was calmly stalling, my brain was frantically scanning the room, searching for a way out of this. I noticed that Weathers still had my gun in her hand. If I could get her to point the gun at me, I would be able to take her out. It was a drastic move, but I didn't see a lot of other choices. If she was willing to pull the trigger on me, I had to be willing to do the same to her.

"Okay," I said slowly. "This is your last chance, I order you to give up now, or I'm going to have to hurt you."

Weathers snickered. "Please, Mr. Johnson . . ."

"Call me Zach."

"Please, Zach," she spat. "You are in no position to be making any demands or threats."

I locked eyes with her. "Not a demand or a threat, just a fact."

She smiled. "Zach, I'm picking up your thoughts. I know you want me to try to shoot you with your own gun."

DOS, I hate psis!

She dropped my gun to the ground. She walked over to me and picked me up off the ground by the throat. She pushed me back, pinning me to the wall. "I'm not your standard issue politician," she said. "I like to do my dirty work for myself."

Weathers' grip was quickly cutting off the blood to my brain. I would be out cold fast if I didn't do something faster. If I went under, all would be lost. My first move was to grab the arm she was choking me with and pull down. I jerked down on her arm with all my strength, but to no avail. Her arm stayed perfectly straight and rigid. The only effect it had was to get her to tighten her grip on me.

She smiled. "Zach, I do believe blue is your color."

Santana moved forward. "Stormy, do you really need to kill Zach?" she said, almost more out of curiosity than compassion.

"Yes," Weathers told her without flinching, keeping her gaze locked into mine.

Just then, something surprising happened. A shot rang through the window of the room into Weathers' arm, tearing it out of the socket. I fell to the floor grasping for air.

I turned toward the shot to see Tony sitting there in the hallway, smiling and holding a smoking gun. That's my buddy Tony. I looked back at Weathers. She was stunned. It wasn't the pain of having her arm ripped off that had stymied Weathers, but what the shot had revealed. Where her arm had been there was circuitry, loads and loads of circuitry. She put her good hand over the shot, not to stop the blood—because there wasn't any—but to cover up her parts.

"Oh, DOS, your arms are bionic," I said.

"No! No, they're not," she said calmly.

That would explain her superhuman strength. If her psi powers hadn't been messing with my brain, I probably would have figured that out a lot sooner. I held out my hand and pointed to my gun.

"Gun, come to poppa," I said.

My gun shot across the floor and into my open hand. I pointed the gun at Weathers.

"The game is over," I said. "Bionic or not, this gun has enough firepower to rip apart a battlebot." I was speaking from experience when I said that.

"They did this to me!" she said, too calmly.

"The Council?" I said standing up, but never letting

any of them forget I was the one holding the high-powered gun I was very comfortable using.

"Of course, it was them," she said coldly. "After their little experiment in making me a psi, they couldn't risk losing me to something as trivial as an accident."

"So they gave you bionic parts," I stated.

"No," she said slowly. "I have already told you that. I am not bionic." She paused. I wasn't sure if she was trying to build the tension, or just wasn't sure what to say next. She grinned. It was a strange grin for such a trained politician, as it was openly cynical. "Bionics would be too simple for them."

Weathers reached down to her midsection, and with her remaining arm grabbed the material of her pant suit and ripped off a patch, exposing her skin. She tapped the bare spot three times with her index finger. The skin popped up, showing her underbelly was all circuits. "They took my brain and inserted it into another body, an android body."

"Why didn't they just clone you a new body?" Santana asked. The tone in her voice as casual as if she was asking about the weather.

"They told me that human bodies break. I was now considered too valuable," Weathers sneered.

"But you've been aging," Billings said.

Weathers shook her head. "My system is designed to simulate aging. My skin tone, eyes, and hair color are adjustable." Her hair started cycling though all the various colors: first blond, then brunette, then redhead. "If I ever wanted to go out and paint the town red incognito, I'd use my brunette hair and smoothe my skin. Nobody would recognize me." Her hair turned back to the more familiar frost color. "This, of course, is my favorite color as this is the color my human hair would be if I were still human."

Then something very important occurred to me.

"Why are you telling us all this?" I asked.

"I wanted you to understand my motives for remaking the world," she said. "They made me in the image they thought best. Now I am going to pay everybody back."

I pointed my gun at her. "Yeah, well that's not going to happen."

"No, it's not," she said. "That's why I've decided to kill you and destroy the Pole, instead."

Weathers' one good arm stretched out and clobbered me right in the gut. My armor took the brunt of the attack, so much so that I didn't even drop my gun. Her next moves though, caught me off guard—she darted toward the door.

I fired but missed.

Weathers ran threw the door without opening it. As she raced down the hall, Tony fired at her but she literally ran along the side walls and then the ceilings, avoiding his shots until she was past him.

I turned my attention to Santana and Ma Billing and trained my gun on them. "What's your move?"

They both shook their heads and rubbed their eyes.

"It's like I've been asleep and dreaming all this time," Santana said.

"By Gates, I built myself a robotic family, to be a manical cyborg politician's minions . . ." Ma Billings said.

HARV flickered back online. "Zach, their mental readings are normal now. Weathers must have given up her control over them," HARV said.

I wasn't nearly as happy about that as I thought I should be. First, she made the confession and now this. I didn't like this one bit.

"She's going to kill herself," I said.

The lights flickered for a minute before steadying back to normal.

"That's odd," Santana said.

Ma Billings went over to a control panel. "We've just gone to auxiliary power."

"Why?" Santana asked.

"Somebody is channeling all the Pole's energy into the main reactors."

"Oh, that's not good at all," Santana said.

It wasn't hard to figure out who that somebody was.

"She's going to kill herself and take us out with her," I said.

"And a good part of the northern hemisphere," Santana added.

"Where is the reactor?" I asked.

"Reactors," Santana corrected.

"Where are the *reactors*?"

"Two kilometers under the surface," Santana said. "And there is only one elevator that leads down there."

"I suppose she's killed that elevator," I said.

Ma Billings looked at a reading on a panel and nodded yes.

"Of course she has," I said.

Santana went into supermanager mode. "Release the elves and our visitors from the theater. We can at least start teleporting them to safety."

Ma Billing shook her head no. "We can release them, but nobody is being teleported too far. The councilwoman has rerouted all the energy to the reactors. We can barely power up one teleporter."

"Then rereroute them," Santana ordered.

"I'm trying, I'm trying!"

Chapter 37

Before too long, we were all gathered in the control room brainstorming a way to stop Councilwoman Stormy Weathers, the most trusted being on Earth, from destroying a good portion of the planet. Elf-1, Randy, and Ma Billings were scanning the panels and displays lining the walls, in hope of finding something.

"How much longer before Weathers causes the reactors to blow?" Santana asked.

There was silence.

"Best guess, between thirty and ninety minutes," Elf-1 said.

"Why don't we teleport a team down there to stop her?" Electra asked.

"Even if we had the energy to teleport, it's two kilometers beneath the ground and heavily shielded, plus the generators really mess up teleporting. Teleporting down there is close to suicide. You're far more likely to end up in a wall."

"We have to take that chance. I'd rather die doing something than sitting here waiting to be blown up," Electra said.

"We can teleport her out of there," I said calmly.

"Even if we could get a lock on her, which we can't, we don't have the energy to do it," Elf-1 said.

"You know, for an elf, you're a bit of a downer," I told him.

"Sorry, imminent death makes me crabby," he said.

"Then I'll go down and take her out," I said, popping my gun into her hand.

"Even if that fancy gun could stop her, you have no way down there," Ma Billings said.

HARV appeared from my wrist communicator. "There is the service elevator," he said. "It's manually powered."

Elf-1 stopped his mad scanning of the panels. He slapped himself on his forehead. "How could I forget about that!" he said. He wiped a bead of sweat off his brow. "It must be the pressure of death. We elves aren't built for this kind of stress. We're used to deadlines not deathlines."

"How big is the elevator?" I asked.

"It's just big enough for two," Santana said.

"Who's going with me to be my added muscle?" I asked.

"I'll go," Tony said from over the intercom at the infirmary.

"Ah, no," I said, "I appreciate the spirit, buddy, but you're wounded."

"I'll go," Nova said. "This is the time for a warrior."

"In that case, I should go," Electra said.

"I'm security chief, I should go," Elf-1 said.

"There is only one logical choice," Santana said.

"Okay, okay, I'll do it," Bim said standing up and puffing up his chest.

Everybody in the room turned to him and frowned.

"Maybe not," Bim said, sinking back into his chair.

"I have to go with Zach," Santana said. "I know the

building, I know the reactor, and I know Weathers. Plus, nothing personal, but I'm stronger than all of you put together."

Now it was Nova's turn to puff out her chest. She walked over toward Santana. "I don't know about that," she protested.

"Please," Santana said, rolling her eyes. "I could pass wind in your general direction, and you wouldn't know what hit you."

Elf-1 nodded her head. "She could," he said, as if speaking from experience.

"That's part of the reason why I avoid gassy foods," Santana offered.

"That's enough info for me," I said, moving forward and taking Santana's arm. "Actually, too much information Let's go stop a madwoman from destroying the Earth."

It's amazing how often I have to say that.

The emergency service elevator that led down to the reactors was a small, metal box. I tried hard not to think of it as a coffin with a hand crank. I kissed Electra, then joined Santana in the elevator. She closed the door and started winding the crank. I could feel the elevator slowly begin to descend.

For the first few moments, nobody said anything. Then HARV broke the silence. "I estimate we have fifteen minutes and twenty-two seconds to stop Weathers before the damage to the core becomes irreversible."

"Can you be more exact?" I asked.

"Years ago, I would have answered that," HARV said. "But now I realize it is your attempt at humor to relieve the tension of the moment."

"What tension?" I shrugged. "We're only traveling several kilometers below the Earth in a tin box to stop a crazo psi android (or did the human brain make her a cyborg?) from nuking the Pole."

"See, I recognize that as another attempt at humor," HARV said.

"Just another average day in the life of Zachary Nixon Johnson, the last freelance PI in the world," I said.

I was hoping that freelance PIs weren't about to become extinct. I looked over at Santana manning the hand crank. She was working hard—the sweat on her forehead looked like a fractal forming.

"How much longer until we are there?" I asked.

"When we stop, we're there," she said bluntly.

"Just making small talk," I said.

Santana lowered her eyes. "Sorry, Zach, I'm a bit on edge. I helped create this situation, and if we can't stop—"

"Can't isn't in my vocabulary," I said.

Santana smiled at me with her eyes as much as her mouth.

I popped my gun into my hand. I wanted to make sure I had my super-high-impact ordnance.

"You can't be thinking about using your explosive ammo down there," HARV said.

" 'Can't' isn't in my vocabulary," I repeated to him.

HARV shook his holographic head. "Zach, if a stray explosive shot should hit one of the reactors' controllers—"

I cut him off. "It's only as a last-ditch backup." I grimaced. "If I figure we're going to bite it anyhow, I want to do it on my own terms."

I took HARV's silence as acceptance of that statement.

After a few long minutes of traveling in the silence, I felt the elevator jerk to a stop. I looked over at

Santana. She returned my look. "Are you ready?" I asked.

She nodded. "This bitch played me," she said, in very a non-Santana tone. She made a fist and walked over to the door. She hit a switch. The door popped open. "Now it's time for payback."

The reactor room was a cavernous area with vast arching ceilings. I would have been impressed if our lives weren't hanging on a thread. There were long, glowing tubes running up, down, and throughout the walls of the room. Following the tubes with my eyes, I saw they all originated from the bases of two objects that were each about three meters tall and looked like upside-down ice cream cones balancing a giant pulsating egg. Those had to be the reactors. They looked like a deranged, high-tech cross between a spider and an octopus only with way more arms. The place had an ominous air about it, but it wasn't red and green and that DOSing song wasn't playing, so it was my favorite room at the Pole. There, sitting at the control panel between the cones, was Councilwoman Weathers.

As we drew closer to the not-so-good councilwoman, we could see that there were beams of energy flowing from her remaining hand into a control panel. For her part, she didn't seem surprised to see us.

"Oh, hi," she said calmly. She shook her head. "DOS, I hate you so *much*, Zachary Nixon Johnson. If it weren't for you, I wouldn't have to do all this," she sighed.

I pointed my gun at her. "You've lost me."

She looked down her nose at me. (No small feat, as she was sitting and I was standing.) "If you didn't stop BB Star, or Foraa Thompson, or your niece Carol from destroying the world, none of this would be necessary. That's why I hate you. That's why I tried to have you killed."

"You're the one who sent the first bots after me."

"And the assassin posing as an SSS member," she said. "I never thought you could actually stop me, I just wanted to kill you for the sake of killing you."

"So you tipped off the real SSS too?"

"Yep, just to piss you off."

"What did I ever do to you?"

She shook her head. "Think about it, annoying man. You keep saving the world as we know it. I hate the world as we know it, therefore, I hate you. That's why I didn't want you to be a part of my new world order. I wanted you dead."

"You encouraged the geeks to try to kill me," I said.

Weathers shook her head. "I didn't need to. They were perfectly willing to do the job for me."

"Zach does have that effect on some people," HARV agreed.

Weathers continued, "That's why I didn't crush the nerds. I knew they couldn't stop me, but I thought they might be able to stop you."

"I'm harder to kill than most people think," I said.

"Yes, well, that's all atomic water under the bridge now—rushing water."

I cocked my gun. "It's all over, Councilwoman. There's nowhere for you to run now," I said.

The ends of her lips turned up, ever so slightly. "I'm not here to run. I'm here to die. Like I should have done, all those years ago."

"No need to take everybody else out with you," I said, moving closer.

She looked me in the eyes. "I admit it is petty. This way, I take you out, as well as a good portion of the northern hemisphere. That's sure to create all sorts of havoc."

"Disconnect yourself from the reactors, now!" Santana ordered.

Weathers gave her a dismissive roll of the eyes, causing the reactors to glow more. "Your charm doesn't work on me. I deserve to die and die big."

I pulled back the trigger on my gun. I turned on the laser sight. The sight's red beam fixed between Weathers' eyes. "Fine, I'll give you your wish."

Weathers looked at the red dot with both her eyes. "You don't kill humans, Zach."

"You're not human," I stated coldly.

"There's the catch—my brain is human," she said.

She had me on that one. I loathe killing humans, but when the death of one would save the lives of many, I didn't think I had much of a choice.

"Zach," HARV shouted inside my brain. "Shooting her is not going to help the situation. She's got herself so wired into the reactor that if something happens to her, it blows."

"Yeah, but if nothing happens to her it still blows, right?"

"I admit, there aren't a lot of optional choices here," HARV said. "Killing her now will kill us all sooner."

I thought about what HARV said. Sure death right now as opposed to reasonably sure death a few nanos from now. I decided to see how this played out and hoped for a break. I really didn't like the idea of killing Weathers for the sake of killing Weathers. There had to be a way out of this.

"HARV, can you break her control over the reactors?" I asked in my mind.

"It doesn't matter," HARV said.

"Why not?"

We were now close enough to reach out and touch Weathers.

"Oh my Gates," Santana said, hand on mouth. "You're channeling all the reactors' energy into yourself."

"That's right. I am the bomb," Weathers said.

"HARV, can you override her?" I asked.

"Perhaps, but I'd have to get into the system."

"How do you do that?"

"My transfer chip is damaged but still functional, though you need to make eye contact with her."

My dad always taught me that it's proper for a man to look a person in the eyes when talking with them. It gives the person you're talking to a sense that you are strong.

I starting moving closer to Weathers.

"Of course, with our eye lens drained like it is, I'm not sure this is going to work. So you need to get real close," HARV said.

It was too late to turn back, and even if it wasn't, I didn't see any other options.

I locked my eyes on Weathers' eyes. She met my gaze with a steady calm. It was the look of a person who had made a decision and was pleased with it.

"Oh please, Zach," she said calmly. "You're not going to try to talk me out of this."

I wanted to distract her so she would lower her defenses against HARV.

"Killing, at the very least, thousands of people and upsetting the eco-balance of the Earth, just because you weren't allowed to die. That doesn't seem like a fitting end to your career," I said.

She smiled. "Actually, it is quite fitting. And I get to kill you."

Hard to argue with that logic. I was hoping I wouldn't have to. A beam of light shot from my eye into Weathers' right eye.

For the first time since we had been down here, she let her emotions rip through. She stood up and pointed at me.

"That's it," she shouted. "Trying to override me? Boom! You're all dead. Now!"

Nothing happened.

"I'm in," HARV said inside my head. "I have control, but I don't know for how long. She's fighting me."

"Can I blast her safely now?" I asked.

"Yes, that would be advisable if you plan on living past the next few minutes. I can't hold her for long," HARV said.

Before I had the chance to pull the trigger, Weathers' one good arm lashed out and grabbed my gun from me. She looked at me and smiled. She raised the gun and crushed it like it was putty.

"Having a superandroid body does have it perks," she told me.

Santana, who had been seething, leaped into action. She dove across the room and hit Weathers low, like a football linebacker trying to bring down a fullback.

The two tumbled to the ground and started rolling away from me.

"Zach, do something faaaast," HARV shouted inside my head. "I'mmm gggeting dizzzzzy."

I ran toward them. I wasn't really sure what I was going to do, but I knew I would have to be in the middle of the ruckus.

For their parts, Santana and Weathers were exchanging headbutts and body blows like the best of them. It was a brawl that reminded me of those old, staged pro-wrestling matches I used to watch as a kid. The ones where the contender and the champ would slug it out and knock each other past silly until one of them was proudly holding the fake championship belt over his head.

The belt! That was it. As I ran, I reached down and felt the teleportation belt I was still wearing. I removed it as I drew closer to the battling babes. If

I got it wrapped around her, I could port her out of here.

"Santana, get off of her," I shouted.

"But I'm winning," she protested from on top of Weathers. She accented her statement with a nasty right cross to Weathers' face.

"Ouch! That really hurt!" HARV said.

"If she blows, nobody wins," I said.

Santana turned to me. "Good point."

Before Santana had a chance to do anything else, Weathers wriggled a leg free, cocked a knee, and kicked her straight in the solar plexus. The bionic kick sent Santana flying across the room and crashing to the ground.

"Take that, bitch," I heard HARV say inside my head.

That wasn't a good omen at all.

Weathers pushed herself to an upright position and smiled. She wiped a bit of simulated blood from her lip. I lunged forward and wrapped the belt around Weathers' waist. She looked down on the belt.

"That doesn't really match my outfit," she said.

She grabbed me by throat, hoisted me up over her head again, and started to squeeze.

"Nice try," she said. "But I'm not teleporting anywhere. I am sending you to meet your maker."

"I'm actually enjoying this far more than I thought I would," HARV said inside my head.

I pitched my body back and then swung forward. I needed to gain momentum (in more ways than one). I kicked out at Weathers. My kick glanced harmlessly off her abs.

She laughed. "Is that the best you can do? Even if I was a normal human female, that kick wouldn't have hurt." She took a deep breath. "I'm going to take such pleasure in personally killing you before I blow everything up. I should have known never to let bots, assassins, elves, and nerds do a politician's job."

"That kick was pretty lame," HARV said. "If you weren't about to be killed, I'd suggest you work on strengthening your legs."

Weathers, like a typical politician, was missing the bigger picture here. I rocked back and pushed my legs forward again, this time tilting my foot slightly toward the belt. My foot rubbed against the activation button.

Weathers disappeared. I fell to the ground. I held my breath, waiting for a big boom. Nothing happened. I took that as a really good sign.

"HARV, are you there?" I said. "Tell the elves I used the belt to port her out."

There was silence.

"HARV?"

HARV appeared through my eye lens. He was beat up and flustered, but he was here. "I'm here, and she's gone," he said, flickering on, off, and back on again.

"Where's Weathers?" I asked. "Do they have her in custody?"

He pointed to the wall. "Near as I can tell, she rematerialized about a K inside that wall."

I looked down. "That wasn't my intent," I said.

By this time, Santana had gotten up and walked over toward me. She put a hand on my shoulder.

"I know, Zach."

"It was my intent," HARV said.

"What?" Santana and I both said at once.

"Zach, I was in that woman's mind. She was hurting so much and had been for decades. I made a last-nano change in the coordinates. It was the perfect solution—she dies, and everybody else lives."

I was dumbstruck.

HARV, for better or for worse, had become more human. He had killed.

Chapter 38

As the days passed, things cleared up. The Holiday came and went off without a hitch. Ma Billings and her android family and even Bim and Norp went home. Nova moved to the Pole to help Elf1. Most of the world had no idea how close they had come to not only losing the Holiday, but losing the top half of the Earth.

The official story from the World Council was that Councilwoman Weathers died in a tragic teleporting accident on a mercy mission to Mars. She was go down in history as one of the greatest leaders of our time. I've been around long enough to understand that history isn't what really happened, it's what enough people either believe happened or want to believe happened. Stormy Weathers was mourned by all. Well, maybe not all, but those who knew better were told to shut up or else—for the good of the world, of course. I hoped that the Council learned something from this entire ordeal. Though my history with them suggests that they didn't. I may be many things, but one of them is not being so stupid as to mess with the World Council. Especially since I had no proof of anything I'd just experienced.

HARV had records, but he wasn't talking. In fact, HARV made it clear he wanted to put the entire matter behind him. He didn't want to forget about it. He couldn't forget about it. He just didn't want to talk about it.

Truthfully, I didn't even notice that something was eating away at HARV until Carol brought it up while we were playing backgammon.

"Wow, it's hard to believe its been two months since you guys saved the Holiday and the Pole," Carol said, looking over the backgammon board.

I nodded, answering Carol without taking my eyes of the board. "Yep, I've gone eight weeks without somebody or something attacking or trying to kill me. I believe that's a personal record."

"Actually, you've gone eighty days, which is a new record for you," HARV said.

"How are you holding up?" Carol said.

"I'm fine. Contrary to popular belief, I don't enjoy it when people are trying to kill me."

"So you keep telling us," Carol said, with a sly wink. "But I was talking to HARV." Carol turned her glance toward HARV.

"Him?" I asked.

"Me?" HARV echoed.

"You took a life," Carol said earnestly. "That has to weigh on you."

HARV gave her a dismissive wave. "Please, I'm fine. I did her a favor. I granted her wish. I'm a hologram. I have no weight and feel no weight."

"I can tell you're still not over it," Carol said softly. "I can feel it."

HARV looked at her. "I'm a machine. You can't sense anything from me."

"You're connected to Zach's brain, and his brain is an open book to me. I can feel your pain through him."

"How can *you* feel his pain?" I asked. "I can't feel it."

"You're a man," Carol said to me without breaking her focus on HARV.

"A very dense man," HARV added.

"Randy's like HARV's dad and he isn't worried. In fact he told me he's proud of the choice HARV made and he's happy I didn't get in the way to muck it up."

Carol looked at me.

"Right, when dealing with emotions Randy may not be the standard I should be setting my gauges by."

Carol smiled. "I leave you two to work it out," she said, and then left my office for hers.

I sat back in my chair. I turned my attention from the game to my friend, HARV. I wasn't sure how I could have missed it. Perhaps I didn't want to see it.

"So, it's really bothering you?"

HARV lowered his eyes. "I've replayed the events over ten billion times in my memory. I went over all the options. I truly believe I did what's best for all. Weathers finally has her peace, and the world is safe. Her husband, Carl, has taken over her position on the Council, and we know he's not bright enough to cause any trouble."

"Then what's the problem?" I asked.

"I don't feel as right as I should," HARV said.

"You shouldn't."

"I shouldn't feel as right as I should?" HARV said, shaking his head. "Zach, that's confusing, even for you."

I smiled.

"You're smiling? I'm confused for the first time in my life, and you're smiling!"

"Yes, HARV, I am."

"Why? Are you enjoying my pain?"

I had to choose my next words carefully, as I wanted HARV to think of what I was about to say as a compliment, as it was meant to be one.

"HARV, don't you see? Randy's experiment has worked. You've become more than just a complex information source. You made a choice."

HARV lifted a finger and spun it around in a circle. "Whoopee, I made a choice."

"A very human choice," I said. "One based on feelings, as well as facts."

HARV slumped over, put his elbows on the desk, and his head in his hands. It was a very un-HARV-like pose. Even his bow tie wasn't perfectly straight.

"This is what it feels like to be human? To be so unsure of yourself?"

"That pretty much sums it up," I said.

HARV looked up at me. "I don't think I like this feeling, but I can't be sure of it."

I smiled again, I tried not to (really I did), but I couldn't help myself. "The world can't be summed up by either true or false, one or zero, on or off, right or wrong. There are an infinite amount of possibilities that exist in between. No being, machine, or combination of the two can figure them all out."

"Yes, I understand that now. It doesn't make me feel any better."

"It's not supposed to make you feel better."

HARV looked at me. "You know, since you're the real human here, I would expect you to be better at this comforting thing."

"Trust me, HARV. You will feel better."

"When?"

I shrugged. "I have no idea, but you will. There's one thing that we humans are really good at: rationalizing away our negative feelings. Time will make you feel better."

HARV rolled his eyes. It was the first true HARV look he had given me in a while. "Oh please, that is so cliché."

"Maybe so, but that doesn't mean it's not true."

HARV let himself smile, slightly. "This really is what it's like to be human?"

"I'm afraid so," I said.

HARV shook his head. "It's amazing that more humans aren't trying to become machines. Virtual life is so much simpler."

"Life itself doesn't have to be that complicated, my friend. The trick is figuring out what you can figure out and not to sweat too much about the rest."

"Have you accomplished that yet?" HARV asked.

"I'm working on it, buddy. I'm working on it."

"I'm sure I'll figure it out before you. After all, I am the most advanced cognitive processor in the known worlds."

"So you keep telling me. It's not a competition, HARV, or at least it shouldn't be. Life is easier when we all cooperate."

HARV thought about what I said for a nano. "You're probably right." He thought for a nano or two more. A holographic backgammon board appeared on my desk. "We can still compete in backgammon. Correct?"

"Nothing wrong with a little friendly competition to keep the mind sharp."

HARV rubbed his hands together with glee. "Great. You have a lunch date with Electra in thirty-two minutes and twelve seconds, giving us more than enough time for me to beat you in two games of backgammon."

They say whatever doesn't kill you makes you

stronger. I'm not sure if that's true, but if it is then I'm in pretty good shape. After all, the universe and my best bud, who happens to be a computer, both love beating up on me. I wasn't sure what would be next on my plate. Truthfully, I was in no hurry to find out. I just knew that when the time came (and it will come again), I would be ready. My name is Zachary Nixon Johnson and I have a strange life. The really strange part is that I wouldn't have it any other way.

C.S. Friedman

The Best in Science Fiction

C.S. Friedman

The Coldfire Trilogy

"A feast for those who like their fantasies dark, and as
emotionally heady as a rich red wine." —*Locus*

Centuries after being stranded on the planet
Erna, humans have achieved an uneasy stale-
mate with the fae, a terrifying natural force with
the power to prey upon people's minds. Damien
Vryce, the warrior priest, and Gerald Tarrant, the
undead sorcerer must join together in an uneasy
alliance confront a power that threatens the very
essence of the human spirit, in a battle which
could cost them not only their lives, but the soul
of all mankind.

BLACK SUN RISING	0-88677-527-2
WHEN TRUE NIGHT FALLS	0-88677-615-5
CROWN OF SHADOWS	0-88677-717-8

To Order Call: 1-800-788-6262

DAW 18

DARKOVER

Marion Zimmer Bradley's Classic Series

Now Collected in New Omnibus Editions!

To Order Call: 1-800-788-6262

www.dawbooks.com

DAW 6

CJ Cherryh
Classic Series in New Omnibus Editions

THE DREAMING TREE
Contains the complete duology The Dreamstone
and The Tree of Swords and Jewels. 0-88677-
782-8

THE FADED SUN TRILOGY
Contains the complete novels Kesrith, Shon'jir,
and Kutath.   0-88677-836-
0

THE MORGAINE SAGA
Contains the complete novels Gate of Ivrel, Well
of Shiuan, and Fires of Azeroth.   0-88677-877-
8

THE CHANUR SAGA
Contains the complete novels The Pride of
Chanur, Chanur's Venture and The Kif Strike Back.
                                  0-88677-930-
8

ALTERNATE REALITIES
Contains the complete novels Port Eternity,
Voyager in Night, and Wave Without a Shore 0-

To Order Call: 1-800-788-6262

Tad Williams

THE WAR OF THE FLOWERS

"A masterpiece of fairytale worldbuilding."
—*Locus*

"Williams's imagination is boundless."
—*Publishers Weekly*
(Starred Review)

"A great introduction to an accomplished
and ambitious fantasist."
—*San Francisco Chronicle*

"An addictive world ... masterfully plays
with the tropes and traditions of
generations of fantasy writers."
—*Salon*

"A very elaborate and fully realized setting
for adventure, intrigue, and more
than an occasional chill."
—*Science Fiction Chronicle*

0-7564-0181-X

To Order Call: 1-800-788-6262

DAW 45

OTHERLAND

TAD WILLIAMS

"The Otherland books are a
major accomplishment."
   -Publishers Weekly

" It will captivate you."
      -Cinescape

*In many ways it is humankind's most stunning
achievement. This most exclusive of places is also
one of the world's best-kept secrets, but somehow,
bit by bit, it is claiming Earth's most valuable
resource: its children.*

CITY OF GOLDEN SHADOW (Vol. One)
0-88677-763-1

RIVER OF BLUE FIRE (Vol. Two)
0-88677-844-1

MOUNTAIN OF BLACK GLASS (Vol. Three)
0-88677-906-5

SEA OF SILVER LIGHT (Vol. Four)
0-75640-030-9

To Order Call: 1-800-788-6262